Dangerous Urges

Konrad Hartmann

I0553931

ForbiddenFiction
www.forbiddenfiction.com

an imprint of

Fantastic Fiction Publishing
www.fantasticfictionpublishing.com

DANGEROUS URGES
A Forbidden Fiction book

Fantastic Fiction Publishing
Hayward, California

© Konrad Hartmann, 2012-2016

CREDITS
Editors: Rylan Hunter, Lon Sarver
Cover Design: Siolnatine
Cover Art: Collage by Siolnatine from photos by fotshot & aitoff @ Pixabay and other public domain sources.
Internal cover design: Siolnatine, D.M. Atkins, and Carol Fiorillo
Production Editor: Erika L Firanc
Proofreading: Todd Michaels

SKU: KH1-1.100016-01 FFP
ISBN: 978-1-62234-306-5

Published in the United States of America

DISCLAIMER

Dedication

Kingdoms rose and fell since first we spoke words
In tongues long forgotten, moon-drunk lost birds
Asleep through the ages, but not by choice
I offer this now, a gift for her voice.

Contents

Foreword from the Editor..1

1. Hunter's Tree..3
Does the hunter wear a mask to cover his face, or to reveal it to his prey?

2. Tomb Brides...26
It was a simple plan: Distract the undead guards with slave-brides. But it got complicated, fast...

3. All Consuming..52
Jacqueline's sexual fantasies are dangerous--as are the lovers willing to fulfill them for her.

4. Lot's Sin...107
Lot and his daughters escaped divine wrath for the sins of others – but what of their own sins?

5. Frogger Says..126
Hannah's an odd girl; she talks to her stuffed animals. But when they talk back, it's so much worse...

6. Glad Rags..159
All he wants is a quiet lay, someone who will do what he says without talking back--and then things go horribly right...

7. Arena Breed...174
Fame in the arena can be hazardous for a gladiator – especially when the fans have money and extreme desires.

Author Notes..245
About the Author..248
About the Publisher..249

Foreword from the Editor

by Lon Sarver

Konrad Hartmann is a weird dude. I don't mean that as a personal judgment — we've never met in person, so I have no basis — but as a literary one. Konrad's work stands firmly in the line tracing from pulp-era weird fiction, the movement that transformed the gothic romances of old Europe and the ghost stories of young America into a literary form to hold the unease of the Great Depression. In doing so, weird fiction laid the groundwork for modern horror and dark fantasy, and the recent New Weird.

If you look at it, there's a clear lineage to be traced from Edgar Allen Poe to H.P. Lovecraft and Robert Bloch, through Shirley Jackson and Stephen King, up to China Miéville and Caitlin Kiernan. Konrad Hartmann belongs in that lineage. Perhaps as Kiernan's odd cousin; both of them write about characters with dangerous urges, sexual and otherwise, that lead them into dark places and life-altering encounters with the Other.

Each of these stories contains some degree of the weird. It's most subtle in Glad Rags, and not subtle at all in Frogger Says. When I first started working with Konrad (on Frogger Says), we got to talking about the weird. To paraphrase Konrad's definition (sorry if I get this wrong, man), the weird is what you get when an alien reality intrudes on the mundane world of the characters, leaving them questioning what this "reality" thing is, anyway. To this, I'd add that, in the best weird, the alien reality mirrors — or actually is — the character's emotional life, forcing them to confront the parts of themselves that they'd

1

rather never admit. The characters are transformed by their encounter with the alien, whether they ever understand it or not.

Mixing this with erotica is a tricky dance. On the one hand, it has to be sexy, on the other, we're dealing with characters the reader would more likely run from than hit on. The ideal emotional response we want from the reader is a progression from "do I want to see?"" to "oh, yeah, I want to see," with an aftertaste of "what does it say about me that I found that hot?"

If you think you see a parallel between that and the weird fiction protagonist's encounter with the alien, you're not wrong. Fiction is an alien world, and by letting it into you, you invite it to challenge and change you.

You've been warned.

If you'll allow me a brief plug for Konrad's other work, I'd recommend his novel Spidermilk to anyone who enjoys the stories in this anthology. It's post-cyberpunk noir erotica about a struggling private eye hired to find a gangster's runaway daughter, in an underworld of junkies who drink drugged breast milk and cultists worshiping spiders from Mars.

But that's enough from me, I'm not the one you wanted to read. Konrad's waiting just around the corner, and he has some surprises for you. Turn the page and dive into the weird.

Hunter's Tree

Chapter 1
The Forest Gives a Gift

Justin pulled the wolf-mask over his head, and it was then the girl started to run. Her first few steps triggered a hammer-pulse in his chest. He knew this one would be good. She might have fallen down sobbing, stood and screamed for help, or tried to fight him. None of these choices would have stopped him, but the chase always provided the best encounter. He felt something waking up inside.

He admired the magnificent swells of her hips and ass as she ran. She was larger than Justin, 303 pounds according to her record. Even from behind, he could see her full heavy breasts swinging from side to side as she ran. *Here you are again. How long has it been, Brooke? Your record says, age 24. Five years? Six? Six long, long years.*

The girl wore trail shoes but the colorful skirt reminded him or eastern European patterns. The sweat of fear and exertion darkened the back of her blue blouse. The colors of her clothing blazed against the backdrop of the trees. Two thick braids of sandy-blond hair writhed about her shoulders and back as she ran. As he ran where she ran, the scent of her sweat lingered, and he sucked it in through his nostrils, remembering her scent.

He recited a verse under his breath.

> *"Run though you may,*
> *and seek safety in flight,*
> *I smell iron in veins,*
> *and fear is my might."*

Justin paced Brooke, taking his time and stepping onto her footprints. He didn't want to catch up to her on the trail, so when she slowed down, he ran faster and growled so she would pick up the pace. He loved the sense of power restraint — the realization he *could* overtake her at any moment, but could also choose not to. He felt his back hunch a bit, and found it easier to run this way.

The mask felt hot on Justin's head, but the innermost layer was made of canvas instead of rubber or latex, so some air passed through despite the fur. And the girl carried no water, so he knew she would overheat long before he would. He also knew that soon the mask would become just another part of his body, his mind slipping past the discomfort and allowing it to become part of his Self.

At the same time, he viewed it as a tool for bringing his Self outward into the world. The firm employed many hunters, but no two were alike. Justin hunted as an opportunity to use what he normally kept hidden.

He began following her three miles back. Most of the people who used the trail only used the first half-mile of it. A day hiker might often see other people, but on a weekday like this, one could sometimes go all day without seeing others. *Did Brooke purposely come here knowing this?*

Justin had studied the trail and knew it well, though he had never before hunted in this forest. He knew this was the most remote portion he expected his prey to reach. And so it was at this point he chose to don his mask. He knew she had been waiting for a threat to appear, but that threat could have come from anywhere. It was time for the revelation.

He had been drinking water, but the girl carried none and would doubtless be dehydrated. He knew he had to drive his quarry from the trail before she collapsed. Her health history indicated nothing to worry about, but like all the others, she failed to carry enough water. They knew something would happen to them, but when they went into the woods, they usually brought nothing.

Justin wanted to take off his shoes and feel the ground on his bare feet, but there wasn't time. Though he could easily track her if he lost sight of her, he loathed the possibility of missing part of the chase. The pacing, the following, formed a link between himself and the prey. As he moved, she moved. He followed, inhaling her fear.

He waited until they reached a point where the woods on the

5

left thinned out to an area of shady pines, a downhill stretch where the semblance of a trail opened up in the trees. Then Justin growled loudly and sprinted towards the girl, and breathed a sigh of relief as she took the bait and stumbled down the poorly marked path, into the pines. He felt like he was bringing her home.

He laughed. They always chose the pines. Few animals would, when chased, enter the open space of the pines. Only humans could be deceived into thinking it was a safe place. But the pines provided virtually no cover. Even better, Justin mused, in a large section of pines, the prey easily becomes lost. He once ran a woman for an entire weekend in the Pine Barrens, letting her run in a huge circle while he attacked and withdrew, attacked and withdrew.

Justin drove Brooke at a slow pace, hiding when he thought she needed breath. He knew she either had no phone or was actually committed to the game enough to not use it. When the targets lost their nerve and went for the phone — and it happened from time to time — he had to make a decision.

If a target successfully phoned for help — in the form of police or friends — Justin, as a hunter, was obliged to leave the scene, if possible. The firm held contracts, collateral, and blackmail against the targets, and if she broke the rules of the game, all of these were invariably used to punish her and protect the hunter.

If a target tried unsuccessfully to call for help, Justin would take the phone and the woman would receive what the firm called an "aggravated encounter." It wasn't pretty, but Justin loved nothing more than when a target made this mistake. Among the hunters, it was referred to as "calling in an A.E." The woman in the Pine Barrens had called in an A.E., and Justin thought of that weekend *every day*.

While all of the women contracted for what the firm offered as a "threshold experience of transformation," none of them knew just what that threshold, experience, or transformation would be. Justin smiled when he thought of it, because they usually thought evading pursuit *was* the experience.

He knew what Brooke had contracted for. She wanted a pursuit with the possibility of capture. She wanted pain without serious injury, excepting the consequences of an Aggravated Encounter. Her request was both simple and vague, but the firm required all prospective clients to complete a standardized test. Brooke's test results correlated highly with those of abuse victims; that wasn't unusual for clients. What was unusual was that the scores also correlated with murderers.

He wondered what Brooke really wanted from it.

For now, the need for restraint became poignant, for he wanted nothing more than to immediately pounce on her, to taste her. To hold back and sit quietly, to keep his body still and his breath quiet, filled him with sweet longing. Now was not the time for an A.E. Yet, his heart pounded, fast but controlled, and every leaf and twig stood sharply outlined in his vision.

Justin stalked her far down into the valley of the pines, traveling to her left and right to guide her to a spring bubbling up from the ground and running in a small stream down the slope. The air felt cool and rich and he sucked it in through his mask.

He hid from her as she approached the stream, and watched as she collapsed on hands and knees before it. Her full and round ass made two luxurious spheres, two massive globes of perfect flesh offered up to him by fate, for he believed that all players, hunter and prey, played out their predestined roles. As she drank, her tongue lapping madly at the clear water, her breasts rested on the stone beneath her, spreading out. A breeze lifted the bottom of her blouse and revealed a plush belly suspended beneath her.

Justin adjusted his erection in his pants, stroking it as he watched her drink. When she finished, she splashed cold water over her red face and over her hair, and then sat down on a flat boulder. Justin listened to her gasp for breath and tried to smell the fear she exhaled. She looked about, and then picked up a grapefruit-sized stone and clutched it in her hands.

Justin stood up, drawing himself to his full height, and approached her from behind quietly, stepping first with the ball of his foot and then rolling his foot to the side. *Now I will be air and move quietly, but soon you will feel me, Brooke.* He enjoyed the quiet stalk almost as much as the outright chase, being able to bypass the girl's hearing.

She turned suddenly when he stood within a few yards of her, and her eyes and mouth became rounded. Justin relished her shock. *Disable one sense and the others follow,* he thought.

7

Brooke quickly drew back and windmilled her arm, throwing her stone at Justin's head. He was glad she was too frightened to take better aim, as he felt it pass over his head close enough to brush the mask.

Justin paused, shocked by the near-miss. Brooke sprang to her feet, about to make a maddened plunge toward escape when Justin grabbed her by the base of her braids. The braids felt smooth in his hands, like ropes of corn silk, and the girl grabbed onto his wrists with sweaty hands. He felt like he had caught a fish, and the adrenaline pumped in his veins.

"No. No. No," she sobbed, turning her head away from him. "Please. Please let me go. Please. You're hurting me. Stop."

"No," Justin said, shaking her. "No, I won't stop. I've caught you, and you will not get away until I say so. Do you understand that?"

"Why are you doing this? You can stop now," she said, tears streaming down her hot cheeks. They never quite knew what they were getting into, and Justin fed on their uncertainty.

"Because the woods and the world gave you to me to enjoy as I see fit. We're going to take your blouse off now," he said. He held both of her braids with one hand as he pulled at her shirt.

"No! No!" she cried out, clawing at his hand. Her body tensed.

Justin froze, staring at her. He growled and yanked her by the braids until she stood up, hunched over and whimpering. He walked her over to a boulder and forced her to lean against it, face down, as he pulled off her skirt. Her panties failed to cover the expansive width of her smooth cheeks. Justin took a handful of the seat of the cotton panties and pulled them down. He pushed her against the rock to keep her in place as he touched the flesh of her buttocks.

It was not enough to stroke or caress their smooth softness. He had to grab and squeeze them, bruise them. The yielding meat filled his hands as he kneaded. He slapped one cheek, watching the quivering wave of impact spread out across the surface. He slapped the other, one stroke soon blending into the next as the smacks resounded through the trees, mixed with sobbing.

Justin drove his hand into the deep crevice of her buttocks, his hand enveloped by the parted cheeks. He found her sweat-moistened asshole and as he introduced a finger, her struggles renewed. The further he slid the finger in, the harder she squirmed. He played with her as if this were a switch, feeling around inside of her rectum, tugging at the ring. He gripped her throat with his free hand and squeezed until she relaxed.

"You are my treat," Justin whispered to her through the mask. "The forest gave you to me. Now. We're going to take your blouse off." He listened to his own voice roughen and grow hoarse. Words felt thick on his tongue as he remembered her.

And Justin did believe what he said, for he had known Brooke long ago. They had lived not far from each other, yet Justin knew little about her except rumors about her family.

Shy and inexperienced, Justin had no real plan with her other than to walk. When they came to an abandoned farmhouse, Brooke stepped closer to him.

They stood outside the house, the ground littered with pieces of crumbled plaster and broken glass from the windows. Thorny wild rosebushes and raspberry bushes surrounded them, in between scrubby trees.

Justin opened the rotting door and stepped inside, feeling Brooke right behind him. On reaching the cellar staircase, Justin felt the first step crumble under his foot, so they decided to stay on the first floor. They peered into the blackness of the cellar staircase, but did not test it.

The ground floor rooms held enough furniture to give the sense of something uncomfortable, as though people didn't have enough time or didn't care enough to take things with them. In a back room, on a broken table propped against a wall, rested a small wooden box with a crude image of a dog painted on it. Justin picked it up and opened it, finding it full of roughly formed lead dog figurines.

Revulsion shook his stomach and he quickly dropped the box on the table and backed away, though he did not know why.

He wanted to leave the house, but when they entered the front room, he felt Brooke's hand on his arm. He turned to face her, and she looked up at him, holding onto his shirt sleeve. When she tilted her face, he realized she wanted him to kiss her.

It was his first kiss. He wasn't sure how he was supposed to do it, but was relieved when he felt Brooke's tongue thrust into his mouth. He wrapped his arms around her, his hands pawing her, awkwardly and automatically seeking her nipples.

She pushed him back a step and he blushed, afraid he'd upset her with his touch. Instead she took his hands, leading him as she sat down on a low wooden chair.

Justin's breath caught in his throat as she unbuttoned his jeans and tugged his zipper down. His penis was limp with anxiety as she pulled it out of his underwear. Justin felt humiliated and afraid it wouldn't harden, that he would finally be with someone and not be able to get it up. What if she told someone? But told who? He had no friends.

But limp or not, her warm mouth felt good around his dick and he almost didn't care if it got hard. As he stopped caring, he felt himself stiffening and listened to the soft slurp of Brooke's mouth. His hands went to her head, but she pushed them away. He held his hands awkwardly in the air for a moment, then put them on his hips while she sucked, and he smiled, not believing it was happening, not believing how good her tongue felt on his cock.

His orgasm took him by surprise, like a sneeze, and he grunted as the pleasure surged through him, feeling himself spurt into Brooke's mouth. She held him inside, letting him finish, letting every drop leave his prick, until it became too sensitive and he recoiled at the pressure of her tongue as it probed his hole.

When he stepped back, he saw them. Outside the broken window, looking in, stood Jimmy Roberts, John Carney, and Scott Williams. They burst out laughing as Justin stood in shock, too surprised to even put away his shrinking cock.

They shamed Brooke in the following week, pretending to suck invisible dicks when they saw her walking by. They sent pictures of pigs to Justin.

Walking home one day, Justin saw Jimmy Roberts and ran towards him, not even sure what he wanted to do. He saw a broken bottle on the side of the road and he scooped it up as he ran. Jimmy's legs pumped, but Justin felt himself overtaking him. Jimmy looked back and saw Justin draw closer.

Jimmy turned suddenly towards the woods lining the road, leaping to hurdle a log. He tripped and fell heavily into a thorn bush. Justin saw Jimmy try to get up, but the thorns snagged his backpack. Jimmy looked up at Justin, and at the broken bottle in Justin's hand, and started to cry.

"Gimme your hand," Justin said.

"No!" Jimmy yelled.

"Do you want me to cut your hand or your face?" Justin asked, swinging the broken bottle past Jimmy's chin.

Jimmy squinted at him, recoiling into the thorns a bit, a trickle of blood running down his forehead.

"Give it to me," Justin said.

Jimmy looked away and extended one shaking hand. Justin grabbed the wrist and pulled Jimmy's arm out straight. He stepped on Jimmy's shoulder, forcing him face down in the thorns. Jimmy whimpered.

Justin saw his own hand shaking, but he jammed the jagged point into Jimmy's palm and twisted, feeling the glass break off inside the flesh. Jimmy shrieked so loud Justin let go of his wrist and threw the broken bottle far away. He looked around to see if anyone saw him, blood covering his hands, his heart pounding.

"Shut up! Just shut up!" Justin yelled at him. But Jimmy continued to shriek and Justin felt he would hurt him more if he had to hear him, had to listen to that screeching wail.

Justin ran, not knowing where or why, but afraid to go home. He sprinted through the woods until he was too tired to run anymore, and he stopped, panting, his hands on his knees. When he looked up, he saw the abandoned farmhouse.

He thought of the wooden box now, with its ugly picture of a dog on it and the stupid, misshapen figurines inside of it. He could think of nothing he wanted to do except to smash the box and its contents to bits.

Justin kicked in the door, knocking it off one hinge so it hung crookedly. He ran inside, the crisp March air now dank inside the house. He ran to the back room, the sunlight fading but still sufficient to see.

The broken table still leaned against the wall, but the box was gone. Justin tried to remember what it looked like. *Were they even dogs? What the fuck were they supposed to be?*

For a moment, Justin considered going back and finding Jimmy, taking his backpack and checking inside of it. But it was a stupid notion and he knew Jimmy would be long gone and someone had probably already called the police.

Justin choked a sob in his throat. He grabbed the table and picked it up, smashing it against the wall, knocking out chunks of plaster until the remaining legs broke off, until he was doing more damage to the room than to the table.

He threw it aside and walked home.

The years passed, and Justin never walked with Brooke again, until the day he chased her in the pines.

Justin lifted Brooke's shirt and she slowly raised her arms as he pulled it over her head. Justin touched the soft rolls of flesh adorning her back. He unhooked the many hooks of her black bra and pulled it from her roughly before tossing the garment aside.

He usually found this to be a crucial moment for the women, the loss of clothing signifying the loss of civilization. As long as they had clothing, they still held onto the connection of the safe world, an anchor to the world of everyday life. Once it was gone, they had to see themselves as they were, possessing the only things they really own, Justin thought. The girl stood leaning against the boulder with her hands and forehead pressed against the stone, her panties tight around her thick, round thighs.

"Turn around," Justin said, removing his belt, wrapping one coil around his hand.

Brooke reached down and tried to pull up her underwear. Justin swung his belt in a flat arc and the girl shrieked as the leather crackled against her ass. Justin felt the belt in his hand as an extension of his thought, the leather alive and warm.

"No! Leave them down!" Justin barked. He strained to control his arm, flexing the muscle to keep it still, to keep it from whipping

Brooke in a frenzy. The belt felt like a snake in his hand. Justin pictured beating her until she collapsed, skin welting, then bleeding in crimson strikes —

Slowly. Slowly, he told himself. You have all day to do this. Brooke is mine. The forest gave her to me.

Chapter 2

Brooke

Brooke turned, standing awkwardly with her panties around her legs. She hugged herself to cover her heavy breasts. Her vulnerability made Justin twitch.

"Arms down!" Justin said, flicking the belt so it stung her arm. She cried out and dropped her arms. A scowl flickered across her face.

Justin stared for a long moment without moving. The girl's breasts were enormous, spreading out to partially obscure her elbows, which were tucked close against her sides. Her belly, soft and smooth hung down almost to the triangular wedge of short blond curls over her pubic mound. Her stomach lifted up and down as she panted and sobbed quietly, and as it moved, the creased hole of her navel opened and closed. He stared at it and felt his prick grow hard and hot, stretching tight against his pants, like a burn, painful in its need.

"Take off your shoes," Justin said. He allowed himself to pace, just a little bit, trying to slow his pulse.

The girl tried to bend over to untie her shoes, struggling to do so without falling over, her legs constricted by the panties. Part of him wanted to make her struggle this way all day, but this wasn't what he was here for, he told himself.

"Take off your panties first," he said.

Brooke looked up at him, and her tears dripped down her face and onto the ground. She looked like she wanted to say something, but then pulled her underwear down and stepped out of them daintily.

"Give them to me," Justin said. The girl clutched the panties in her hand like a lifeline, a last vestige of dignity. She hesitated, and then handed them to him, her shoulders sagging. She leaned her ass back against the boulder as she bent over to take off her shoes. The flesh of her rear spread out against the stone, leaving a faint shadow of sweat on it after she stood up.

Brooke stood before him naked now, her red-rimmed eyes pleading with him, her lower lip curled, and her forehead creased. Her expression pulled anger out of Justin's chest and he wanted to hurt her as much as it aroused him. He pushed down within himself, seeking control.

Justin took a water bottle out of his backpack and held it out to her. Her eyes went back and forth between it and Justin's wolf-mask, until finally she took it and drank deeply, draining the bottle. Nervously, she spilled some down her chin and it trickled down her body, water trickling through sweat.

Justin pointed to a flat boulder that rested almost flush with the ground but rose higher to one side.

"Lay down," he said, pointing to the stone.

She winced and looked back in the direction from where she came. Justin growled from deep within his chest and pointed again to the stone. Within the mask, he licked his teeth.

Staring at the ground now, she lowered herself to one knee and then sat down, her belly transforming into creamy rolls. The shape of the boulder let her lay so her upper body was higher than the lower. She held her legs closed and her arms rested on the stone, palms down, and she stared at Justin as he unbuttoned his shirt and dropped it. Her eyes widened, and he knew she was trying to memorize his tattoos, the images of wolves and the runes and symbols. *They weren't there the last time you saw me*, Justin thought. He took off his shoes and his pants, letting his swollen cock jut out and cool in the air under the pines. From his pants pocket, he took out a small bottle of lubricant.

As he approached her, a soft shaking took over her body. He squatted, feeling his balls dangle, and he pulled her legs open. The flesh was thick around her pussy, and the folds of her labia protruded between them. She whimpered as he touched her, feeling the fleshy lips wet, at least with sweat, and she tensed up as he circled the area of her clit. He savored the way her scent changed as he drew closer to her, changing not just in intensity but also type, as though he passed through layers. He smelled her hair shampoo first, then her sweat, then her breath, sweet like fruit, and finally her sex.

Justin put both hands on the tops of Brooke's thighs and slid his palms upward, feeling the flesh yield to his pressure. He felt her tremble beneath his palms, and he himself tried not to tremble, the tension seeming to flow into his palms and up his arms. He slid his hands up until they framed her pubic mound, and used his thumbs to spread the fleshy lobes apart from her lips, opening her cunt and exposing the thick hood of her clit.

He slid his hands up to her belly and the blood pounded in his ears. He let the softness fill his hands, rolling it gently back and forth, before he allowed himself to touch her navel. He pressed down and spread the flesh to expose the hole. Slowly and tentatively, as though it might burn him, he stroked in slow circles around it, looking at the way it contracted and dilated as he pulled it open and squeezed it closed.

Taking the bottle of lube, he drizzled fluid into and around the hole. The girl stared and swallowed hard, then exhaled. Justin moved his finger in a spiral, drawing closer and closer to the navel pit. He slipped a finger inside and slowly began probing it, feeling its tightness around his finger. The girl's hands rose as though to stop him, flexed in the air for a moment, and again lowered to the stone.

Justin breathed hard inside his mask, but watched as the breasts of his prey rose and fell a bit faster now. He watched as something in her face relaxed, became submissive. He wanted to stab his finger deep into her belly, until it bled, until he would have to remove the mask and taste her.

Breathe, he told himself.

"Hold your belly for me," he said. Brooke frowned and held the sides of her stomach lightly.

"No. Like this," he said, making her press her belly together so that it formed a vertical fold. The hole now lay deeper within the flesh, and Justin sighed as his finger was enveloped. He reached up and lightly stroked the young woman's large nipples with one hand, feeling the tiny bumps, circling the nub under his finger tips. His head felt light and he resisted the urge to jam his finger into her belly. But the frenzy flowed to his other hand and the light strokes on her nipples

continued to fuck Brooke's belly for a long minute.

He lifted himself off her and looked down. Brooke relaxed her hands and her stomach spread out, the come puddled inside her navel running out now. He smelled his own sweat in his mask, but also the smell of his ejaculate, and something else. Dog-like, Justin crouched down and spread Brooke's legs, leaning in and sniffing at her crotch. Her cunt looked pinker now. He slipped a finger inside and found her wet.

"What are you afraid of, Brooke?" he asked. His voice sounded strange in his own ears and he wondered if she understood him.

"That you'll kill me. That I've made a mistake. That I've paid for my own executioner," she said. Her words sounded hollow in Justin's ears and he didn't believe her.

"A minute ago, you were afraid I would rape you," Justin said, slipping another finger inside. He slid them in and out, slowly. His thumb made wide circles around her clitoris, never quite touching it. "You said you were afraid I would rape you, but now, you are afraid I will kill you. Why?"

"I don't know why. It's just fear," Brooke said, her voice thick.

"Really?" he asked, his thumb moving above her clit, making the hood slide up and then down. "Were you really more worried about being raped than dying?" He moved his fingers inside of her faster now. "Touch your nipples."

Her hands moved slowly to her chest, and began to roll her nipples between her fingertips. She rolled them fast. Justin tickled her clit harder. There was a heat to the girl that made Justin feel dizzy as he smelled her arousal.

Brooke whimpered and Justin kept moving his hand until he felt her cunt open up, and minutes later tighten again. She was blushing and soon grunted as her hole clenched down on his fingers. She let her hands fall to her sides again, spreading out her fingers.

"What if," Justin said, "you knew I was going to kill you? Maybe you'd pick up another stone and try to hit me with it. But what if you knew that wouldn't work, Brooke? What if you knew, no matter what you did, I was going to kill you and you only had an hour left?"

"Why are you asking me these stupid questions? No one said anything about an interview," Brooke said.

Justin grabbed his belt and whipped it across her thighs. She sucked air into her mouth between clenched teeth. He whipped her again.

"Every time you answer a question with a question, I will hurt you," he said, crouching closer.

"Okay, okay," Brooke said, blinking tears and rubbing her thighs, frowning.

"Answer," Justin said, feeling irritated. He didn't want to hear the answer. He wanted to fuck her and bite her and taste her blood.

"If I only had an hour left," she said, her voice growing quieter. "If I only had an hour left, I would remember everything good that ever happened to me. I would think of the people I love. I would think of everything I did that made me happy."

"Wouldn't you be angry at me?" Justin asked.

"Yes. I would be angry at you, because you would be taking away my choice."

"What choice?" Justin asked, trying to focus.

"My choice of when I want to die," Brooke said.

"Were you angry when I used you?" he said.

She was quiet for a moment, and Justin wondered if she was thinking of now or of the past. *But you must be thinking of now. You do not recognize me.*

"I was afraid you would hurt me. That's it. I'm angry you're asking these fucking questions." She clenched her teeth.

Justin got up and squatted next to her head. His own embarrassment surprised him. He wanted to hurt her but he saw the wall she was already putting up against the pain.

"Listen. You're going to suck me until I'm hard again. If you bite me, I will break your neck. Do you understand?"

"Yes. I understand," she said, her voice hardening, the tremor gone now.

Justin knelt and she turned to face his cock. It stood half erect. She wrapped her hand around the base and pulled him closer, opening her mouth as it approached.

When she closed it, she sucked it hard, her cheeks collapsing in and out and he felt his cock swell instantly. He held onto her braids and thrust until she gagged slightly. He pulled out and spit ran down her chin. He caught himself leaning forward to lick the spittle, catching himself as he remembered the mask.

"Lay back," he said.

Brooke lay back and stared at him. Justin dipped his fingers into the come and lube surrounding her navel. He smeared it between her breasts.

"Push them together," he said.

Brooke placed her hands on the outside of her breasts and pressed them together, adjusting them as they rolled. Justin straddled her belly and slipped his cock between the large spheres. He started fucking her tits, making her wheeze when he rested his weight on her. He reached back with one hand and found her navel, probing it.

"Brooke. Have you ever been fucked when you didn't want to be fucked?" Justin asked, sliding in and out.

"Yes," she said, coughing.

"I don't mean you had sex because you felt obligated, or bad for your boyfriend."

"I — know," she said.

"Who was it?" he asked. Stepbrother, he guessed.

Brooke's eyes turned to slits. Justin watched as something welled up within her, her face reddening.

"What is it you want to know?" she asked, her voice bitter. "You want to know who got to me? Who left the big scars on me? Is that it? My brother. My half-brother," she said, staring at her cleavage, an emotional kaleidoscope on her face.

"Did he fuck you?"

"Yes," she said, her voice strained not only from Justin's weight. Hot tears started to flow fresh down into her hair and onto the stone. "It was my birthday. Last year. My — eighteenth birthday. He said it was my birthday present. I was eating lunch. I was sitting at the dining room table, eating lunch, and he came in and said, 'Oh, little piggy's eating her lunch.'

Justin thought of Jimmy, screaming and bleeding.

"I was afraid of him, so I didn't say anything. I just looked down. Kept eating my lunch. He said he thought I had enough. Said I was big enough to go to market. Said I was old enough to go to market. I could hear him pulling his zipper down, but I just stared at my plate.

'Hey!' he said. 'Don't think you can just ignore me.' And he slapped me. Slapped me hard enough to make my lip bleed."

Justin felt himself growing excited by the story, both disgusted and aroused.

"I turned to look and he grabbed my hair and shoved his penis in my mouth. Like you did. So I sucked it as best I could. But he kept ramming it in, making me gag. Like you did, except harder, until he made me throw up on myself. And on him. He slapped me again and made me keep doing it, until I threw up again."

Justin pounded harder into the slippery press of her breasts. Brooke pressed tighter, staring past him. Justin wanted to either bite her or kiss her, but he wasn't sure which he wanted more.

"He made me stand, then made me bend over, onto the table. He pushed my dress up, pulled my panties down and stuck his dick inside of me. No spit. No lube. Just dry. I screamed because it hurt so bad. So he pushed my face down into a bowl, a dish of mashed potatoes. He said, 'Eat piggie,' and if I didn't eat, he would push my face down in it again.

"He came right inside of me then. He told me to clean up the mess and then he left."

Justin watched the scene in his mind in perfect clarity. He wanted to kill her brother, but also imagined himself as the brother. He wanted to both hurt and save Brooke. He pulled his prick out and pumped it, feeling the liquid course through his shaft as he spattered her neck and chin with come. When the tension left him, he leaned forward and placed his palms flat on the stone.

"So, now it's happened to you again," he said.

"What?" she asked, frowning and looking at his mask.

"First your brother. Now me," he said, realizing too late he was fishing for a denial.

"No. It's not the same," she said, shaking her head.

"Because I didn't fuck your pussy?"

"Because you're not my brother. Because you're not my family. Because you're a stranger out in the woods. Things can happen out in the woods. Things shouldn't happen at home. Nowhere to run. I didn't sign for that."

Brooke stared up at the sky for a moment, the corner of her mouth crooked. Justin wanted to see what she was seeing. Part of him wanted to hear more of her story. Part of him wanted her to try to run away. No more stories. No more talk. Just the hunt and catch.

"And because I don't know you. I don't know you enough to hate you. And you don't know me enough to hate me. Even if you did kill me, you'd just be killing for the sake of killing. Or because of the game. Or maybe because I remind you of someone. But not because of me. Not because we know each other," she said, her voice turning into a whisper at the end.

Justin felt something twist in his belly.

"Do you want me to feel bad for you? Pity you because your brother fucked you?" Justin asked.

Brooke's face contorted and grew red. She punched him hard in the liver. Justin suppressed a wheeze and grabbed her wrists.

"Fuck you!" Brooke said. "You asked me a question and I gave you an answer."

Justin felt himself falter, felt uncertainty. *Step up*, he told himself.

"You're still mine for now," Justin said. "And I'm not finished with you." He slapped her face, hard enough to sting but not draw blood. Brooke winced, but not without the hint of a smile.

"And if you go home and see your brother," Justin said, fondling her breasts, mashing them roughly in his hands, "will he fuck you again someday?"

Brooke smiled openly now and laughed softly. Her fingers made lines in the dirt.

"He won't fuck *anyone*," she said. "He had a hunting accident during the winter. Not far from here, I think." She stared off in the distance, her eyes unfocused.

"So you killed him?" Justin asked, now really curious.

"He liked pills a lot. The autopsy proved that. He climbed his tree stand and tried lifting his rifle up with a rope. It went off somehow. His wife is trying to sue the manufacturer of the rifle," Brooke said, chuckling. "Anyway, the bullet managed to hit his femoral artery and a kidney, too. He didn't even fall off his stand. He was just hanging there from his harness when they found him. Blood all down below his stand, on the tree. The guy who found him said he saw a coyote licking the blood in the snow."

"What was his name?" Justin asked, crouching into a squat.

"He doesn't have a name anymore," Brooke said, glancing at him.

"Why did you choose here, today?" Justin asked.

"This morning, I told his wife about what he used to do to me. There was the time I told you about. That was just the last time. There were a lot of times before that. I told her about all of them. She called me a whore and a liar.

"So I choose here because, I don't know. It's where I think about things. I don't know exactly."

"You came to visit the place where...he died," Justin said.

"Yeah," Brooke fixed him with a cold eye. "Yeah. Where, *he died.*"

Brooke wrapped her arms around the tree and held onto it, her feet spread apart, her lush ass stuck out behind her. Justin looked up at the tree, at the faint markings left where the tree stand had gouged the bark. He slipped his hands between her thighs and found them wet even before he reached her cunt.

Justin worked the head of his cock into her as she reached down and spread her thick lips. His hands explored her as he pounded into her, squeezing her buttocks and breasts. He held onto her belly, his finger deep in her navel.

With the other hand, he lifted the mask just enough to expose his mouth. He licked the salt from her back and then took skin into his mouth, nipping it at first, then biting harder and harder. He heard Brooke muttering, and he listened closely.

"Surprised to see me, Chuck?" Brooke said, grunting. "I thought you might have wanted your *other* rifle. *This* one. The .30-06. Careful, Chuck. You're not supposed to point a gun at anything you don't want to shoot. Oh. You want to shoot *me*? Huh? Well, what's wrong with the .243 then? All I hear is click. Yeah, that's it, try another round. Not working? Hmm. Do you think *this* piece is missing from the trigger assembly?"

Justin panted inside his mask, soaked with sweat. Brooke reached between her legs and rubbed her clit, rubbed her lips against his hard prick. She continued to mutter through clenched teeth.

"Well. Well, let's see, Chuck. Let's see if your .30-06 works. No, hold still. I held — still — while you — tried."

She cried out and wept at the same time, shaking and clenching.

"Oh, yeah, Chuck. Yeah, it works just *fine*. Stings? Yeah? Why don't I just wait around for a little bit? Make sure you're OK? Maybe you should try direct pressure? Chuck? Not looking so good now, Chuck. Not looking good at all.

"Pretty sure you're dying. Anything you want me to tell Cindy? Like, how you raped your sister? That'll be a *good* story to tell. I look forward to *that* one.

"I'll leave you *this* gun. Maybe, if you feel better, haha, if you feel better you can pull it up with the rope. Let me go ahead and take the .243. You won't need it anymore.

"Happy hunting, my brother."

Justin waited until she was silent, and then pushed her down on her knees. She turned and grabbed him, taking him inside her mouth. She held onto his ass, her fingernails digging into his flesh. As he fucked her mouth, drool hung from her lip.

One of her hands moved and he felt her finger press against his anus. She pushed it in, up to her knuckle, slowly. He felt her tongue scouring his shaft as her finger wiggled inside him. When he came, he felt hot tears on his own cheeks.

Brooke held him in her mouth until he was finished, and then stood up. She looked up at the tree and then down at the ground, looking for something. She stood still, staring at the ground, and then opened her mouth and let Justin's semen spill out onto the ground.

Brooke looked up at Justin, staring at him, her expression calm. Justin felt his fingers go the bottom of the mask, felt them slipping inside.

Brooke looked away. Justin stared at her, frozen, gripping the bottom of the mask. When she did not look back, he let his hands slowly fall to his side, turned, and slowly walked away.

If you enjoyed this story, you can sign up for a free membership at
ForbiddenFiction and discuss it with other readers
and the author at the *Hunter's Tree* story page
at http://forbiddenfiction.com/story/KH1-1.000045.

FORBIDDENFICTION
SHORT STORY

Tomb Brides
Konrad Hartmann

Tomb Brides

Chapter 1

Unnr

Folkvardr retched as the wolf barked its corpse-breath into his face. His hand still gripped a spear, but the beast's paws pinned his arms to the stone beneath. He kicked, but the wolf's body felt like wood against his feet.

The fetid vapor in his lungs, Folkvardr remembered falling into an open tomb, and worse, falling into the rotting corpse within. The smell now blasting from between the wolf's fangs recalled that night.

Was this then the revenge for plundering? Was the curse that he should smell his own decay while his heart still beat? The creature's breath fell in a pattern, making strange sounds. Folkvardr realized these sounds were words; not words in any language, but recognizable only by the way they plucked and gnawed at his mind.

"What would you here?" the wolf asked. The muzzle shot down to his shoulder, nipping his skin. Folkvardr felt the cut and the rasping of a tongue. "You be not jotun nor Aesir nor Vanir. You be not light alf. You be not dark alf. You. Must. Be. Man," the wolf leered as it grated out the words. "And man comes not to Ironwood."

Folkvardr opened his mouth to speak, but the vapor of the breath rolled across his tongue and down his throat like an oily cloud. He gagged and closed his mouth.

"You give me many thoughts," the wolf said. "And many choices. I could devour you now, gulping down your meat and blood while it yet steams in the night air. I could gut you alive, let you die slowly, and later, when decay softens your body and sweetens it with rot, I could savor you then.

"Or," the wolf continued, a rasping chortle in his throat, "I could have you as bitch. Would you like that?"

Folkvardr braced himself. If he could not speak then he would at least scream once in defiance. But when he opened his mouth, the wolf drooled slime in a sticky rope between his lips, and Folkvardr convulsed, coughing and retching as the ooze burned his tongue.

"I can do exactly as I wish with you," the wolf said. "Because you are in Ironwood. You would like a quick fight, wouldn't you? You would fain die on your feet, like a — like a man. Ask for mercy. I will let you stand and fight with your spear. I will tear you apart before you take two steps. But you have to beg for this. No? You won't beg. You don't know where you are. I offer you the easiest fate in all of Ironwood. But still, I wonder what brings you here. Why don't you speak? What is your name?" the wolf asked.

And Folkvardr now felt the dank night air as a fresh breeze, the corpse stench no longer filling his nose.

"My name is Bane-of-Trolls and Lament-of-Curs!" Folkvardr shouted at him.

The wolf's teeth grew large.

"Tell me, oh, Bane-of-Trolls," the wolf said, leering, "what business brings you to Ironwood?"

"To see how high one may stack dead ettins," Folkvardr gasped.

"But you've already failed, oh, Lament-of-Curs. You cannot even start with one."

"Let me stand and I'll start the pile now," Folkvardr said.

"Beg me," the wolf said. "Beg me like a bitch. Beg to be let up. I vow this is the kindest doom in all of Ironwood. You cannot leave now. You cannot go back to Midgard. You are in Angrboda's woods. My name is Skrati."

Folkvardr felt a burning wetness on his stomach. The wolf leaped off from him and was gone. Folkvardr rolled to his feet, his spear in hand, trying to ignore the filth that ran down the front of his tunic.

His heart pounding, he ran in circles through the woods, blood raging, his only thought to find Skrati. He ran aimlessly until the moon set, when he crawled beneath an overhanging boulder and collapsed.

Folkvardr felt the darkness and gasped, feeling a ringing in his ears. He stumbled over something and fell down backwards. Lurching to his feet, he felt a wall of stone and dirt with his hands. He turned at the sound of clicking, and when he saw sparks, realized someone was lighting a torch. The flame lit the room, and Folkvardr saw he was again in the grave mound, the barrow of Alrekr, son of Osvaldr.

The torch spluttered in Unnr's hand. Despite the illumination, her black dress made her blend into the shadows at the end of the chamber. For a moment, Folkvardr saw only her blonde head, and her hands, and the torch floating in the air.

Huld, Unnr's slave, stood with her arms crossed and shoulders slouched, turned half away from her mistress. She stared at the wall or the floor, but rarely at Folkvardr, and never at the body of Alrekr.

An oblong stone, of a mineral different from the others in the local soil, bore runes carved into its face. Folkvardr pointed at them.

"We should leave," he said. "This is a fool's game. What? We bring Alrekr back in vague hopes he will tell us where his gold lies hidden? We face uncertain loot, but certain curses."

Huld glanced at him, at the runes, and stared hard at the ground.

"And why say you that, Folkvardr?" Unnr asked, her head cocked to one side.

"Did you not read the runes?" he asked.

"No. Why don't you read them for me?"

"You can read them at least well as I," Folkvardr said. "And your slave can read them better than you."

At this, Unnr scowled and Huld stared harder at the floor. Unnr walked over to the stone, glanced at it, and then stared at Folkvardr.

"If you won't read them, I will. They say," Unnr said, her stare never leaving Folkvardr's eyes. Her voice grew loud. Hard. Hollow. "I call against the spirit of the dead, against the stalking dead, against they who ride, against those perched, against they who plummet, against the wandering dead, and against those in flight." She stepped close to Folvardr, staring up at him.

"All shall decay and die away," Huld said, finishing the inscription. Her voice crept quietly from where she stood in the shadows.

"Are we dead?" Unnr said. "No. Not at all. What concern is it to us?" She turned and walked towards Huld, grabbing the slave by her thick, black braids. Unnr pulled her towards the center of the room, forcing the young woman to bend over as they walked. Folkvardr noticed the swell of Huld's thighs and breasts beneath the dress as she staggered. He felt his apprehension now mixed with excitement, lust now blending with fear until each offered equal measures.

"Those who fear, should fear," Unnr said, smiling at Folkvardr. She forced Huld to her knees.

"I feel no shame in fearing the rune-master Gyril, only wisdom. I say now before all witnesses here that I take no willing part in this, and what happens, happens not of my will," Huld panted her words out, writhing as Unnr twisted and pulled at her hair.

"I trust you are more willing, Folkvardr?" Unnr asked.

He nodded, a glazed look in his eyes as he stared at Huld. Huld looked up at him, her large dark eyes moist with a silent appeal. She looked at him, he realized, with a desperate hope that immediately hardened his cock.

"Ah, so much for your rescue, my girl," Unnr said. "Your hero's intentions just became visible."

Folkvardr reached for a sack on the floor, and pulled out a length of rope from it. Huld's eyes darted from the rope, to the corpse lying not far away on its bed, and back to the rope. Her body convulsed as she made a sudden struggle to escape.

Unnr pounced on her, strong despite her lithe form, and soon the slave laid on the floor with Unnr's knee in her back. Still, she tried to crawl for the opening, even with her mistress straddling her.

Folkvardr slipped a noose around the girl's neck, and Unnr fastened it like a leash, slipping the knot tight against the neck and pulling the rope with the other hand. Huld's face turned red, and then purple, before she went limp and ceased struggling.

"Give her air, Unnr! If she dies, your efforts come to naught," Folkvardr said.

Unnr stared at Folkvardr, smirking and taking her time in loosening the knot. Huld gasped, sucking in air and coughing, the dust on the floor swirling in an eddy. She grabbed her by the braids again, pulling hard to lift the girl's head from the floor. Huld reflexively reached up to hold Unnr's wrists for support.

Folkvardr clutched Huld's wrists then and wrenched her arms

behind her back, making her squeal. Huld knelt now, and as the man held her arms behind her back, crossing her wrists, she went limp, sagging forward in Folkvardr's grip.

Unnr worked quickly, the rope sliding through her hands like hempen snakes coiling around and around the slave's wrists. Unnr's long fingers wove patterns faster than Folkvardr's eyes could follow, knots weaving upon knots.

Folkvardr eased Huld forward to lay on the stone. Huld wept silently, her tears mixing with the dust.

"Ah, so gentle," Unnr said as she tied the girl's ankles. "She must look forward to kind treatment from you."

Folkvardr ignored Unnr and reached forward to stroke the girl's hair. As he held up the braids, he watched how they shone in the torchlight, almost blue-black in their luster. He stroked Huld's cheek, wiping away the wet dirt. A tug at his belt turned his gaze back to Unnr, who now held his seax in her hand, pulled free from his belt sheath. Huld's ankles were now securely bound. Unnr grinned and Folkvardr wondered if he could actually hear her grinding her teeth. She swept her arm forward in a fast arc, the blade descending towards Huld's bottom.

Folkvardr grabbed Unnr's wrist, stopping the swing only with effort, surprised at the blonde woman's sinews.

"Why would you kill her?" he hissed.

"I. Am not. Killing her," Unnr whispered leaning close to him. Steel shone in the corner of his vision. Too fast to be stopped, Unnr tossed the knife through the air, catching it with her free hand. She slashed towards Huld.

Folkvardr's hand clutched Unnr's throat, only to feel sharp steel against his own. He relaxed his grip, but Unnr did not drop the blade from his neck. She smiled.

"You misunderstand my intentions, dear Folkvardr," Unnr said, her eyes motioning towards Huld. Unnr looked down at Huld. Her dress was now slit to right below her bound wrists, the cut in the linen revealing the swell of one olive-skinned buttock. "However, do remember she is my slave, and I will do with her as I will," Unnr said, again leaning close to Folkvardr.

He stepped away from her and she crouched down, cutting away

Huld's dress in a spiral, rolling the girls across the floor as she pulled away the fabric in one piece. When Unnr finished, Huld lay face down and naked on the floor.

Folkvardr stared at the voluptuous symmetry of Huld's form, at the curve of her full thighs and bottom, the gentle dip of the small of her back, and her narrow waist. He crouched and helped her to her knees. Huld stared up at him, her legs folded beneath her. Tears trickled down and pattered in drops on her full breasts, heaving as she panted, the nipples large and dark.

Folkvardr looked over at Unnr, who was fastening a rope to the support beam overhead. Unnr tied the end of the rope to Huld's wrist bindings.

Folkvardr lifted Huld to her feet. When Unnr finished tying off the rope, Huld stood with her bound ankles together, the rope leading from her wrists to the ceiling mercifully slack.

"You enjoy this, don't you, Folkvardr," Unnr said, circling her slave, running her fingers over the smooth skin. Standing behind her, she cupped Huld's heavy breasts and lifted them, stroking the nipples gently at first. They hardened quickly and Huld stared at the wall, frowning. She winced as Unnr pinched them tighter and tighter. One hand slid to down to the lush black curls of Huld's pubic hair, the fingers plunging in to grip the hair and pull as Huld gritted her teeth.

Unnr released her and walked behind Folkvardr, circling him with her arms. She pushed him forward to stand closer to Huld. He stared at the girl as he felt Unnr's fingers untying the waist of his breeches, reaching in to pull out his stiffened cock as she tugged down the garment.

Huld's face reddened and she looked away.

"Would you like this, slave?" Unnr said, pumping the penis in her hand and rolling back the foreskin. "No, don't look away!" Unnr's free hand darted out and hit Huld's face with an echoing slap. Huld stared now at Folkvardr's cock.

Unnr grabbed Huld by the hair and forced her to bend over, so she leaned forward, her arms stretched behind her by the rope. Folkvardr felt fire course through his brain, and now he grasped the girl by the hair, filling his hand with the silky coils as he pressed his prick towards her mouth.

"Please, no!" Huld gasped, "Not here! Not in the barrow!"

"Your defiance shortens your days, my cunting slave," Unnr said, going to a bag lying nearby.

Folkvardr felt a hot shame as he ran his hands over Huld's body but his penis throbbed painfully. He felt her breasts, unrestrained now as he squeezed and fondled them.

Unnr lifted her dress and slipped it over her head. She was slender and willowy, contrasting to Huld's voluptuous form. Folkvardr stared at her small, upturned breasts and blonde-haired pubic mound as he groped Huld. Unnr smirked and held up a stone phallus, smooth but massive in its dimensions. She wiped grease over its surface.

Huld tried to turn to see what Folkvardr stared at, but the man held her head so she could not see. Smiling coldly, Unnr rested the polished cock against Huld's bottom. The slave squirmed but could not avoid the dildo as Unnr pressed it against her anus. Unnr held it like it was her own penis, and Huld shrieked as Folkvardr watched it sink between her parted ass cheeks.

"Suck, slave!" Unnr barked. "Suck or I will tear you in twain!"

Huld stared up at Folkvardr with wide, tear-soaked eyes and opened her mouth, sticking out her flattened tongue. He shoved his penis into the girl's mouth and moaned as Huld sucked, obedient and fearful. Folkvardr felt control slipping away as he held the girl's face in his hands, feeling the warm scrub of her tongue. He started fucking her mouth hard now, watching as Unnr violated the slave's other end, the stone cock penetrating the hole with a barely audible slick sound. Unnr's eyes were half-hooded, and Folkvardr vaguely realized she quietly muttered strange words as the torches burned dim.

He felt Huld spluttering and gagging around his cock, but the fever in his nerves drove him onwards as he plunged deep and came, ramming his penis into her throat and holding her hair. She coughed and gagged on bile, blowing fluid from her nose as he forced the last drops of his sperm into her gorge.

As he slid his penis out and Huld retched, he listened to Unnr. Her face was tight with effort and she spoke her strange words quickly, her hair hanging in her face as she rhythmically penetrated Huld's rectum.

Folkvardr walked over to the bag lying on the floor, searching it until he found the small pouch within. He held it in his hand for a moment, weighing it. When he looked up, Unnr has staring hard at him. She nodded quickly, never breaking her stream of words.

Folkvardr walked over to the corpse of Alrekr. He stared down, and it felt as though he stood on the edge of a very deep pit, that the floor could shift at any moment, causing him to plunge down to where the dark blue cadaver lay. He forced himself to steady his feet, feeling the stone beneath him. Behind him, he heard the monotonous drone of Unnr's voice, but now there was a swishing sound, a cracking sound, and the squeal of Huld.

He ignored the sounds and forced his fingers to untie the knot cinching the pouch closed. His hands shaking, he untied the cord and opened the pouch. He reeled for a moment, the pungency of the powder making his mouth water sickly. He spat, and tried to avoid smelling it again. Holding the pouch away at arm's length, he slowly began to sprinkle it over the corpse, taking care not to let it fall onto him.

The grains fell like powdered rot; green, the color of a wound turned foul. He winced, and when finished, tossed the pouch away.

He turned to look at the women. Unnr held a lash in her hands, whipping mercilessly at her slave. Huld wailed, twisting and writhing at the end of her rope to avoid the beating. Red streaks, many of them trickling blood into sweat, covered her buttocks and thighs. Sometimes she fell to hang painfully by her wrists, and when this happened, Unnr drove her to her feet by lashing her breasts. When this no longer forced the girl to stand, she dropped the lash and picked up the seax.

Unnr's arm swung in a perfect arc, and the blade slashed the suspension rope. Huld fell uncontrolled to the floor. Rolling the slave onto her back, Unnr straddled her face, the knife poised over Huld's stomach. Grunting and grinding her hips, she force Huld to lick her. Unnr leaned forward over the girl's body. She held the seax by its blade, and Folkvardr heard Huld's muffled whimpering as Unnr began to cut runes into the thighs of the slave.

Chapter 2
Alrekr

Three rows she cut into each thigh, afterwards using the dull edge of the knife to scrape up blood onto the flat of the blade. Unnr rose, careful not to spill the blood. Over to the corpse of Alrekr she walked. She looked Folkvardr in the eye for a moment before she turned the blade, allowing it to spill the blood onto the chest of the corpse. Unnr flicked her wrist shaking as much blood as possible onto Alrekr before turning and walking back to Huld.

Unnr stepped over the slave's inert form, straddling her, with one foot on either side of Huld's hips. Crouching slightly, she held the blade of the seax beneath her crotch. Folkvardr saw Unnr's body grow tense, and then a thick stream of urine fell, steaming in the cool air as it washed the blood from the blade. Huld writhed as the acrid fluid washed the blood from the runes carved in her skin, wincing at the burn.

After the last drop fell, Unnr began to sing her galdr-song. She stared at the body of Alrekr as she sang. Folkvardr felt his skin crawl as the words clattered against the stone walls of the tomb, clanging like steel, jarring in their crispness. Beneath her, only Huld's shoulders shook as she sobbed without sound.

Huld looked up at Folkvardr.

"It cannot be undone. Not now." Folkvardr heard the words, but he saw Huld's lips did not move.

"Awake. He is awake now," he heard her say.

Folkvardr saw movement from the corner of his eyes and recoiled from the grave slab. He felt himself backing into a corner as the figure of Alrekr twitched where he lay. The corpse moved in a way that reminded him of a head-wounded fighter, one mortally wounded, but not dead yet, dancing like a puppet before life seeps out completely.

Breath hissed out in a rattle from between the dead warrior's swollen blue lips. The figure sat up, struggling, stiff muscles and joints crackling as he rose. Alrekr's head swiveled in quick jerks, turning to face Folkvardr. Folkvardr tensed himself. His spear rested against the wall, out of reach, and he cursed himself for leaving it so far away.

A laugh like the rustling of leaves escaped Alrekr's mouth as he opened his eyes and stared with milky, half-deflated orbs at Folkvardr. But now a nearly continuous wail filled the barrow, and Folkvardr saw the mound-dweller turn to stare at Unnr and Huld. Unnr's face was set into a hard grimace, and Folkvardr saw her white form grow paler. She stood with one foot on Huld, holding the slave in place only with effort. Huld's eyes rolled and the girl slobbered and convulsed in her fear, writhing and straining at her bonds. Folkvardr wondered if she would have broken her own back, had Unnr not held her down.

Alrekr stood, his body swelling, growing larger. Folkvardr fought the urge to run, to discard any pride and flee screaming into the night. Only the fact that Alrekr turned away from him kept him in place, for he would have to run past him to reach the opening.

Folkvardr stared at Alrekr's back as the walking corpse turned towards the women. The fabric of the garments stretched tight, pulled taut by the expanding flesh, the blue skin puffing out around the cuffs and neck of the tunic.

As Alrekr stepped forward, the garments began to tear at the seams, each step signaled by a ripping sound, audible only in the gaps between Huld's hoarse shrieking.

Folkvardr could see the sweat glistening on both women—on Huld in her struggle to free herself, on Unnr in her struggle to hold down her slave. While total panic convulsed the slave's face, Unnr's face was set into a mask of stone. Folkvardr could see her limbs shaking with more than the effort to restrain the other woman. He thought of a sailor holding the steering of a ship in a brutal storm, holding onto the only means of survival.

The corpse man stood before the women now, his clothing in shreds on his mottled, dark skin, his body misshapen in un-death. Unnr stood her ground and Folkvardr admired her, for he knew he would have run. She stood with her feet apart for support, the sinewy muscles of her lean legs and arms flexed, as though restraining not only Huld, but also herself. As he watched the interplay of Huld's shapely form writhing in chaos, and in Unnr's slender figure standing almost motionless above her, he realized he was watching a strange formula working itself out. This was the magic Unnr knew and craved, and Huld knew and feared.

Folkvardr felt helpless, as though he wasn't even in the chamber, but his heart pounded and a thrill pumped through his veins as he watched the women, watched their breasts heave with exertion, watched Huld's legs open and close in her struggle, bound at the ankles but moving like wings.

Alrekr, the size of the man while he laid in his tomb, now stood so large his head almost reached the eight-foot ceiling of the barrow. Folkvardr realized he gripped his spear in his hands. When had he reached it? Parts of the tomb now seemed closer than they should be, and was that a voice now whispering in his ear? As he looked up, he saw Alrekr was looking back at him, a parody of a grin revealing his yellow teeth. They were the teeth of a beast, he thought, stained with the blood and fats of his prey. What would a spear do against this being? Instead of a weapon, Folkvardr used it as a staff, preventing himself from collapsing. Words poured into his ears now, trollspeak, words of a strange language, giving him cravings that made no sense.

Folkvardr watched as Alrekr ripped away the rest of his ruined grave clothing. The cadaver's penis jutted out towards the women, a coal-black monstrosity glistening in the torchlight. Huld closed her eyes now and pressed her face to the floor, no longer screaming but babbling incoherently into the dust. Alrekr stepped forward and Unnr stepped backwards, releasing her grip on the girl, staring blankly at the creature before her.

Alrekr reached down and gripped the rope binding Huld's ankles. Pinching the strong rope between his fingers, he pulled and the rope snapped with a loud cracking sound. Free now, Huld's legs thrashed, her feet seeking purchase against the floor as she tried to scramble to her knees. And then her legs churned uselessly as Alrekr lifted her in the air by her waist. Folkvardr could see the whites of her eyes half-concealed by the black tresses clinging with sweat to her face. Her large breasts swung freely as she struggled in mid-air.

Alrekr gripped her around the waist and lifted her above his swollen penis. As he watched, Folkvardr felt the space between the creature and himself grow somehow thinner. He tried to back up, but felt hands pressing him from behind, and he dared not turn, dared not look at the owners of those hands. Still, the space between himself and Alrekr shrank, until he felt himself very close. He felt something breaking inside of himself, and felt he must somehow be pulled into Alrekr.

His vision grew dark and the pushing of the hands against his back grew stronger. He felt himself pushed against a wet and very cold wall. The hands pushed him into it, pressed him inside of it, and the cold made him scream, the fear gone now, replaced with pain. The cold burned and shrieked in his ears, until he felt himself pushed into warmth. He sobbed, joyful in his relief, and was answered by dry laughter.

He was inside something, now. He was inside something, but he could see everything in the room. He saw Unnr, and she stared back at him, shaking, surrounded by a frosty blue corona. Things moved in the corners of the room, but when he saw a sheep-sized spider with a woman's head, he stopped looking. Something pressed against his groin, he felt warmth against his belly, and as he looked down, he saw he was gripping Huld with his enormous blue hands.

He was inside Alrekr, and yet he could feel the woman pressed against the belly of the giant corpse. He could feel what the dead man felt, but when he tried to move the body, he could do nothing. He shared perception with the thing, but not control.

"So you want to feel death?" a rasping voice croaked. Though Folkvardr could hear with Alrekr's ears, this voice was inside his mind, his mind captive within Alrekr.

Folkvardr hungered for the warmth pouring from Huld. The shared flesh of Alrekr ached and Folkvardr felt something crawling within the muscles. He felt anger for the heat Huld had and he did not. He craved her and felt a hunger to consume her.

"Do not kill her!" he heard a voice shouting at him, but realized he was screaming at himself as Alrekr laughed and mocked him. The craving for Huld deepened.

He felt Alrekr's hands moving over the girl, groping her, squeezing her heavy breasts as she kicked and struggled, her hands yet bound behind her back. His heavy cock slipped between the girl's lush thighs as she flailed, and the pressure of her thighs against his shaft maddened him. Folkvardr felt his hand holding his cock, lifting the girl by the waist with the other arm.

He felt the foreskin rolling back, the crown of the penis pressing against the girl's slit now. Folkvardr wanted to be in her and he howled now within his prison. The organ was impossibly large to fit into her, but Folkvardr would have driven it into her, uncaring in his desire.

Instead he felt a shudder, and he realized the cock was changing shape, growing flexible enough to writhe its way into the girl's cunt. He heard someone sobbing uncontrollably. And then he was fucking her, feeling her flesh wrapped tight around his shaft, absorbing her delicious warmth into himself. He held her under the top of her thighs as he pounded into her, suspending her above the floor.

Folkvardr felt Alrekr's hands and arms growing longer. He felt one finger enter Huld's rectum, pressing in through the tight ring, now wet. A finger of the other hand went towards her clitoris, stoking her with the delicacy of rose petals. Though still mewling in terror, Huld was coming against her will, the muscles of her cunt convulsing around the black shaft that spread her lips wide.

When Alrekr set the girl down on the floor again, Folkvardr begged him not to stop fucking her, but the undead thing only laughed and turned towards Unnr, who was now running for the opening. And now Alrekr held Unnr in his iron grip, her nails digging furrows in his skin. Folkvardr heard the sound of Unnr's nails scraping on stone. It was Unnr that Folkvardr now craved, and a deep relief shook him as Alrekr carried her to the grave bed.

Dropping her so only her head and upper back rested on the stone, he held her by the legs, spreading her open wide to expose the flushed pink of her vagina.

Unnr tried to cover herself, putting her hands over her slit. Folkvardr laughed to see and feel the black organ of Alrekr, now slick with Huld's moisture, become like a serpent as it writhed and pushed between her hands. He felt his penis push deep into her cunt, her tight hole almost pushing it back out. Unnr's eyes rolled back and she gasped.

Folkvardr felt panic rise for a moment as he felt the flesh changing again, this time forming tiny tongues above, around, and beneath his cock. He could even taste Unnr as the tongues scoured the edges of Unnr's stretched labia, her clit, her asshole, each tongue giving a different flavor.

He was going to come now, and he almost feared what would happen, as if he were slipping off a cliff. A smell like the air before a lightning strike filled his nose, and soon he felt himself spinning, a euphoric glee stabbing him in the brain as he felt come surge through his cock and into Unnr's pussy. The woman was convulsing and smiling, but all sanity was gone from her eyes.

Folkvardr woke to coldness, and as he opened his eyes, he saw the milky predawn light in the sky. His heart raced for a moment and he quickly looked at his hands, relaxing when he saw that they were his own. He rose and checked his weapon, noting a fine speckling of rust on the spearhead. He sharpened the blades and ate a meager meal, but did not linger long in his shelter, for the rocky outcropping overhead reminded him too much of the barrow. He craved an end to that memory. It could only end with Alrekr's destruction, or, perhaps, his own. The women were surely dead. How many more would die because of the creature? And Folkvardr would bear the shame, for he and Unnr awakened him.

The sun rose as he walked, casting a diseased light through the branches of Ironwood's dead trees. Dry leaves crunched under his feet and he watched carefully, his spear ready.

"Ah, well, one of us is lost," a voice spoke and Folkvardr whirled in his steps, spear aimed at the source of the words. An old woman walked behind him, bent almost in two as she walked with a cane. She looked up and smiled at the weapon that almost pierced her. Folkvardr saw her lips bore odd scars.

"Then it be not I," Folkvardr said, feeling sweat chill on his brow.

The old woman walked forward, ignoring the spear as it slid across her, tangling in her garments before Folkvardr recoiled and pulled the weapon free.

"Come. Let us walk," she said, never pausing in her step.

Folkvardr paced her, never taking his eyes off of her and maintaining a safe distance.

"Do white-haired ladies claim many warriors where you come from?" she asked, laughing softly.

"No. But ettins do," Folkvardr said.

"Really?" she asked. "Be they so common in your land?"

"We make certain they never become common," he said.

"Ah. So you must be the ettin-slayer, so famous in these parts. I smelled Skrati on you."

Folkvardr stopped. The woman did not.

"Come on," she said, and Folkvardr felt a quick pressure against his knees so he fell heavily in the leaves. He lurched to his feet.

"Come on!" the woman called out, neither turning nor stopping.

Folkvardr walked, and the woman reduced her pace until he caught up with her.

"You doubt me, but trust at least these words: do not tarry in this spot. Those who wish to meet you here are less desirable traveling companions than myself," she said, chuckling.

"Who?" he asked.

"I will do you the favor of not answering that."

"And what do you want?" he asked.

"I want to see how far you will get," she answered.

"I will go as far I need to."

"You cannot go far enough to destroy Alrekr. He has gone to a place you cannot go. Truthfully," she said, turning and smiling, showing teeth that should not belong to an old woman.

"What do you know of him?" Folkvardr said, grabbing her shawl as they walked.

"Knowest thou, how to put to sleep?" she said, cackling. "No. That you did not know. Only how to bid. Ha ha! You knew only how to wake him up. Did you like walking with Alrekr? Did you like being one who walks after death, tasting the blood of your people on your lips and doing all the things that crawl about in your black heart? Ha ha!"

Folkvardr was trying to shake her, but she was unmovable, only walking on.

"But now, if you see Alrekr again it will be by his choice and to your disadvantage. There is nothing to be gained of it for you," she said. "But you might be interested to meet friends of yours in Ironwood."

"I have no friends living," Folkvardr said, his teeth clenched.

"Ah! Would you speak so cruelly of those with whom you have shared so much? Would you truly say that of Huld and Unnr? The slave and her mistress, though I know not which is which?" she asked.

"They live?"he gasped. He found himself more relieved for the sake of Huld than of Unnr, and the thought surprised him.

"Oh! Naturally, they live! Here in Ironwood even! They are guests of a most prominent lady here, none other than the very lady of Ironwood!" she said, mocking astonishment.

"Angrboda!" Folkvardr cried out, choking on the name. Angrboda, bearer of Loki's seed, mother of the wolf Fenrir, mother of the Midgard Serpent, mother of Hel, mother of countless wolves by hordes of giants. Ever did her womb bear foul fruit.

"Though, I must say that Alrekr brought them here in a shameful fashion. No matter."

"You are she!" Folkvardr shouted.

"No," the old woman chuckled, standing up straighter now, growing taller, and younger. A beard sprouted from her face, and soon a powerful young man, fair of face and bearing stood in her place, still walking. He still bore the scars around his mouth.

"No. I am not she," the man said, laughing. He slapped Folkvardr hard on the back, sending him sprawling in the mud. "But find Angrboda and you will find your ladies!"

Folkvardr wiped mud from his eyes and when he blinked, the man was gone. But a fat lazy fly circled the air thrice above him and flew in a straight line towards a small mountain that poked its head up above the tree-line in the distance.

Chapter 3
Angrboda

Folkvardr walked until hunger overtook him. He stopped long enough to eat a bit of his cheese and bread. The food seemed to spoil quickly in the fetid air of the forest, but he did not like the looks of the game he saw in Ironwood.

He remembered the mountain and kept his course until nightfall. Though he hated the way the trees seemed to suck all of the light and warmth from the sunlight, he hated it worse when Sunna abandoned her hopeless effort to light the forest, and left on her path beyond the mountains. Then the stench of decay seeped up from the soil, befouled by the poison fungi that sprouted like disease from the flesh of the earth, and in the dimming light drained energy from him.

What do I seek? he asked himself. *I came here to destroy Alrekr. But I believed the women to be dead. What if I can save them, yet, even if it cost me a chance to slay that undead thing? Should I even save Unnr, whose will made all of this manifest? But then I am just as guilty.*

When he found an area with a small cave-like shelter, he wondered for a moment if he'd only walked in a circle and arrived at the previous night's camp. But it was dark now and he did not favor walking far by night in these woods.

Huld wanted no part in this, Folkvardr thought. *I must at least bring her out of this place, and out of whatever torments she now suffers. I will bring her and Unnr out, and then worry about Alrekr.*

As fog rolled in and damp sunk into his bones, he decided to make a small fire, though the light might bring unwelcomed visitors. Did the trolls not know he was here already, anyway? What did it matter? If he was a fey man, then so be it, he reasoned. Better to perish by a warm fire than to die shivering in the dark.

By the light of the fire, Folkvardr saw he lay not in last night's shelter, for the stone in this one was marked by an unknown hand. Lifting a firebrand and holding it closer to the boulder, he saw it was covered with runes, if runes he could call them, for their shape and order were completely alien to him. He puzzled over them until sleep overtook him.

He heard babbling and wailing, and realized he was lying on the floor of the grave. He sat up in time to see the massive bulk of Alrekr walking towards the opening, the flailing form of Huld under one arm, and the cackling form of Unnr under the other. Folkvardr rose to his feet, but his legs failed and he crumpled to the floor, watching as Alrekr carried them off. He called out to them, but heard only the sound of heavy hooves beating the ground outside.

He stared at a torch lying on the floor until the light burned out. Then he screamed at the darkness and plunged headlong towards the opening.

Folkvardr woke to find himself standing in the forest, the miasma reminding him that he was in Ironwood. Mani, the moon, stood high in the sky and Folkvardr silently thanked him for the little light he gave now. He looked about for his campfire. He had built it incautiously high before falling asleep, and it should still have been visible if he had not wandered far from the camp.

He crouched as he heard hoof beats and reached for his spear before realizing he'd left it at camp, or lost it somewhere in the darkened woods. He knelt behind a fallen tree as he tried to place the direction of the sound, his knee sinking into the black mud.

Was it many horses? The noise came from one direction, and then the other, but it never sounded like more than one horse at a time, until the horse appeared mere yards in front of him, thundering down upon him.

Folkvardr ducked, and the mare leaped over him and the fallen tree, the animal's bulk blocking Mani's light as the beast flew through the air. It landed behind him, spraying him with mud as it ran away, churning the muck with her hooves. The pounding on the earth shook him, making him want to hide.

He stared at the horse as it ran into the forest, his heart thumping with fear that grew hot and melted into rage.

Folkvardr rose to his feet, grinding his teeth and wiping mud from his soiled clothing. But when he turned he saw a maiden standing between the trees, staring at the moon, her white shift gleaming in the silvery light. She tucked her dark hair behind her ears.

"One day," he heard her say as she stroked her belly.The words skittering along the leaves and into his ears. She was fair of form, her limbs perfectly shaped, her full bosom heaving as she sighed deeply before turning to look at him.

Folkvardr leaned against the tree when her eyes met his. He saw her clearly, in a way that defied the night's shadows. Her eyes were black, and no white showed surrounding her irises. Yet they glittered and shone with a light that was not light.

"You found me," she said. "Fárbauti's son said that you would." She held out her hand.

Folkvardr walked towards her. He heard something inhuman scream far away to his left, and something far away to his right answered it. He took her hand. His skin tingled under her fingers. He realized it was actually moving ever so slightly, every inch of skin delicately twitching. The thought of tiny animals came to mind, but he pushed that thought away. Her eyes stared into him. A musky smell made him feel dizzy, made him want to be with her.

She held his hand and led him as they walked, and the forest no longer seemed so dark. Where Mani's light failed, the fungi illuminated the way. When they walked through streams, the water felt cool and refreshing on his feet and legs.

And wherever they walked, shapes slipped in and out of the darkness, pacing them. The realization they were very large wolves startled Folkvardr for a moment, and the laughing howl of one of them made the beauty of the forest shimmer for a moment, and almost collapse. But the woman stroked his cheek and smiled with her white, pointed teeth. He watched a frog, shining and silver in the light, as it ate a smaller frog. He laughed and no longer cared about the wolves as they walked.

"You have traveled far," she said to him.

"Indeed, I have," Folkvardr said, happy to speak with her, eager to hear her talk.

"Why?" she asked, pivoting to stand in front of him. She looked at him, he thought, like a farmer looks at a hog before cutting its throat.

Folkvardr searched his memory. Why had he come to Ironwood? It was hard to remember now. He grinned as he found an answer, for he hoped to please her.

"To find you!" he said.

"How do you know that you have found me?" she asked.

"Of course I have. You are next to me and I am holding your hand," he said.

"But how do you know who I am?" she asked, smiling in a way that sent a tremor through Folkvardr's heart, for he feared if the smile should leave her lips.

"Who else could you be?" he asked. "I can feel it."

"Then, you know my name?" she asked.

"Yes. You are Angrboda," he answered.

"Am I?" she asked. "What if she is Angrboda?" The maiden nodded her head in the direction of Folkvardr's other side.

He turned to look. A woman walked on his other flank now. Her hair was like red flame, her eyes like icy-blue sapphires. She was naked save for a string-skirt. Folkvardr felt himself shaking. As he watched, something dark rippled over the woman's body, and he realized it was fur growing and covering her entire body. She hunched low, on all fours now, and ran away, her shape changing completely into that of an enormous wolf.

Folkvardr turned back to the dark-haired girl, and she flickered in the corner of his vision before he saw her completely. But now she smiled again, pulling him along by the hand as they walked.

"Come," she said, laughing in silver. "If you would like me to be Angrboda, then I am she. And why would you seek me then?"

"To slay Angrboda and rescue his women!" Folkvardr heard, the voice of a giggling girl pealing next to his ear, but when he turned to look, no one was there; only the wolves, still walking along in the woods around them.

"Yes. That is so," Folkvardr said, his stomach sinking as he remembered. "I did. I did come to kill you. But," He tried to remember how he felt. It seemed he'd come to kill her, to destroy Alrekr, or at least put him to sleep again. "But that was so long ago," he trailed off.

"And what of Huld? What of Unnr?" the woman asked.

The names startled him.

"Yes! But," he stuttered. He knew they were important to him once, but could not understand why now. The path felt hard beneath Folkvardr's feet, the ground stony. . He looked up and saw huge jagged stones, larger than halls, rose out of the earth around them. Like massive teeth, the stones jutted from the soil. Folkvardr thought some of them must surely fall over, for the angles seemed all wrong. The stones stood where they should have fallen, and hung precariously on the slope of the mountain rising before them.

The wolves no longer followed them here, but other shapes lurked in the shadows of the stones. Folkvardr wondered where they were going, but it was enough simply to follow her and watch how Mani's light danced in her shiny black tresses. He felt things touching him now as he walked, sometimes caressing him, sometimes jabbing him roughly, but he ignored them all and walked on.

"You will see them again," she said.

He frowned, irritated at being reminded of them, and of his original idea of slaying Angrboda.

"But who first told you my name?" Angrboda asked him.

"One who wore many skins told me. She, or he, told me to find you here, in Ironwood. And then I would find Unnr. And Huld," he said, slowly remembering.

"Ah. Perhaps you met an ancestor of mine," Angrboda said, singing the words.

"Perhaps," Folkvardr said.

He felt her pulling him hard by the wrist now, and looked back. The slope pitched down steeply beneath them. The rocky ground rose steeper and steeper, and soon Angrboda was more lifting him by the arm than holding his hand. He staggered and lost his footing often, sending stones rattling down the mountain, but his guide never released her grip. Though she kept him from falling to his death, he struggled to keep on his feet, for when he fell she only dragged him up and over the jagged stones. He felt himself bleeding from a dozen small cuts, but she never stopped the ascent. When he looked where she stepped, he saw the once-dainty feet now bore horny, black talons that scraped and gripped the rock.

He struggled to breathe now as the air thinned, the cold stinging him as he gasped to fill his lungs. Mani rested on the far side of the mountain now, taking the light with him. The stars in the sky felt very close to Folkvardr, and he wondered if they would soon be able to touch them, for the mountain seemed to have no end.

Folkvardr felt himself pulled over a ledge, his arm nearly yanked from its socket, and he waited to fall over a precipice. Instead, he found himself on flat stone. He no longer knew if he would fall or ascend, but collapsed instead, and shut his eyes.

When he opened them again, he found he was burning with cold, the wind cutting and ripping at him. But there was a hole in the rock wall above him, and somewhere within, flames flickered.

He remembered everything now, and cursed himself for his weakness. He'd been close enough to strike Angrboda, yet he did not, could not. He could not descend the mountain without dying, for he had little clothing, no rope, and it was night. Perhaps it was always night here, he thought. He did not know where Huld or Unnr were, and the cold wind would soon kill him.

He rose, his body aching, and gripped the rock face before him. He climbed slowly, using the small openings to inch his way up. He reached the ledge and pulled himself up and into the hole. He curled up and closed his eyes, eager to at least die in warmth. A new wave of pain swept him then, as his numb limbs now coursed with warm blood, burning his nerves.

Folkvardr opened his eyes. He was in a cave, and fire burned in many pots resting in niches in the walls. He rose and followed the passage forward until it forked. Taking one turn and then another, soon he no longer remembered his path.

Emerging into an open chamber, he saw a large fire burned from a pit in the center. He heard stone grinding behind him, and found the passage behind him no longer existed: only a stone wall. Exhausted, he collapsed and sat with his back to the wall. Hunger twisted his stomach, but the fire warmed him and sucked the last vestige of cold from his bones.

Something moved within the flames, and as they parted, Folkvardr felt the fire pulling the breath from his lungs. Angrboda stepped out of the curtain of flames now, and his breath returned, burning like cinders within him. She stood naked before him, larger now, her breasts heavy and full. He felt her black eyes somehow pressing into him.

And now wolves walked into the room from somewhere beyond the pit, skirting the fire and approaching Angrboda, each of them massive. They sat down next to her, licking their yellow teeth, firelight dancing in their eyes as they stared at Folkvardr.

All the wolves sat but two. These last two wolves carried ropes in their teeth, and at the end of one rope crawled Huld, at the end of the other, Unnr. Both women wore heavy iron collars, and the mark of the birch decorated their backs and buttocks with spidery lines of crimson. Huld crawled on hands and knees, and looked at Folkvardr with a mixture of relief and fear. But Unnr walked on hands and feet now, her rear posed high in the air, and feral intensity blazed in her pale eyes.

Folkvardr rose to his knees as Angrboda approached him. Her arms encircled him, and the hunger burned hotter in his stomach as she pressed him to her breast. He opened his mouth and took her large nipple into his mouth, sucking. He felt tears on his cheeks as warm milk spurted into his mouth, honey-like in its sweetness. His hunger felt endless as he drank and drank, feeling his cock swell.

Angrboda pulled him to the floor as she laid down, holding his head fast to her breast as she nursed him. He felt his tattered clothing being pulled from him and looked to see the red-haired woman from the forest undressing him. As he knelt over Angrboda, kneading her breast, he felt a tongue on his anus, licking and penetrating him as a warm, slimy hand pumped his cock.

Folkvardr felt the flesh shifting under his hands, as Angrboda's belly swelled and rippled. Her torso stretched, a row of breasts swelling out from her distended form. He was almost pushed aside as the wolves pressed in against him, each of them seeking their own teat, snapping and biting at each other. All around him whirred flashing fangs and hot wolf's breath, until the winners took their spoils and lapped hungrily at the milk flowing from Angrboda's nipples.

Folkvardr fought desperately to maintain his place, clawing and biting at the snarling forms around him, feeling come pumping out of his penis as the ettin-woman's long tongue fucked his rectum. But he held his own place and when he had drunk his fill, he stood, a buzzing in his head.

He saw Huld on all fours, trying to bear the weight of an enormous wolf now mounting her. The beast's forelegs were clenched tight under her arms, and he growled as his hips pumped furiously. As her shoulders sunk lower, Folkvardr saw she was pushing back with her broad ass, using her hips to bear the wolf's weight. Folkvardr watched as she first winced and bit her lip, but soon her mouth was opened and she was yelping, her face flushed as she cried out. The wolf leered at Folkvardr, and he recognized Skrati now.

Many of the wolves now dozed before the fire, but two others yet stood. Unnr crouched, her head under the belly of one, suckling the creature's red penis as it licked its lips. Behind Unnr, a wolf bitch licked the fluids dripping from the blonde's cunt, her long tongue licking the crease.

Folkvardr felt himself pulled to the floor by strong hands, and then Angrboda was on top of him, pulling his penis into her slit. He felt his body quiver involuntarily, and an orgasm shook through him, the giantess's vagina clenching and milking the sperm from him.

He wanted to run away then, away from the black mirrors of Angrboda's eyes. She smiled at him then, her teeth sharper and whiter now, and held him by his shoulders, pinning him to the floor.

He struggled to push her away, to climb out from beneath her, but she only laughed, clenching his prick inside, forcing him to stay erect.

She leaned forward, and as he felt her teeth biting into his shoulder, he felt his will slipping away. He no longer felt the floor beneath him, only Angrboda as she milked him of sperm again and again. He heard howling and smelled blood as her teeth nipped and nicked his skin.

Darkness fell over the fire like a curtain. Folkvardr felt himself falling, seeing nothing but blackness. Cold air buffeted as he fell and he willed himself to feel nothing.

He remembered the sensation of being on a horse, and when the blackness left him, he found himself lying in cold grass, his limbs locked with a warm body. He stared into Huld's eyes as they embraced.

Laughter devoid of sanity rattled in his ears, and he looked up to see Unnr dancing next to them where they lay outside of the barrow mound. Strange runes, freshly carven, trickled blood down the skin of her stomach.

Huld and Folkvardr rose and stared at the rising sun. An old woman walked by them and looked at Unnr, pausing for a moment to watch the blonde woman's mad dance.

"Ah, well, one of us *is* lost," the old woman said. She cackled and turned away, and Huld and Folkvardr watched as she disappeared into the woods.

If you enjoyed this story, you can sign up for a free membership at ForbiddenFiction and discuss it with other readers and the author at the *Tomb Brides* story page at http://forbiddenfiction.com/story/KH1-1.000176.

All Consuming

Chapter 1
Bait

Jacqueline clutched the heavy fishing rod and waited for a shark to hit the bait. She sat on a folding beach chair, digging her toes into the sand as she stared at the moon. Jacqueline fingered the megalodon tooth hanging on a cord around her neck. She untangled wind-blown strands of her curly blond hair from the cord. *One year since you left, Genesis,* she thought. *How did you do it? Did you try to swim out? Or did you just keep walking in?* The waves crawled towards Jacqueline's feet, moving in as high tide approached.

Jacqueline sat with her knees wide apart, because between her legs rested a complicated contraption. She wore a fighting belt and harness with a back belt. Used for bringing in big game fish like tuna, the belt held a sort of hard plastic codpiece, with a socket to hold the butt of the fishing rod. The device made the rod steadier, allowing the fisher more power in reeling in, and preventing fatigue.

Jacqueline's fighting belt, however, contained a secret. A prong protruded from the base of the socket, and this prong would fasten into the butt of the rod. But the other end of the fitting, the part behind the codpiece, ended in a flexible silicone curve, which fastened to a vibrator, which rested inside Jacqueline's vagina, held in place by the codpiece of the fighting belt.

Donning and inserting the device required privacy, which Jacqueline found only by driving her jeep to an isolated part of the beach, late at night. The better parts of the beach for fishing unfortunately attracted fishermen, and Jacqueline wanted no human company if her contraption worked as planned. If it worked, as it worked when she tested it, inserting the rod butt into the socket with pressure would turn on the vibrator. The movement of the shark would move the vibrator inside.

In the sand next to her rested an arsenal of equipment. A hefty tackle box held an assortment of hooks, sinkers, ball swivels, and various hardware. A second fishing rod rested in a sand spike. Two smaller rods, which she used to catch bait fish, rested next to her kayak. Both of her main rods were short for surf fishing; one was five feet long, the other was seven. But longer rods would give too much leverage for a big fish to use against her.

Most of Jacqueline's equipment represented the extreme end of what one would need to fish for sharks; most fishermen she knew would use much lighter equipment. As a short woman, she received many comments and strange looks regarding her stature and equipment. Each of her two rods held over 1000 yards of line. Each line ended in a wire leader, which served to prevent a shark from slicing the monofilament fishing line. Each leader consisted of #19 single-strand wire doubled up and attached to a 500-pound-test crane swivel, crimped to six feet of 500-pound-test monofilament line, with another 500-pound-test crane swivel at the other end of the monofilament. At the end of each leader hung a 20/0 circle hook, with a mullet—a bait fish—impaled on it. The circle hooks reduced the likelihood of the shark swallowing the hook and lodging it in its gut. The circle hook was designed to hook the fish with minimal injury, allowing the fisher to release the shark back into the water. One hook rested about two hundred yards out from the beach, the second, about four hundred yards.

Such ranges would be unreachable by casting, and so, next to her other equipment rested her surf kayak. Jacqueline didn't fish from the kayak; she only used it to paddle out the bait, a few hundred yards off the beach, where the water could be fifteen feet deep, which was deep enough for a very large shark. Jacqueline originally planned to fish from a boat, but the expense of an adequate boat proved far beyond her means. Her rod and reel setups alone cost her over $500 each, the kayak close to $600 to get a good one with a back rest.

She practiced fishing and paddling out in the daytime, spilling her kayak many times before she got the hang of it. But being hundreds of yards out from the beach, with oily bait fish with her in the surf kayak, by moonlight, proved both nerve-racking and exhilarating. Tonight was her first experience paddling the surf in the dark, and a half hour after she was back on dry land, her hands still shook with adrenaline. She wore a flotation device, a suspenders-like harness, which would inflate with carbon dioxide if she pulled a ring. A strap secured her thick glasses in the event of a spill. She wore a wet suit, too, when she paddled out. The water wasn't terribly cold, but she read most hypothermia cases occur in the summer. She knew if you floated long in any water below 98.6 degrees F, it would eventually leech away body heat. She was glad she brought a hand-held GPS because it looked like a mile when she was only four hundred yards away from the beach.

But back in the beach chair, she sat in a different world. Out there, she only worried about getting out far enough, about dropping the bait in the right place, about not spilling the kayak. It was a world where only survival mattered, where you have to make correct decisions. But back here on land, she was in a world where people like Genesis walked into the surf because nothing mattered anymore.

Jacqueline reached into the gear bag next to her chair until she found the vodka bottle. She held it up, reading the name "CZAR," the moonlight reflected in metallic letters on the label of the flask-sized bottle. Jacqueline unscrewed the cap and sniffed the contents.

"Ugh," she said, exhaling the solvent-like fumes. She put it to her lips and swigged like she was drinking spring water. "Oh, fuck," she gasped, choking on the taste. "How did you drink this all the time, Genesis?" Jacqueline rarely drank alcohol, and never straight liquor. She coughed at the burn, trying to spit out the aftertaste. She hated everything about vodka, especially the way it seeped out of Genesis' pores in the morning, after the woman had been drinking the night before. She hated the way it smelled on her partner's breath, promising tears and arguments later. But on the anniversary of her lover's death, what the authorities called an 'accidental drowning', Jacqueline had to know what taste Genesis last knew. The police found an empty Czar bottle next to Genesis' clothing in the sand. Jacqueline had to know what it tasted like. And it tasted like death.

How exactly did I get to this place? It's weird isn't it, my interest in sharks? Genesis let me know it was, at least towards the end of things. Who could I explain this to? I thought I could share it with her, the only person I ever did try to share it with, and I let her die. With Genesis gone, the beach might as well have been a desert island with no one to ever share her life. *What I care about makes me a monster.*

Jacqueline thought about the time, at the age of twelve, when her passions first made her feel monstrous. In the pre-Internet days of her childhood, she began nosing through the boxes of her Uncle Greg's things, the boxes stowed away and forgotten in Jacqueline's grandparents' attic. On one hot and sleepy summer day, Jacqueline was bored enough to sort through a big box of sports and motorcycle magazines. At the bottom of the box, two types of magazines startled her and made her look to see if the attic door was closed.

One type consisted of dirty magazines, with glossy pictures of women posed and exposed. The second was composed of lurid shark attack magazines, rough looking publications with grainy photos on pulpy paper. Both types fascinated her, but in different ways.

She had always loved sharks. She knew the dirty magazines were forbidden, but she didn't know about the shark ones. Both types offered Jacqueline a look into people, sometimes literally into people, in very intimate ways. The anatomical displays of the skin mags contrasted with the many black-and-white photos of shark attack victims. Sometimes, they were alive and well, showing off their huge, bite-shaped scars. Sometimes, all that remained were some shredded remains on the beach. Jacqueline spent hours staring at open human orifices, open bite wounds, and the open, gaping mouths of sharks. While she owned a number of shark books, posters, and paraphernalia from her parents, she knew these magazines were different, pornographic in the luridness of the illustrations. Her parents bought educational books, striving to direct the wide eyes of their little curly-haired daughter towards healthy knowledge, while trying unsuccessfully to prevent her from seeing any of the *Jaws* movies. They said the movies would give her nightmares, but instead they only fed her dreams.

It took a number of trips, but by her thirteenth birthday, Jacqueline completed moving her treasure trove into her room in her own house, a few magazines at a time hidden in her backpack. Not knowing if her parents would take the shark mags, which she valued more than the other type, she hid both kinds of publications.

As early as she could remember, sharks gave her a particular thrill. She remembered visiting an aquarium for the first time. In one section of the aquarium, the thick glass walls curved overhead to form the ceiling. When the sand tiger and lemon sharks swam overhead, she pictured the glass falling away and imagined herself swimming in the water with the sharks, their eyes like strange marbles, the jagged blades of their teeth jutting out. She had a falling feeling in her crotch, the way riding on a roller coaster made her feel.

It was at this time when she first dreamed of the bull shark. Though she dreamed often of sharks, one night she dreamed of walking down a set of steps from the beach. A stone staircase began in the sand and descended into the surf. Curious, she followed it, the waves knocking her back as she tried to follow them down. But once beneath the surface, the water was calm, and she could look down a rocky slope littered with bones of many creatures. Stones appeared to be piled into certain formations, not just randomly scattered. Jacqueline was aware of neither being able to breathe water, nor of drowning. She could see clearly underwater, an act successful in waking life only with an awkward arrangement of her thick glasses under a pair of old scuba goggles, but now she needed no glass barrier before her eyes.

Then She appeared. She didn't know how she knew the bull shark was female, but in her strange dream logic, it seemed obvious. Jacqueline could neither swim towards Her, nor swim away, but could only remain where she half-stood, half-floated. But she could look at nothing else but Her as She pulsed through the water. Jacqueline wanted to cry or laugh or somehow express the emotions twisting inside of her. The creature looked the normal size for Her species, yet a vastness about Her crushed Jacqueline. Her dark eye fell open her and Jacqueline shook, the shark's mouth opening just enough to reveal teeth. She looked perfect but seemed old in the way that mountains are old, and Jacqueline was allowed to be with the beast for that moment, just a moment before the shark turned and disappeared into the darkness. Jacqueline panicked, fearing she would never see Her again, and she launched herself from the steps to swim after Her, but she could not swim, and only sunk deeper down the staircase before waking up from the dream.

Growing up, she dreamed of Her again and again, and her obsession with sharks never faded. She begged her parents for every vacation to be at a beach. She watched every TV show she could about sharks. She found them all interesting, including the nurse sharks, the whale sharks, and the basking sharks. But the man eaters she held in a special awe. Whites. Bulls. Tigers. She learned that Jacques Cousteau regarded the Oceanic white-tip shark as the most dangerous of all, though its location in the middle of the ocean prevented much contact with humans.

Jacqueline wanted to swim as often as she could. Her parents tried to interest her in the swim team, but she refused, year after year. Her parents saw an excellent swimmer who spent hours in the pool, and even longer out in the ocean during beach vacations. What Jacqueline saw was a home in the water, where she fantasized about swimming with sharks, even about being a shark. Knowing she shared the water with them excited her. She wanted to see one up close, not trapped behind a Plexiglas wall, but free. She wanted to feel its hard body against hers, flexing, maybe even raking its teeth along her thigh, just enough to cut, just enough to share that most basic of exchange with the godlike creature.

Lost in reverie, Jacqueline often looked at the other girls in the water, swimming near them, smiling and talking, but also seeing how close she could get. Her poor vision prevented her from seeing their expressions without her glasses, which she never wore while swimming. Instead, she had to judge their attitude by body language. It made the process feel primal to her, predatory.

Jacqueline, like her mother, never grew beyond five foot one, but developed a compact and attractive figure. Her parents wistful questions about boys grew fewer and fewer, replaced with brittle queries about the female friendships their daughter seemed to almost hunt. And it was a hunt, as far as Jacqueline was concerned, as she collected secrets shared in nocturnal swims with her friends. She preferred moonless nights, when the shadows evened out the disadvantages of her vision. The less light, Jacqueline found, the more experimental her companions became. The darker the night, the deeper the secrets.

On a class trip to a museum, she bought a megalodon tooth, hanging it on a necklace when she got home. From that day on, she wore it daily, feeling the fossil sliding on her skin.

And as Jacqueline traversed adolescence, the victim photos always hung in the back of her thoughts, providing both pleasure and shame. The magazines took on a different role in her life. She had her favorite victims, and their pages grew especially worn over the years. On page 43 of *Jaws of Blood* magazine, surfer Becky Milligan showed off the giant oval of railroad track stitches covering her ribcage. On page 6 of *Killer Great Whites*, an unnamed dark-haired girl — Jacqueline called her 'Sally' — displayed the stump of her arm. On page twenty three of *Bloody Jaws of Death* magazine, the mangled remains of an unidentified female swimmer lay next to the slit open belly of a bull shark in South America. Often, she pictured the victims as her friends from school, or as herself.

By the time she reached adulthood, the Internet had arrived, opening up endless images of sharks, sharks attacking other sharks, sharks attacking other animals, sharks attacking humans, human remains of shark attacks, and every variation of shark-inflicted injury. Moving into a dorm and away from her parents' eyes allowed her to pursue both her shark obsession and her interest in girls with greater devotion, her secret world now expanding. She even, for a time, considered trying to meet survivors of shark attacks, and fantasized about women bearing the curved, jagged scars.

But with the freedom to pursue her interests, Jacqueline also gained the confidence to share her thoughts with another biology major named Sarah. A pixie-like blonde with freckles and braces, smaller than Jacqueline, Sarah was the first girl she ever kissed in public. Sarah made her feel like she could be herself, that the sky wouldn't fall just because you did the unusual thing, because you liked something people said you weren't supposed to like. Out in public, people asked if the blondes were sisters, and the thought both flattered and turned Jacqueline on. She grew very close to Sarah, closer than she had to any other girl.

One rainy day, she lay with Sarah in the upper bunk bed of Jacqueline's dorm room. Jacqueline's roommate had gone home for the weekend, leaving an opportunity for the girls to enjoy some time alone. Sarah's slim little body rested half on top of Jacqueline, her freckled cheek laying against her chest, her breath tickling Jacqueline's broad nipples. The room smelled like sex, and Jacqueline smiled, feeling the opiate-like, post-orgasmic fuzz clinging to her brain.

"Can I show you something?" Jacqueline asked, trailing her fingertips down Sarah's spine.

"Mmm. Long as I don't have to get up," Sarah said, twitching with a shiver of pleasure, nuzzling closer.

"Then I can't show you," Jacqueline said.

Sarah sat up and smiled. She threw her leg over Jacqueline's waist and straddled her, leaning over her. Her wet pubes brushed Jacqueline's belly, her small breasts hanging slightly. Jacqueline was used to being the assertive one with girls, at least in private. Sarah was different, more like how she thought of guys behaving. Sarah dipped her head and kissed her suddenly, mouth wet and open, before rolling off of Jacqueline to sit cross-legged on the bed.

"Show me, then," Sarah said.

Jacqueline got up and put on her glasses. She climbed down the ladder to the cool linoleum floor, opened up her closet and pulled out a box. Sarah hung her head over the edge of the bed to watch her. Jacqueline thought of telling Sarah to come down from the bunk to see, but decided to bring it up instead.

Jacqueline lifted the box and handed it to Sarah.

"Should I open it?" Sarah asked.

Chapter 2
Sharing Secrets

"Wait," Jacqueline said, clambering back up the ladder. She sat down cross-legged across from Sarah, the box between them, and opened it. Jacqueline took out a few of the slightly yellowed tabloid shark magazines. Each one was bagged in a clear, protective sleeve.

"Ha! Jaws of Death!" Sarah laughed. "Diver Survives Deadly Ordeal with Monster Great White! Where did you get these?" Sarah upended one, letting it slide out of the sleeve and flop on the bed.

"Careful!" Jacqueline said, smoothing the cover. "My uncle."

"Oh, are these, like, collectible?" Sarah asked, flipping through the pages. "Ew. Gross. It's like shark attack porn. Are these all like that?" Sarah started digging through the box.

Jacqueline felt herself blush, regretting her decision to share as Sarah started to pull out the various images printed from online photos. A female surfer lying dead on the beach from blood loss after losing a buttock. A woman hauled onto a dock, minus several limbs. A close-up of a gashed thigh from a victim with a hairy vulva. A woman missing one breast and one arm, the healed skin pulled tight. Various pictures of sharks, either swimming sleekly or attacking bait with yawning maws.

"What are you showing me?" Sarah asked, frowning. "Your uncle printed these off?"

"Yeah. I guess," Jacqueline said, clearing her throat. "Yeah, pretty fucked up, right?" She forced a laugh and started quickly boxing the images and magazines back up.

"Wait," Sarah said, digging into the box again.

"No, c'mon," Jacqueline said, trying to push Sarah's hand away, but the blonde was faster.

"So," Sarah said, pulling out the clear Tupperware box, the dildos and vibrator within it rolling around. She grinned as she looked at it. "Why didn't you just show me these?"

"Well, yeah, I was going to!" Jacqueline said.

"These aren't your uncle's?" Sarah asked.

"No! They're mine!" Jacqueline laughed, eager to move the topic away from the images.

"How old is your uncle?" Sarah asked.

"He died when I was really little. He was in his twenties."

"But the pictures are his?" Sarah asked.

"Yeah," Jacqueline said, opening the lid to the sex toy box and smiling at Sarah.

"So, that's a pretty good printer for the early 70s," Sarah said.

"Yeah, I guess." Jacqueline took the vibrator out of the box and turned it on, sliding it along Sarah's thigh, feeling awkward.

"Really?" Sarah said, taking the vibe from Jacqueline's hand and turning it off. "He didn't print them, did he, Jacqueline?"

"No."

"You did," Sarah said, lightly circling Jacqueline's nipple with the tip of the vibe. "Right?" Sarah turned on the toy and the buzz in her teat made Jacqueline jump. Sarah put her other hand on Jacqueline's back, guiding her down until she was on all fours. Sarah picked up a photo of a white shark erupting from the water, attacking a hunk of meat. She set the photo on the bed in front of Jacqueline, and next to it, a picture of a bloodied, dark-haired woman being pulled from the surf.

Jacqueline's body tingled. Excited from the anticipation of what Sarah would do, she stared at the images, the pink maw of the shark, the teeth about to penetrate the meat, the eruption of power from the water, the torn woman, whose flesh knew the might of those teeth, becoming one with the beast as it tore her apart. She gasped as the tip of the vibrator buzzed directly on her clit.

"Easy!" Jacqueline whispered. It was too much all at once, and she squirmed.

"You don't like that?" Sarah said, not relenting, but pressing harder.

"Just, go easy!" Jacqueline squealed.

But Sarah wrestled her as she tried to squirm away, using her knees to keep Jacqueline's legs open, using her free hand to push Jacqueline's head down into the bed. Jacqueline felt angry and hurt, the vibration overwhelming her nerves. The forced orgasm twitched through her body, Jacqueline's face mashed into the crumpled print-out of the shark as warmth pulsed through her body. The mixture of the climax and humiliation confused her, like she was eating cake while people laughed at her. The vibrator penetrated her vagina, still buzzing on high, making her groan as it sunk deep inside. Sarah let go of her and the vibrator slid out, rattling wetly on top of a torn magazine.

Jacqueline spun around, wiping tears from her eyes under her fogged glasses. Sarah climbed down the ladder and began tugging on her clothes.

"Why did you do that?" Jacqueline sobbed, trying to understand what just happened. "Where are you going?"

"Thought you'd like it. You know, getting off on dead people and everything," Sarah shrugged, her expression cold. "Enjoy your shark porn," she said, turning and leaving.

Pain stabbed into Jacqueline's gut as the door closed behind Sarah.

"Fucking bitch!" she yelled, punching her pillow. Sarah could've simply left, and Jacqueline didn't understand why her lover did it the way she did. "I'm a fucking idiot. Fucking idiot," she sobbed.

Despite the humiliation, Jacqueline still tried to call Sarah, who ignored her from that point on. The experience left Jacqueline hardened and cold. And the small lesbian population of her college reacted differently to her now, the well apparently poisoned by Sarah's snickering whispers.

Isolated with her passions, her masturbation took on an almost religious ceremony. If the world chose to reject her as a freak, she chose to turn inward, embracing her fantasies. She imagined the pain of the victim, flesh torn in a frenzy of violence by the most perfect creature on Earth. Sharks had survived for four hundred and fifty million years. A form older than dinosaurs, any human taken seemed like the merest sacrifice to ultimate beauty.

Upon graduation and getting her own house in a shore town, her shark adoration increased. Shark artwork, books, and artifacts filled the home. On her twenty-fifth birthday, she declined a parental invitation to go out for dinner, and decided to celebrate as she celebrated many nights.

Living alone, she enjoyed not having to lock her bedroom door, though habit coaxed her to close it. Her collection had only grown over the years. Though she had thousands of electronic images, the hard copy remained crucial for her, nurtured by habit. She set printouts of her most recent and favorite pictures at the foot of her bed.

The magazines lay open to her favorite photos, several propped on music stands next to the bed. And on a table pulled alongside the bed sat the jaws of a mako shark, a full twenty inches wide. Smaller sets of shark jaws surrounded the mako. The smaller ones she bought over the years at shore-town and boardwalk tchotchke shops. The size of the jaws increased as Jacqueline grew older. She slipped off her clothing as she looked at her relics, her skin tingling, her nerves growing more sensitive.

Jacqueline gazed at the array of images. A bull shark coasted through murky water, massive in its streamlined bulk. A white shark erupting from the water, carrying a seal yards above the surface. A woman smiled at the camera, her one arm proudly holding a surfboard, the other arm missing below a scarred stump close to her shoulder. A redhead crumpled on her side on the beach, sand clinging to her black wetsuit, except for the part where the suit was torn away, exposing a deep red gash from thigh to lower back, flesh torn into the shape of folds.

Jacqueline imagined parting those folds with her hands, reaching into the still warm flesh, slick with blood. She imagined being the woman at the same time, imagining herself reaching into herself. She knelt on the bed, running her hands down her body, imagining the wounds of various victims on her own body. She sat back into the nest of pillows arranged behind her. Her hand immediately went to her slit, dipping her fingertip inside. Her secretions were thick as egg whites this week, and her index finger reached her fattened clit, slipping the hood up. She circled the bump once, twice, three times, changing direction just as the sweet crush started to pulse through.

Her free hand went to one nipple, then the other, squeezing, tugging as she climaxed, an electric tingle rippling through her body as she imagined herself spinning underwater.

Jacqueline collapsed back into her nest, letting herself grow heavy and sink. She focused on the painting on the wall of a hammerhead, its underside silvery, a cloud of fish silhouetted in the water above it. Its smooth angularity confounded her, fascinated her, the beast's body sleek and smooth. She realized she was cupping her hand over her wet vulva, rubbing herself again. She wasn't finished, yet.

She reached behind her pillow nest, fumbling through an assortment of sex toys. She felt the cool smoothness of her stainless steel dildo, and it felt right in her hand. She hefted the heavy toy, a hook-like curve with a round knob on either end. She leaned back again, tilting her hips. Pressing the head on the dildo against her wet folds, she let the steel slide in under its own weight, letting gravity penetrate her. The hook slid in and she moaned as it followed her contours, as if making its own way to her G-spot. Cool at first, the metal quickly warmed as she let it lay in place, feeling the pressure of the knob inside for a moment before sliding it in and out. Jacqueline only needed the slightest movement for it to feel good, the slick hook rubbing and pressing inside her pussy, the curve sliding up and down, just beneath her clit.

Blood throbbed in her temples and she craved release. She touched her swollen clit as she pressed the steel deep inside, no longer gently circling her nub but rubbing it. Pressure rose in her chest and she fucked herself hard, watching her lips tighten around the rod, taking it deeper and deeper as she came, grunting. A thousand little jolts of pleasure rocked her body, and she clenched tight, feeling herself squirting fluid. She looked at the hammerhead painting and felt surrounded by salt water, inhaling it, letting it fill her lungs. She closed her eyes and for a moment, she was the hammerhead, and before her, she saw Her, the bull shark, the one her dreams never abandoned. The image lasting fleeting seconds before leaving her to collapse into her nest again.

Jacqueline's solitary pleasures continued, hidden from the world. She retreated socially, haunting the beach and her own imagination, meeting the bull shark again and again in her dreams. She interfaced with the outside world as needed, like eating or excreting, activities necessary for survival. But it would be Genesis who would breach that barrier.

Jacqueline had been in no way looking for a partner. A tiny art gallery in town featured work by various painters, none of them known to her. One oil painting, lit by a shaft of sunlight, caught her eye through the window. She stepped inside to look closer. The painting depicted two boys swimming in a creek, their eyes wide with terror as they pointed at something outside of the viewer's perspective. The painting was titled *Wyckoff Dock*, by an artist named Genesis de Jesus. Wyckoff Dock seemed somehow familiar to Jacqueline, and she searched the term on her phone. She smiled as Matawan appeared in the search results. Wyckoff Dock on Matawan Creek was the scene of several deaths during the 1916 New Jersey shark attacks.

The featured artists would be appearing at the gallery the next night. The painting reached Jacqueline deep inside, a moment of communication with someone who might at least touch upon her own world. She decided to attend the event, if only to get a look at Genesis in person.

That night at home, she found a few photos online of Genesis. She expected Genesis to be a man, but was pleased to find the artist was female. The woman's hair was a mass of long, black curls, her skin a creamy light brown. She seemed to be of mixed race, perhaps mostly Hispanic, but with an exotic Caribbean look suggesting ancestry from many lands.

Jacqueline forcibly suppressed her excitement. She could expect no special connection with this woman; she was just an artist who painted a shark related painting. Nothing more, she told herself.

The next night, Jacqueline pulled on a snug, green dress and arranged her curly blond hair to frame her face, calling herself stupid the entire time. *Who are you trying to impress?* She pushed her feet into a pair of high heels, adding a few inches to her height. *Really, do you think it will matter to anyone? Inside, you are still a monster to everyone else.*

Her compulsion to meet the artist overrode her self-loathing and carried her to the gallery. Jacqueline spotted Genesis immediately, the artist engaged in conversation with a couple in their mid-30's. Her hair looked every bit as wild as it did in the pictures. The woman wore a long pleated black skirt and a tight top. She was much curvier in real life, with full breasts, and a round bottom filling out the back of her skirt. She stood a few inches taller than Jacqueline. Jacqueline pretended to look at the other artwork as long her patience could bear, but when she found herself within range of Genesis, she waited for her chance.

"*Wyckoff Dock*," Jacqueline blurted out as Genesis faced her. Genesis's expression seemed different as she smiled, as though emitting light and energy. Jacqueline could look at that smile all night. But Jacqueline stumbled over herself, having nothing to say, her mind blanking.

"You like it?" Genesis asked, her voice warm and soft, a little deep and husky. She stepped closer to Jacqueline. Jacqueline nipples hardened and she clenched her fists to stop from shivering. She smelled flowers in the woman's perfume. "I painted that last year," Genesis said. "Are you aware of the story behind it?"

"Yes," Jacqueline said, happy to have something to hold onto in the conversation, trying to focus as she stared into Genesis's big brown eyes. "Matawan Creek? 1916?"

"The shark attacks?" Genesis said, her smile broadening as she put her hand on Jacqueline's arm. Jacqueline felt light-headed, her vagina opening with excitement, becoming wet even as her mouth grew dry with anxiety.

"Yes!" Jacqueline said. "I'm convinced that it was, in fact, a white, the white caught by Schleisser in Raritan Bay. I mean, it had human remains inside of it. So if that wasn't the shark, or one of the sharks, involved, then we'd have to be looking at multiple types, which makes a statistically rare event even more rare. It seems more parsimonious to go with the white as the likely suspect."

Genesis looked at her with what Jacqueline knew must be amusement. She knew she was getting carried away, but still she prattled on about sharks, unable to stop, unable to anchor herself.

"This is fascinating," Genesis eventually said, cutting her off at one point as other people waited impatiently. "Listen, I'd really like to talk more another night. Can I get your number?"

"Sure," Jacqueline said, wanting to punch herself, hating herself for wanting this connection. She gave Genesis her number. Since the other woman did not give out her own, Jacqueline knew what that meant. She was just some weirdo annoying the artist.

When Jacqueline received a text later that evening at home, she almost passed out.

Free on Friday? Genesis had texted.

Definitely, Jacqueline wrote back.

When they met for dinner that Friday, Jacqueline asked about buying *Wyckoff Dock.*

"I'd be lying if I said I wasn't hoping you'd buy it," Genesis grinned, sipping her wine. "I have it in my trunk."

Jacqueline forced herself to not talk about sharks constantly, and managed to ask questions about Genesis's artwork, and about the woman. The entire conversation pivoted carefully around the subject of dating or about men.

"Would a check for the painting be all right?" Jacqueline asked Genesis as they prepared to leave the restaurant. Jacqueline had already paid the bill, including a bottle of wine mostly consumed by Genesis, who made a token effort at offering to split the bill. Jacqueline didn't mind, and was happy for the company. Her job paid well, and she never went out. But now having paid for the wine, Jacqueline began to wonder about Genesis's ability to safely and legally drive.

"Of course!" Genesis said, a little loudly.

"Are you okay to drive?" Jacqueline asked, knowing she wasn't.

"Oh, I know I'm okay to drive," Genesis said, deadpan. "But the judge seemed to disagree." She burst into laughter.

"What do you mean?" Jacqueline asked, laughing along nervously.

Genesis leaned across the table, as if to tell a secret.

"Suspended license!" she whispered loudly.

"Oh," Jacqueline said. "Look, I'll give you a ride."

"I live four hours away," Genesis laughed. "I can't make you drive that. I'll be fine."

"Why don't you stay at my place?" Jacqueline said. Part of her thought it was a bad idea, the part of her that wondered what kind of problems Genesis might have. But the loneliness within devoured these concerns. Jacqueline pictured another year of celibacy and loneliness. How long had it been since she last got laid? And here was someone who could get hurt or arrested, someone who really needed help. Someone who now had her bare foot sliding along the inside of Jacqueline's calf under the table.

"You don't mind?" Genesis said, reaching out and taking Jacqueline's hand. The artist trailed a trimmed fingernail across Jacqueline's palm.

Chapter 3
Temptation

Not gonna do anything because she's drunk and that would be wrong, Jacqueline told herself as they got up from the table. Out in the parking lot, she helped Genesis move the painting from the woman's battered 20-year-old Isuzu to the trunk of Jacqueline's new Toyota Avalon hybrid. She opened the passenger door for Genesis, climbed into the driver's seat, and had just hit the start button when she smelled perfume and felt breath close on her cheek. Jacqueline turned her head, and Genesis cupped her chin, pressing her full lips to Jacqueline's. Jacqueline put her hands on Genesis's shoulders sliding her tongue into the woman's mouth, tasting her, melting into her as she cursed being alone. Genesis sunk her fingers into Jacqueline's hair, cradling the back of her neck as she kissed down Jacqueline's neck. Jacqueline throbbed between her legs, craving this woman in a way she never knew before, but forced herself away.

"Genesis, look, you're drunk. We should at least wait until you're sober," Jacqueline said, pushing her glasses up the bridge of her nose.

"Wait for what?" Genesis said. "We're just kissing. That's nothing, right? I wanted to kiss you when I first saw you."

"Yeah, but," Jacqueline said, putting on her seatbelt. "Put your seatbelt on."

"Okay, there it's on," Genesis said, buckling up as Jacqueline pulled out of the parking lot. "Sorry."

"For what?" Jacqueline asked.

"For kissing you. I didn't want to make you uncomfortable. I think I just misjudged the situation," Genesis said, a slight slur tugging at her words.

"Misjudged how?"

"Like I thought you might be into messing around."

"Well, maybe I am but not when you're drunk," Jacqueline said.

"Okay, girl scout."

"Girl scout could be taken a couple different ways," Jacqueline laughed.

"Yeah, well, so can I," Genesis said, smiling as they pulled into the driveway. "Oh, nice house."

As Jacqueline took the painting from her trunk, it suddenly hit her she was allowing someone else into her world. Visitors to her home had consisted almost entirely of family members, never a lover or date.

"What's the matter?" Genesis asked.

"Nothing, just trying to remember something," Jacqueline said. She braced herself as they walked inside and turned on the light.

"Oh, wow!" Genesis said, looking around the living room at the various shark decorations and paraphernalia. She walked over and picked up a set of shark jaws from the top of a bookshelf, eying Jacqueline between the teeth.

"I know. It's weird," Jacqueline laughed nervously.

"Weird, huh? Is that what you call it?" Genesis wasn't laughing or smiling. She set the jaws back on the shelf and walked over to Jacqueline. Jacqueline took a step back, intimidated. Genesis took a step forward. "Let me tell you something." Genesis put a hand on each of Jacqueline's cheeks, staring down at her, paralyzing her with her gaze. "Weird is the word I heard growing up. You're weird, Genesis. Why you painting that fucked up painting, Genesis? Shit's weird. Are you high? Why you like girls? That's weird. Fucking weird-ass dyke."

Jacqueline felt her throat closing with fear, not knowing where Genesis was going with this.

"I hate that word, Jacqueline," Genesis said, sliding her hands down Jacqueline's body, brushing her breasts on the way down to rest on her hips, pressing her to the wall. "And I especially hate to hear someone like you say that word. Because I think, no, I *know*, you know what it's like to not be like everyone else." Genesis's mouth moved closer to hers, the woman's hands slowly lifting the skirt of Jacqueline's dress. "To not think like everyone else," she said, her mouth close enough to taste her breath. "To not feel like everyone else."

Genesis's fingers slid into her panties and any thoughts of responsibility or sobriety vanished from Jacqueline's thoughts. Jacqueline widened her stance as Genesis hugged her to her breast. The artist's fingers darted back and forth along her slit, just barely reaching her clit before sinking one, then a second finger inside. Jacqueline moaned, the initial first rub of penetration dousing her brain with pleasure. She had to do nothing, could do nothing, as Genesis held her tightly with one arm, up against the wall, fingering her quickly, her thumb now circling Jacqueline's nub. Genesis's fingers curled inside her, rubbing forward, energy pulsing inside and outside her body. Jacqueline muffled her cry against Genesis's chest.

Genesis slipped her fingers out and kissed Jacqueline, still holding her tightly.

"Show me where we sleep," Genesis said.

Over the next weeks, Genesis's visits grew longer and longer. She seemed to dread the long drive home to her mother's apartment, where she lived. And Jacqueline dreaded the nights alone. When Genesis mentioned not having enough gas money, Jacqueline began giving her prepaid cards. When Genesis began talking about the new apartment her mother wanted to move to with her daughter, Jacqueline knew she wanted Genesis as more than a visiting lover. But she also knew she didn't want a repeat of her college experience.

When Genesis arrived one night, Jacqueline was ready for her. *Here we go. All or nothing,* she thought, climbing out of bed in a long nightshirt. She let Genesis in, her lover clad in black tights and t-shirt. When they kissed, Jacqueline tasted iced tea and a hint of some kind of alcohol. *She doesn't seem drunk.*

Once Genesis poured herself a drink, the women settled onto the couch.

"Remember what you told me that first night?" Jacqueline asked.

Genesis raised one eyebrow.

"About being weird," Jacqueline said, wondering if Genesis had forgotten.

"What about it?" Genesis asked.

"I have to show you something. And I have to know, honestly, how you feel about it."

"So mysterious!" Genesis said. "I'm excited. What?"

"Come on," Jacqueline said, walking to the bedroom.

Genesis followed her in, drink in hand. In the bedroom, Jacqueline had arranged her items just as she always had before a solitary ritual. Images of gaping jaws and wounds lay on the foot of the bed or propped on music stands. The mako shark jaws, and other teeth lay on a small table to the side. A small assortment of sex toys lay on the bed. *Wyckoff Dock* hung on the wall, as it had since the night Genesis first slept there.

"I don't know how to tell you this, but this is what I'm into," Jacqueline said.

"Well, I already knew you were into sharks," Genesis said.

"Yeah, I know, but it's kind of more than that."

"So, it's a turn-on?" Genesis asked, sipping her drink.

"Yes," Jacqueline said, waiting for the worst. "Seeing the sharks, seeing the people afterward. It's hard to explain, but it's something I always liked. I know it's strange, but it's who I am."

"Then that's what you do. And I'll be here with you to share it," Genesis said. She drained her glass and set it on a shelf. The woman knelt on the bed and opened her arms wide.

Jacqueline fought back tears as she rushed to the bed to hug her lover. Genesis held her, planting hot kisses all over her face and throat. Jacqueline pulled off her nightshirt, pressing herself against Genesis, groping, not even trying to be graceful.

Genesis grabbed her ass with both hands, pulling her close, then smacking her bottom playfully before letting go. The brown-skinned woman leaned back, peeling off her shirt. Jacqueline slid her palms over the woman's breasts. The bra looked too small, squeezing them. Jacqueline slid her palm across the fabric, feeling Genesis's large nipples harden behind the material. Genesis grinned and ducked her head down, her tongue darting in and out as it circled Jacqueline's nipples before sucking them. It almost felt like too much, but not quite, as she enjoyed the pull on her teats.

Jacqueline unhooked the multiple clasps of Genesis's bra, slipping off the straps and letting the woman's breasts sway. They felt so
full and good in her hands, and she kneaded them as Genesis sucked.
She let go and slipped her fingers into the waist of Genesis's tights,
tugging them down. Genesis sat up and shimmied out of them. Her
tiny G-string barely covered the bump of her pubic mound, and her
trimmed pubes peeked out along the edges of the garment.

Genesis smiled and turned around, getting on all fours and showing her plush ass. Jacqueline crouched and pulled the wet fabric of the
thong out of her lover's crease. She pulled it aside, where it dented
into the soft brown flesh of the Genesis's ass cheek. Genesis spread
her knees a little farther apart.

Jacqueline leaned in, inhaling her lover's earthy scent as she spread
the woman's cheeks apart. She lapped at her, driving her tongue along
Genesis's thick labia, up and down dipping in, then sliding up to lick
her puckered anus. Genesis grunted as Jacqueline reached for the
woman's swollen clit, teasing the organ until Genesis bucked impatiently, then stroking it with her fingertip as her tongue explored ass
and pussy. Jacqueline loved to feel her twitch and moan, loved tasting
her. Jacqueline played with her, feeling how Genesis's labia engorged
when she got hot, puffing into thick, rubbery petals, slick with juice.
Jacqueline sunk her fingers inside, always surprised at how rough her
lover liked it. Jacqueline slid in and out quickly, tongue on sphincter,
rubbing Genesis's clit with her free hand. Genesis came fast and wet,
yelping a little as she shook through the orgasm, bumping into Jacqueline and smudging her glasses with fluid.

"Fuck me," Genesis begged, her hips twitching in an almost involuntary motion.

Jacqueline picked up a purple vibrator from the bed, the base of
the toy studded with nubs, and tugged Genesis's thong down, sliding
it off. She parted Genesis's fat lips and eased it in as her lover pushed
back. Once it was all the way in, Jacqueline turned it on and listened
to Genesis gasp.

"Oh, yeah, fuck, in, in, in," Genesis panted. She squealed when
she came again, pressing her face into the bed before collapsing.

Jacqueline ran her fingertips over Genesis's dusky skin, and the
woman shivered. Jacqueline ached for release, unable to stop touch-

ing Genesis, groping, stroking.

Genesis sat up suddenly, as if just waking. She looked at the photos and the shark teeth, and blinked, confusion and desire mixed on her face.

Jacqueline watched her, waiting for Genesis's move. Jacqueline knew what she wanted, but she wanted to experience Genesis without guiding her too much. Genesis looked over at the selection of toys, her hand hovering for a moment before closing on a glass dildo. She looked up at Jacqueline, staring into her eyes. A hot pulse throbbed between Jacqueline's legs, her body burning.

Genesis moved quickly. Jacqueline fell backwards onto the bed, half-pushed, half-startled, Genesis's control and power melting her. Genesis landed kisses all over her face and neck, down to her breasts, squeezing her nipples with her lips, tongue pressing them, sucking them. Jacqueline pushed her fingers through Genesis's thick, wild hair, pulling her down to kiss her, sliding her tongue into the woman's mouth.

Genesis ground against her, breasts mashing down on hers. Jacqueline opened her legs and thrust at her, grinding against her, needing her, but unable to form her animal grunts into words.

"What do you want, baby? You need me to fuck you?" Genesis cooed in her ear.

Jacqueline reached over and grabbed a smaller set of shark jaws from the table.

"Like this, while you fuck me," Jacqueline whispered. She pressed the jaws, the teeth filed sharp, into the outside of her thigh, just deep enough to draw blood.

Genesis's eyes grew wide as she lifted to her knees, and took the jaws from Jacqueline's hand.

"You sure about this?" Genesis asked softly.

"Please," Jacqueline said. Jacqueline grabbed Genesis's wrist, the one holding the dildo, and pulled it towards her pussy. Genesis slid the tip along her folds; the glass felt cool as it slipped along her lips. Jacqueline tilted her hips and Genesis let the toy slide into her cunt, sinking deeper and deeper.

"Say stop when it's too much," Genesis said. Jacqueline wasn't sure if she meant the dildo or the teeth, but didn't care. The teeth weren't breaking the skin yet, and Genesis seemed to be afraid to press down.

"Harder, please!" Jacqueline said.

'Which?" Genesis asked.

"Everything," Jacqueline said, almost regretting it for a split second as the dildo suddenly plunged in, stretching her pussy, pleasure and pain taking turns confusing her nerves. An electric burst popped in her thigh as she felt the teeth finally sink in. "All over," Jacqueline hissed, touching Genesis's jaws-hand and waving her own hand all over her body.

Genesis's hands never faltered, the glass dildo pumping in and out, the hardness pressing and stretching her in a steady rhythm. Jacqueline felt her juices running down into the crack of her ass as Genesis moved the shark jaws with the other hand, biting into Jacqueline's inner thigh. Jacqueline heard herself moaning through the ringing in her ears. She reached down for her clit as the jaws bit into the side of her breast. She was floating now, inhaling brine, teeth biting her from all sides, and as she rubbed herself, she felt herself sinking, Genesis's dark eyes staring into hers as the orgasm popped inside her brain. Jacqueline closed her eyes now and saw Her, the bull shark, coasting through Her rocky lair, as the hard cock pumped into her.

Jacqueline opened her eyes. Like surfacing from water, she saw Genesis, sweating, heard herself moaning. Jacqueline reached over and grabbed the large set of mako jaws. This was real. With her other hand, she grabbed the dildo from Genesis. This was happening, her nerves changing, opening, feeling everything. She pressed the mako jaws around her side, then placed Genesis's hands on them.

Fucking herself with the dildo, she rubbed hard on her front wall, closing her eyes as the big jaws sunk into the skin of her flank. The jaws twisted and turned as she writhed, and now She had Jacqueline in Her embrace, consuming her, fucking her. Jacqueline rubbed herself as she pounded the cock into herself, letting the scream slip from her lips as she came, a rushing sound like static in her head.

When she opened her eyes again, Genesis hovered over her, frowning. The jaws were back on the table, Genesis's fingers tracing over Jacqueline's body, both fingers and skin covered with a light blood-smear. Genesis laid down next to her and hugged her tight until Jacqueline fell asleep.

"I would love to!" Genesis said, coffee slopping over the top of her mug as she set it down on the table. She reached over and grabbed Jacqueline's hand, squeezing it. They sat in the corner of the cafe, the midday sun shining through the window. "Only..." A shadow darkened Genesis's face.

"Only what?" Jacqueline asked, a little too quickly she realized. She badly wanted Genesis to move in with her, but didn't want to be too pushy.

"Honestly, I don't know how I could split the rent with you," Genesis said. "I can get a job here, but I doubt it would cover whatever it costs to live here. I know it's expensive."

"Don't worry about it," Jacqueline said. "I'm already covering the mortgage. And you already have a job."

"What, painting? I mean, I sell one here and there but it's not steady. And it's not much," Genesis said, biting her lip.

"Listen," Jacqueline said. "You're a painter. That's what you are. That's who you are. You can live with me, paint, and you can work on selling your art. Genesis, your work is brilliant. It will sell. Give it time. But, I'm not trying to push you into anything. But I would love it if you moved in."

Genesis moved in the very next weekend. The women set up the guest room as Genesis's work room.

"This is beautiful," Genesis said, her big eyes filling up with tears as she set up her easel. "At my mom's, I had to cram everything in my little bedroom. I love you, Jacqueline! Thank you so much!" She turned and threw her arms around Jacqueline, squeezing her tight.

The warmth soaked through Jacqueline, and she wanted Genesis to hug her forever.

"I love you, too, baby," Jacqueline said.

"Genesis, listen, you *cannot* drive," Jacqueline said, holding the bill for court costs in her hand. "If you get pulled over, they could *arrest* you! And you've been driving all this time like that," Now that Genesis changed her mailing address to the house, Jacqueline was alarmed at the amount of trouble her lover racked up.

"I *know*," Genesis said. "I just really wanted to see you." She was sitting on the couch, drinking vodka and juice. She wore shorts, and sat with her legs crossed, bouncing her one foot.

"And I appreciate that," Jacqueline said, sitting down and writing out a check. "But can you promise me not to drive until you get your license back?"

"If I have to, sure," Genesis said. She raised one eyebrow and drained her glass.

Jacqueline watched her, trying to remember how many drinks Genesis had that day.

"What?" Genesis asked.

"Well, Genesis, do you ever think there's a connection?"

"Connection?" Genesis asked, frowning.

Chapter 4
The Swim

"Between this," Jacqueline held up the bill. "And that?" Jacqueline pointed to the bottle of Czar vodka on the table.

"Maybe," Genesis said, cocking her head and setting her glass on the coffee table. Her voice grew soft, just loud enough to hear. "But Jacqueline, if you're going to try to micromanage my life, I can go back and get that from my mom just fine. Yeah, I know I drink too much. Never hid that. But I didn't move in here to get lectured. Okay?"

"Yeah," Jacqueline said, clearing her throat. "Fine." The threat of Genesis moving back with her mother stung. It would take time, Jacqueline thought, but she would figure out a way to sober her up. If she was too pushy now, she might wreck everything.

The next Saturday, Jacqueline found herself sitting on the couch watching TV with Genesis. To Jacqueline, it felt like Genesis was drinking away their hours together with each glass of vodka and juice.

"It's a perfect day outside," Jacqueline said, looking out the window. People rode by on bicycles, beach chairs strapped to their backs, coming and going.

"Mmm-hmm," Genesis said, flicking the remote control buttons.

"Hey, why don't we go to the beach?"

"Oh," Genesis said. "But, I thought we'd re-watch Walking Dead. First season."

"Why not tonight? We haven't been to the beach all week," Jacqueline said.

"I just got comfortable, though, baby," Genesis said, snuggling up to Jacqueline. Her fingertips brushed along Jacqueline's inner thigh. The blonde felt her body responding immediately.

"Yeah, but it's perfect out, Genesis!" Jacqueline said, squirming away and standing up. She knew she had to move, or they would end up laying around and messing around all day. *And Genesis will keep getting you off as long as she can keep getting drunk*, she thought, regretting the notion and trying to forget it.

"Aw, really?" Genesis said. She smiled and stretched languidly, letting her skirt ride up until the crotch of her panties showed, the bulge of her vulva visible through the fabric.

Jacqueline looked away, out the window.

"Oh, fine," Genesis said, getting up. She swatted Jacqueline's butt as she walked by to get changed.

Soon they made their way to the beach, Genesis stuffed into a colorful tankini, frequently plucking at the bottoms as they crept up. The woman carried out a small drink cooler. Though Jacqueline didn't see her fill it, she assumed it contained something mixed with vodka. Still, Jacqueline was happy to get them out of the house. Genesis's brown skin seemed to be growing too pale, and Jacqueline wondered how long her lover would stay inside, left on her own.

The beach wasn't as crowded as Jacqueline expected, and she was happy they found a spot close to the water. Glistening with lotion, Genesis quickly settled into her beach chair and poured a drink. Jacqueline still stood.

"Come on," Jacqueline said.

"Nah, I'm cool here," Genesis said sweetly.

"Just come in with me real quick," Jacqueline said.

"No. I hate the water," Genesis said.

"Oh, come on."

"We just got here," Genesis pleaded.

"Please?"

"Oh, Jesus Christ, Jacqueline! Can I finish this first?" Genesis said.

Jacqueline waited impatiently. Genesis rolled her eyes and tossed back her drink.

"Okay, okay, just a little bit," Genesis said, standing up with effort. "I'm not going in far."

"Fine," Jacqueline said. She scanned the landward horizon for a few recognizable shapes of buildings to use as a guide, then took off her glasses, checking to make sure she could still make them out. Satisfied, she set the glasses carefully inside her beach bag and took Genesis's hand as they made their way through the short maze of towels and beach umbrellas. When they reached the water's edge, Jacqueline looked back again, noting the colors of the umbrellas as a guide.

"Oh, shit, it's cold!" Genesis said as they waded in mid-thigh. They staggered as the waves hit them on the hips.

"Really? Feels perfect to me," Jacqueline said, enjoying the cool embrace of the water.

"Ugh."

"Oh, c'mon. Just jump in and get it over with. It won't feel so cold then," Jacqueline said, tugging Genesis along.

"No way!" Genesis laughed. "Slow down."

"C'mon. Don't be such a baby." They were up to Jacqueline's navel now. Genesis clutched Jacqueline's hand, shivering as she held her elbows up above the water.

"No!" Genesis whined, giggling half-hysterically.

"One."

"No!"

"Two," Jacqueline laughed.

"Oh, fuck."

"Three!" Jacqueline pivoted, pulling Genesis with her under water as a wave rolled over them. They surfaced, Genesis gasping.

"You bitch!" Genesis laughed. "Oh, my fucking God, that's cold!"

"C'mon out with me," Jacqueline said.

"Uh, no, Jacqueline. I'm not a swimmer like you. I like walking, having shit under my feet, you know?"

"Just a little bit," Jacqueline said.

"Oh, shit. Okay, just a little bit," Genesis said, shaking her mane of curls. "But don't you let go of me, promise?"

"Yeah, sure."

Genesis clutched her hand tighter as they stepped deeper, treading water now.

"Okay, I'm done! I'm done!" Genesis said. "Oh, shit. Lifeguard's blowing his whistle. Jacqueline, we gotta go back! We're out too far!"

"Okay, okay, let's go in," Jacqueline felt the tug of a riptide, felt them moving. Genesis clutched tighter now, sometimes using both hands, kicking her feet. "Listen, Genesis, don't get upset. I just need you to float on your back."

"Jacqueline, why the fuck is he blowing his whistle?" Genesis asked, panic stretching her voice. "There's no fucking shark is there?! Jacqueline! Fucking look around! Is there a shark? Shit! We're going out further!"

The riptide wasn't strong, barely even brisk enough to call it such. Alone, Jacqueline had dealt with much stronger currents. But now Genesis was starting to make Jacqueline dip under water, holding tighter. Instead of treading water herself, Genesis was clutching onto Jacqueline. And the current continued to pull them out.

"Genesis!" Jacqueline said, trying to quell her own panic. "Listen! You'll be okay. Just, let go a little! I can't swim for both of us! It's just a riptide. We just have to float on our backs, let it spit us back on the beach further down, okay?"

"We're gonna fucking drown!" Genesis yelled.

"No!" Jacqueline cried, regretting taking her out into the depths. "No! Listen!" Water splashed into her mouth as Genesis pulled her down. She spit out water. "Genesis! Let go!"

"Help! Help!" Genesis screamed.

And now Jacqueline fought for breath, having to pry Genesis's strong arms from around her throat, kicking at her lover as she fought for air. *We're both going to die and it's my fault!*

"Genesis! Let up!" Jacqueline gasped when her face was above water. "Can't swim like this!" But now Genesis was on top of her, climbing her, pushing her under. Knees drumming into Jacqueline's back, fingers clawing into her hair, she had to get Genesis off of her. Jacqueline's head went under, and she struggled to not inhale the water she swallowed. Now fighting her own panic, she let herself sink down in the hope of getting Genesis to let go.

She let herself drop. Genesis clawed harder for a moment before letting go, but not before slamming a heel down into the base of Jacqueline's skull. Jacqueline couldn't tell up from down now. Pain blossomed in the top of her chest, spreading out and down. She pounded her limbs into action, focusing all of her thought into making them move, swimming toward the lighter area in the hope of it being sky. Erupting from the surface, she gulped air, shaking violently with relief, and then pain as she breathed again.

"Jacqueline!" came the shriek behind her, full of rage and terror. Genesis could swim, at least enough to get to the surface and tread water, Jacqueline realized. She turned to look. Without her glasses, Jacqueline could not make out Genesis's face, but she could see the woman's arms thrashing towards her. Jacqueline tried to swim away but Genesis latched onto her once again.

This time, Jacqueline knew she could not go under again. When Genesis dug in her nails, Jacqueline clawed back. Up close, Jacqueline could barely make out the widening of Genesis's eyes and the white of her teeth, the clawing now mixed with punches and kicks. But Jacqueline fought back, the fear of going under greater than any intimidation from Genesis. And within Jacqueline's mind something woke up, a strange and intoxicating feeling of excitement, of being alive, a celebration of still breathing. Every nerve now engaged, blood pumping through her veins, she was alive in a primal moment of frenzy.

Genesis lurched forward, surprising Jacqueline by clutching a handful of her blond curls. Genesis pulled her head under, pulling herself over top of Jacqueline at the same time. Jacqueline did not have to think of what to do next, an energy millions of years old now clattering inside her brain. She locked her teeth into what may have been a leg, clenching down until her mouth hurt, snapping her head from side to side, tasting blood. Something pounded against her skull and then Genesis was gone.

Jacqueline bobbed to the surface, and something soft and red bounced off her head. Before her, a gray shape loomed, and she recognized the shape of what had to be the lifeguard's row boat before her. The guard leaned over the edge, saying something. To her right, Jacqueline saw the shape of Genesis, clutching a red float which would be tethered to the boat. Jacqueline could hear Genesis sobbing.

"Take the float!" the lifeguard shouted at Jacqueline. Jacqueline reached out and grabbed the red shape before her, holding on as the guard rowed back to shore. As they approached the surf, two more lifeguards swam out with floats, guiding Jacqueline and Genesis in through the breakers. Jacqueline felt no riptide now, and soon they reached the shallows.

Back on the beach, Genesis argued with the lifeguard. Jacqueline didn't know what to expect, what to say, or even to think about what had happened.

"I fucking said, I'm fine!" Genesis shouted. "You okay?" She pointed at Jacqueline.

Jacqueline nodded. A crowd gathered. Genesis's inner thigh was bleeding, though Jacqueline couldn't tell if it needed stitches. Jacqueline knew it should at least be seen by a doctor. But she felt ashamed of having done it, and now just craved getting home. She didn't want to sit in an emergency room for hours, nor did she wish to answer questions about the marks and wounds she and Genesis had inflicted on each other.

"Then let's go. No, leave us the fuck alone, we're fine!" Genesis shouted, marching back towards their things, her gait a little unsteady.

Jacqueline followed her, nervous about facing her, but eager to leave the beach. They quickly packed their things in silence, Jacqueline hoping to leave before any emergency responders arrived. She was glad when Genesis wrapped a towel around her hips, concealing the leg wound. Both women ignored the stares of onlookers, and Jacqueline sighed with relief when she felt sidewalk under her feet again. They walked in silence all the way home. It had all been panic, Jacqueline told herself, over and over again. That was all it was. But she dreaded what they would say when they got home.

But back home, they said nothing. An hour after walking through the door, both women were showered and sitting on the sofa, silently watching the first season of The Walking Dead. The blinds were drawn, blocking the sight of the people riding bicycles to and from the beach, with beach chairs strapped to their backs. Genesis was on her second or third drink, depending on how Jacqueline counted the refill. Genesis's bathrobe covered the bandage on her leg. On the screen, a zombie bit into the flesh of a victim. And Jacqueline tried not to think of how Genesis's flesh had felt in her mouth.

Any window for discussing the day at the beach seemed to grow smaller and smaller for Jacqueline. Mostly, she did not want to talk about it, or even think about it. And with each passing day, it became easier to push it back in her mind, though at moments it came rushing back as she laid in bed or let herself daydream at work. Genesis painted more, and that was good for justifying the silence, but the woman also drank more.

After a week of quiet tension, Jacqueline came home and found Genesis sitting in her usual nest on the couch. Instead of a bandage, the scabbed over wound was now visible on Genesis's inner thigh as she crossed her legs, her cotton dress riding up.

"Genesis, we need to talk," Jacqueline said, a knot twisting within her chest. She needed to say something, but didn't know what or how. She just wanted something to say, something to relieve the pressure.

Genesis's expression flickered from stupor to confused panic, just for a moment before setting into something like hunger. She stood up, shaking her mane out over her shoulders.

"Do we?" Genesis asked softly, walking towards Jacqueline. Jacqueline couldn't tell if she was trying to be intimidating or seductive, and in turn felt both effects. Genesis reached out, slowly, and took Jacqueline's hands. Jacqueline tried to keep them from shaking as Genesis lifted them above her head, softly pinning her to the wall as she leaned in. Genesis's lips tasted of vodka and lemonade as she pressed them to Jacqueline's, her tongue sliding in to invade Jacqueline's mouth. Jacqueline felt herself opening up, very wet now, her body responding, losing control as her lover pressed against her.

Genesis slid her hands along Jacqueline's body, guiding her towards the bedroom, kissing her neck and ears as they walked. In the room, the site of her images, magazines, and shark jaws, her items prearranged, startled her. Genesis had done this without asking, and it felt invasive, but Jacqueline couldn't find the words to protest. Genesis pushed her down on the bed, yanking down Jacqueline's pants now, and then pulling off her blouse. The intensity both excited Jacqueline and made her wonder what would happen if she said no. But now Genesis's fingers were down the front of Jacqueline's panties, stroking alongside her folds, tickling around her clit and numbing any silent objections. Genesis's thumb fluttered over her organ, and another finger penetrated her, rubbing her like she knew Jacqueline's body better than she did.

"Tell me what you want, baby," Genesis whispered into her ear. "Tonight we make it happen. Tonight we make you feel it."

Jacqueline's mind staggered at the brink of orgasm, Genesis's words pouring into her ear. She felt like a puppet, the fingers driving her, overwhelming her. She felt Genesis's eyes on her, too intense to meet.

"Tell me. Tell me, don't hide anything," Genesis whispered.

"I can show you," Jacqueline grunted. It was something she fantasized about, but held back.

Genesis moved away, and Jacqueline sat up, pulling off her bra and panties as Genesis undressed next to her. Jacqueline opened the dresser, her body throbbing, and pulled out a set of straps. Then she plucked a picture from her collection, a photo of the remains of a young woman. Only the woman's torso remained mostly intact, the limbs apparently severed in an attack.

"Bind me like this," Jacqueline said, setting the image on the table beside the bed.

Genesis took one of the straps and frowned, looking back and forth from the picture to Jacqueline.

"Like this," Jacqueline said, laying back on the bed. She bent one leg, took one of the straps, and wrapped it around her folded limb, buckling it in place. The band was wide enough to spread the pressure, allowing circulation. Her leg folded beneath her, she could now imagine her knee as a bloody stump. Jacqueline throbbed between her legs, excited to be sharing this new game with Genesis.

Genesis smiled and leaned in, her heavy breasts swaying beneath her as she picked up another restraining band. She grasped Jacqueline's other leg spreading the blonde open as she folded the limb, strapping it firmly but not too tight. Jacqueline's head grew light as Genesis trailed her fingertips along the inner thigh, up to her labia. Genesis raised her fingertip and slowly set it down on Jacqueline's clit, circling one way then the other. Jacqueline's orgasm slid out of her throat, the throbbing rush heavy and sweet.

As Jacqueline panted, Genesis used the remaining bands to fasten Jacqueline's arms. Jacqueline writhed on the bed.

"I found you," Genesis said. "I found you like this, washed up on the beach. Destroyed." She picked up a small set of shark jaws, just barely brushing Jacqueline's side with the teeth tips. The pressure rippled through Jacqueline's body. Genesis climbed down, sucking and licking at the skin around Jacqueline's vulva. Jacqueline arched her back.

"Please!" She begged, aching for Genesis.

Genesis jammed her tongue inside Jacqueline's slit and Jacqueline wriggled, unable to grab her lover's hair or wrap her legs over her shoulders, unable to do anything but surrender. Genesis drove her tongue in, frenzied, lapping deep into her cunt. The shark teeth raked Jacqueline belly and thighs, electricity lacing the pumping heat inside her body. Genesis sucked hard at Jacqueline's clit, merciless in intensity. Jacqueline could only take it, could only give up and come and cry out to keep conscious, grunting as the orgasm punished her.

Genesis got up, leaving Jacqueline to catch her breath, sweating into the sheets. Jacqueline stared at Genesis's painting of a tiger shark on the wall, a new painting. She felt herself tumbling through the water, imagined the beast taking the last of her limbs as she sank.

Chapter 5
The Test

Genesis reappeared before her eyes. Teeth protruded from her mouth. Genesis had apparently modified one of the small sets of jaws, rigging them somehow to fit to her mouth. On her hips, Genesis wore a strap-on harness, her large and smooth blue dildo set in the hole. Genesis stood over Jacqueline, her image unearthly as her hair almost seemed to move on its own. Her large dark eyes probed Jacqueline as she gnashed her pointed teeth, phallus aimed like a horn. Genesis looked no longer human. A rushing filled Jacqueline's head as she gave herself to Genesis. The monstrous lover climbed over her, teeth nipping lightly all over Jacqueline's body, her stumps, her breasts, her neck. The dildo was too large for Jacqueline's vagina, and she had only ever used it inside Genesis. But now the thick toy burrowed inside of her pussy and she groaned at the stretching throb. Genesis pounded into her, squeezing her nipples as she thrust, then reaching down to turn on the vibrating egg embedded in the toy.

Jacqueline's control slipped away as the vibe buzzed inside her, coming hard and clamping her muscles. Genesis groaned and pounded into her. Jacqueline gasped for air, blood rushing to her head. She rode the aftershock, catching her breath as Genesis slowed down, whimpering through her own climax, pressing the base of the toy against herself.

But when Genesis's eyes cleared, she pushed deep into Jacqueline, laying her weight on the smaller woman. Never stopping her rhythm, pumping into her, Genesis placed the palms of her hands on the sides of Jacqueline's throat. Jacqueline stared up into her lover's face, Genesis's eyes now opening into black wells a thousand feet deep. The throb coursed through Jacqueline's entire body as Genesis slapped her hips against her. Jacqueline's bound limbs now ached, and the long dildo jabbed into her cervix from time to time, but she felt the pain barrier melting, the hot rub of the dildo inside her, the buzz filling her core.

She whimpered as she started to come, and Genesis's hands pressed on the sides of her throat, pushing harder, the woman's thumbs now pressing against her windpipe.

"Don't kill me!" Jacqueline tried to say, but could not speak, could not breathe, spots of light flickering in her vision. The orgasm felt like the push of a roller coaster drop on her stomach. Her ears rang and she was under water again with Genesis, who now fucked her while drowning her. She heard a popping rush and for a moment, She appeared in the green water before her eyes, the bull shark, majestic as She swam towards Jacqueline. There was no fear now, for she was with Her, always.

But now she felt air rushing into her lungs and saw Genesis crouching over her. Jacqueline was back in the room. The woman no longer wore the shark teeth, but grinned a white smile of her own as she unstrapped Jacqueline's aching limbs.

Jacqueline woke up alone in bed early the next morning. She got up and looked around the house for Genesis, who was nowhere to be found. It was odd, since Genesis always remained in bed until after Jacqueline got up for work. Genesis's purse was gone, but her phone remained plugged into its charger. Jacqueline found no note, and had no message on her own phone.

A headache kicked into gear, and Jacqueline began to pace. She looked out the window into the small yard. She walked outside and checked both her car and Genesis's car. She found nothing. She restrained herself as long as she could before checking Genesis's phone, but there were no recent messages.

She went inside and wondered what to do. The realization of how isolated she'd become sunk in. Jacqueline had a few casual friends, but no one to call and ask for advice on a missing girlfriend. Jacqueline didn't know any of Genesis's friends, and Genesis's mother had been extremely cold when Jacqueline showed up to help Genesis move. Nor did Jacqueline know what she would say to her own family.

And what would she say to anyone? That Genesis had gone out, locked the door behind her, leaving her phone and no note? She couldn't call the police with that. It didn't make sense to panic. But she felt a sick sourness in her belly and wished Genesis would come back. What if she never came back?

Jacqueline forced down a piece of bread and followed it with naproxen and water. Her head throbbed and her vagina felt slightly tender from the night before. It was getting late, so she called out sick from work. She kept asking herself why Genesis wouldn't tell her where she was going. The naproxen made Jacqueline drowsy, but when she started to doze, she imagined Genesis at the hospital, injured in a car crash. Jacqueline got out of bed and checked to see if the car was still there. After the same dream and the same checking again, she stayed out of bed.

She paced as long as she could stand it, then put on a pair of jeans and walked to the beach. The sky was overcast and the air chilly enough to make Jacqueline wish she wore a sweatshirt. She walked the beach, hoping to distract herself. She checked her phone every so often, and often caught herself looking for Genesis, though she knew this was the last place her lover ever went. She walked past the beach crowd, the ranks thinned out from the cool weather. She walked far enough to arrive at the section used only by fishermen, an area where vehicles were permitted. Three men had set up with massive rods and a huge amount of equipment.

"Catching anything?" Jacqueline asked, not caring, but somehow wanting to exchange words with another person.

"Nothing," one man with a bandanna said, shaking his head in disgust.

"Not like last week," his friend, a small man, said.

"Yeah, last week, this guy caught an eight foot bull," the third man said, puffing on a cigar.

The trio quickly had their phones out, eager to show Jacqueline dozens of photos of themselves posing with the creature, making goofy faces next to the magnificent being.

"Did you keep it?" Jacqueline asked, clearing her throat, trying to hide her anticipated indignation.

"Oh, hell, no," the short one said. "What are you gonna do with something like that? Eat it? Put it on your wall? Nah, we had him right back in the water, so we can catch him again!"

When the man with the bandanna asked for Jacqueline's number, so that he could send her the pictures, she decided it was time to go and politely excused herself.

When she returned to the house, her heart leapt into her throat as she saw the lights shining. Relief washed over her when she saw Genesis in her usual spot on the couch, wearing a short skirt, her smooth legs folded beneath her.

"Hey," Genesis said, glancing at her before turning back to the TV.

"Hey, no note? No text? What the hell?" Jacqueline asked, her hands on her hips. She wanted to shake Genesis.

"Oh, baby, I'm sorry. I forgot," Genesis stood up. "I had a doctor's appointment."

"So why didn't you tell me?"

"Because I didn't remember until early in the morning," Genesis took Jacqueline's hand and led her to the couch. They sat down. "Couldn't sleep, and then I thought, didn't I have an appointment coming up. So I checked my phone and, sure enough, there it was on my calendar. I had to hurry up and go. Actually, I'm lying. I had to hurry up and go so I could get something to eat at the cafe before my appointment. Anyway, planned to call you but forgot my phone! I'm such an idiot!"

"Okay, so after the appointment?" Jacqueline asked.

"I had to pick up a few things, and then I came home," Genesis shrugged. "You went out? Mmm. You smell like fresh air! No work today?" Genesis snuggled up against her, warm, her perfume fresh-smelling.

"Yeah," Jacqueline said, not sure if she felt more relieved or resentful. "Yeah, I went for a walk." She thought about pressing the discussion, asking Genesis more questions, but she suddenly felt tired.

They sat in silence for a long hour. When Genesis returned with another drink, Jacqueline felt irritated with her.

"Genesis, do you ever think about not drinking? Or even drinking less?" Jacqueline asked.

Genesis sighed and swirled her ice. She raised an eyebrow and looked out the window.

"Yep," she said, finally.

"And?" Jacqueline asked.

"Tell you what," Genesis said, putting her hand on Jacqueline's thigh. "Since I already know where this is going, and we're going to talk about rehab."

"I didn't say that," Jacqueline said.

"Yeah, no one's talking about rehab, except, they're talking about rehab. Yeah, yeah, I get it. I know. So let's make a deal. Tomorrow, I go to rehab or see a counselor or, listen, whatever it is you want me to do. But you gotta do one thing." Genesis raised one finger and put it to Jacqueline's lips.

"Fine. What?" Jacqueline asked.

"You gotta have a drink with me."

"Fine," Jacqueline said, surprised but relieved at the request. "There's a little chablis left in the fridge." She started to get up.

"No, no, no, no, no," Genesis said, putting her hand on Jacqueline's shoulder, pulling her back down. "No, I mean a big girl drink." Genesis raised her glass and clinked the ice.

"Ew, vodka? I hate vodka!" Jacqueline said.

"Fine. Deal's off," Genesis said, pursing her lips. She stood up and stomped out to the kitchen.

"What the fuck?" Jacqueline hissed, punching the couch. She got up and walked out to the kitchen.

"Okay, fine!" Jacqueline said. "If that's the little game we have to play. Go ahead. Pour me a drink. But we take you to see someone tomorrow, no matter what. Promise?"

"I promise," Genesis said, pouring a drink into a large glass. She used a lot of lemonade, but Jacqueline also winced at the amount of vodka Genesis poured. They returned to the living room, and Jacqueline took her drink slowly, wondering if Genesis was just bullshitting her.

"I think most of the programs are thirty days," Jacqueline said.

"Mmm-hm. Yeah, I'm sure they can tell me all about it tomorrow," Genesis said. "Mind if I watch this?" She turned up the volume on the TV.

Jacqueline wanted to smash the remote control, but instead she took a drink. By the end of the show, she felt the alcohol buzzing in her skull, and it felt good. She felt very good. She didn't remember it feeling this good to be drunk, but it had also been a long time since she had more than a couple glasses of wine. When she finished the glass, Genesis quickly brought her a second one. She tasted the vodka more and made a face, but it was drinkable.

As they sat and laughed at the next show, Jacqueline understood why Genesis drank. At that moment, everything felt fine. The worries of the day melted away. Jacqueline felt warm and cozy, snuggled up with her lover.

Jacqueline had to pee, and when she stood, she realized how drunk she was, tilting a little on her feet before stumbling towards the bathroom. *Could I really be that drunk on two drinks?* Jacqueline asked herself as she sat on the toilet, then laughed because she wasn't sure if she'd said it out loud.

"Can I really be that drink on two drunks?" Jacqueline laughed as she walked out of the bathroom. Genesis stood before her in the hallway.

"Yeah, sweetie, you really can be that drink," Genesis smiled as she walked Jacqueline into the bedroom.

"Mmm. Bedroom," Jacqueline laughed suddenly aware of how horny she felt. She stumbled and the floor rose up to hit her, then stopped. Genesis caught her. Jacqueline laughed.

"Careful, baby," Genesis said, helping her back up. "Oh, did you get drunk, Jacqueline?" she said, walking her to the bed.

"Um, think I may have," Jacqueline chuckled.

"Well, that's naughty, Jacqueline," Genesis said, unsnapping Jacqueline's jeans.

Jacqueline felt herself immediately get wet. Sober, she felt like she had very few defenses against Genesis's advances. Drunk, she felt like a raw nerve waiting to be touched.

"Really? Am I naughty?" Jacqueline laughed. "What are you gonna do about it?" She heard the slurring in her own voice.

Genesis yanked Jacqueline's jeans down around her knees. Jacqueline tumbled forward and found herself across Genesis's knees now, the woman pulled down Jacqueline's panties. Jacqueline's glasses fell off somewhere next to the bed.

"Hey!" Jacqueline laughed, then a palm smacked across her bottom and she yelped. "Ow!" Again Genesis spanked her. "Stop!" Jacqueline yelled. It stung, and Genesis wasn't stopping. Emotions sprung into Jacqueline's heart. She felt anger with each swat on her bottom, insult at being controlled, but also an intense arousal, a fiery heat blossoming between her legs, mixed with resentment of her own excitement. She loved the feeling of being controlled by Genesis, and hated it at the same time. Each smack on her ass fanned the fire, made her crave release.

Genesis stopped suddenly, sliding her finger down the crack of Jacqueline's ass, slipping into her pussy. Jacqueline lifted her hips as Genesis slid two fingers inside her, each one writhing in its own rhythm. Genesis slid her fingers out again and swatted Jacqueline's butt, more playful now, but it made Jacqueline feel unhinged, aroused with a manic intensity. Genesis let her up, and Jacqueline quickly peeled off her clothing as her partner undressed.

Jacqueline fell on the bed next to Genesis, her hands crushing the woman's breasts, kneading, squeezing, while Genesis penetrated her. The woman licked along Jacqueline's neck, her breath hot as she gently nipped her shoulder. The touch of Genesis's teeth maddened her, and she licked her way down to the woman's heavy breasts, moaning at the pleasure of the thumb brushing her clit. The soft brown flesh before her eyes awakened something within her, and she remembered the feel of it in her mouth, the rich taste of blood mixed with seawater.

Jacqueline's jaws opened reflexively, and she clamped down, biting the side of Genesis's breast. Genesis shrieked, the sound reverberating through the ribcage beneath Jacqueline's ear, and then something cracked into Jacqueline's eye, stars flashing in her vision. She rolled backwards in time to see the blur of Genesis's fist before it hit her in the jaw.

"What the fuck was that?" Genesis screamed in her face, gripping her by the hair.

"Genesis, I'm sorry!" Jacqueline said, shaking with fear.

"Oh, you're sorry? Yeah, you better be fucking sorry!" Genesis got up. Jacqueline saw the woman at the dresser, and heard the drawer yanked open.

"Genesis, stop, please. Let me get my glasses," Jacqueline said, crawling to the edge of the bed. Her face throbbed.

Genesis grabbed her wrists and flipped her on her back. A ringing filled Jacqueline's ears as she felt a strap being fastened around her wrists. Genesis secured her wrists and pulled them over Jacqueline's head. Jacqueline tried to move them, but they were fastened to the headboard.

"Look at this! Look at this!" Genesis yelled, apparently gesturing to her breast. "Oh, you can't fucking see it because you're blind. There," she said, wiping something wet on her Jacqueline's face.

Jacqueline squirmed, trying to turn away.

"Oh, don't you fucking dare kick me!" Genesis said. "Do that and I will fuck you up. I promise that shit."

"Genesis, listen, I'm sorry. I just, I feel really drunk. I don't know why I did that," Jacqueline sobbed.

"No, no, no, that's fine, lover," Genesis said, her voice mocking calm and sweetness. "You just want to play rough. You just want to bite me and drown me and lock me away in rehab, but that's cool. Here's let play some shark games, yeah?"

Genesis moved away and came back with something, holding it up close enough for Jacqueline to recognize the large set of mako jaws. Then Jacqueline heard a buzz and felt a wand vibrator jammed between her legs. She grunted at the intensity, but could do nothing but feel it pulse into her.

"You keep your goddamn legs open," Genesis said, grinding the vibrator against her. With the other hand, she pressed the jaws against Jacqueline's side, hard, making quick side to side motions.

Jacqueline squealed at the pain and the vibration and the terror.

"Genesis," she grunted.

"There, you like that, don't you, you fucking freak?" Genesis said, her voice sharp, unhinged. "That's it. You're gonna come while you bleed."

The pain at her side and breast alarmed her, and when she looked down, she saw red. At the same time, she started to come, reflex clenching her pussy as she panted through the climax and the pain.

She felt light-headed.

Let go, she heard the voice say, in her voice, but not in her voice. Genesis tore at her, a beast devouring her flesh, yanking nerves to and fro. But it hurt less and less, the air swirling around her, pulsing thick like clear jelly. The jaws were gone from her side now, and though her vagina still throbbed the vibrator was gone. Instead, she felt something being wrapped around her neck.

Genesis was on top of her now, her fingers jabbing into her, pushing, pushing. Pain blossomed from her crotch as she felt the woman's hand entering her. It grew hard to breathe, the band about her neck tightening. She no longer felt the Genesis's weight on top of her, only the pressure of the hand inside.

Chapter 6
Recovery

Surrender, the voice said. And Jacqueline let go, let herself open, feeling the tight pressure of the hand, the knuckles rubbing into her G-spot. She couldn't breathe, but plasma fireworks erupted in her vision, burning underwater with her and Genesis. She felt stone beneath her back, and looking up realized the presence of Her, The Bull Shark, The Lady of the Sea. She was there, gliding above them, blocking the moonlight with Her huge form. The shark circled once, then dove at Jacqueline, jaws open wide. Jacqueline raised her arms and shouted in joy as the teeth closed upon her in consummation.

Jacqueline woke groaning in pain. A headache throbbed in her skull. Her face, especially her left eye, hurt and felt swollen to the touch. Her neck felt bruised. The sheets were brown, and Jacqueline had to pick carefully to separate the fabric from where it had dried and stuck to the considerable scabs on her side and breast. Her wrists were chafed, though no longer bound. Her vagina was sore. She felt very light-headed. And nausea coiled in her stomach.

She looked around the room for any blur resembling Genesis, then reached along floor next to the bed until her hands found her glasses, the frames cracked and bent. Once she had them on, she looked around the room. Little squiggly shapes of broken blood vessels danced in her vision. The stain on the bed was unmistakably dried blood, and lots of it. She examined her body. Dried blood caked her one side, and she knew it would have been a good idea to get stitches, judging by the cuts Genesis made. She also believed the drinks Genesis made her definitely contained more than alcohol, judging by how impaired she had been, and the way she felt now.

Jacqueline listened for the TV, or for any sounds in the house. She picked up an obsidian carving of a tiger shark, holding it in her hand like a weapon. She wondered if Genesis was out there, waiting for her, waiting to attack.

Jacqueline thought about the mirror for a long moment before she found the courage to look into it. When she did, she sobbed reflexively. Her left eye was swollen almost completely shut, the flesh purple, the eye itself, bloodshot. Another bruise decorated her jaw and cheek on the right side, and blood was smeared on her forehead. A purple band circled her neck. She felt stupid, ashamed, and afraid. She thought of calling the police, but then imagined the conversation about how, yes, she had bitten her partner, but hadn't meant to hurt her, and yes, she did enjoy being cut with shark teeth, but not like that, and yes, she did like being restrained but not like that, more like when she wanted to feign amputated limbs. No, she decided she did not want that conversation.

She clenched her fists and shook, hot tears pouring down her face.

"Alone," she said through gritting teeth, facing the mirror. "I can only be alone. I can only be alone. I can only be alone." She repeated the words over and over again, until they became gibberish in her ears.

Jacqueline pulled on a bathrobe, and made her way quietly out in the hall, wielding the shark statuette. She went room to room, but did not see Genesis. The woman's purse, keys, and phone were gone, and when Jacqueline looked out the window, she saw the Isuzu was gone as well. It was almost noon. Jacqueline made an awkward phone call to work, citing injuries and illness. She took a chef's knife from the kitchen, and carried it, the statuette, and a kitchen chair with her into the bathroom. Jamming the chair under the knob of the locked bathroom door, Jacqueline turned on the shower.

Under the spray, she watched the caked blood break apart, a map on her skin washed away by rain. *What will I do now?* Jacqueline asked herself. She wanted Genesis out of the house, but questioned herself. The violence of the night before had reached a new level. She couldn't take that degree of punishment, and didn't want to walk around with a battered face. And maybe next time, it would be worse. She feared Genesis now, but wondered if it was fair to not talk to her first. After all, she thought, they had rough sex before, never discussed limits, and had too much to drink last night.

Too much to drink. The thought shook her. There was simply no way Genesis hadn't put something in her drink. Genesis had drugged her, left her vulnerable, and then when Jacqueline lost control, attacked her. *But I was trying to force her into rehab when she wasn't ready. And I had introduced the shark teeth and the rough sex. So is it really Genesis' fault? Or did I bring it on myself?*

Jacqueline's face burned with confusion, and she turned the water to cold, sobbing loudly, pounding the heels of her hands against the tiles. She swallowed water, and her thoughts turned to the day at the beach, Genesis pulling her under water, drowning her. And she remembered the moment when self-preservation made her bite Genesis to get free. Jacqueline grew calm, her thoughts suddenly clear. *Many creatures bite to survive. There is no choice. Fight or die. Biting Genesis last night was just another way to break free, to not drown. If we stay together, Genesis will consume me. And Genesis is not my Mistress. She will not devour me.*

She finished her shower, her mind focused and clear, and examined the cuts. Many of them were deep, exposing the white fatty tissue underneath the outer skin. She'd dressed her wounds often before, but never anything this severe.

Jacqueline doused the wounds with hydrogen peroxide, grinding her teeth with the sting but glad the wounds didn't foam, which meant they were still clean. She used butterfly strips and skin glue to close the rents, and hoped for the best.

Once showered, bandaged, and dressed, Jacqueline felt slightly better. It was time to prepare. She would call the police if it came to that, but she wanted to face Genesis herself, wanted to tell her to leave. The police were part of the world outside, and Jacqueline wanted badly to expel that world, including Genesis, from her own world, a world she could share with no human.

Jacqueline forced down food and painkillers, and left the house. At an outdoor supplies store, she bought pepper spray. At a home supplies store, she bought new locks for her doors.

When she returned home, her stomach squirmed as she saw the Isuzu parked again in its place.

"I will be alone!" Jacqueline said as she climbed out of her car, the pepper spray in hand.

She walked into the house cautiously. The TV was off, but the light in the spare bedroom, Genesis's painting room, was on. Jacqueline made herself walk in, her limbs feeling wooden. Inside, Genesis sat on a chair behind an easel, the back of the painting towards Jacqueline.

"Well, hello, there, Shiner!" Genesis said, cackling. She was swaying in her chair, a bottle of Czar vodka next to her. "Painted you a picture!"

Jacqueline wanted to scream at her, but the words stuck in her throat, seeming to choke her.

"Well, don't you wanna see it?" Genesis asked, slurring badly. "Here!" She clenched her paintbrush between her teeth and stood up crookedly. She picked up the canvas and turned it around.

The image, apparently recently and hastily completed, consisted of a crude, cartoonish image. An unflattering caricature of Jacqueline, with frizzy hair and extremely thick glasses, was surrounded by anthropomorphic sharks in a gangbang. Huge penises penetrated the cartoon Jacqueline's mouth anus, and vagina.

"Get the fuck out of my house," Jacqueline said, voice shaking. She thought about going over to Genesis and dousing her with the pepper spray until it was empty.

"What the fuck?" Genesis asked, shaking her head. Then her gaze rested on the pepper spray. "Oh, for real? You have got to be fucking kidding me! That's the most fucked up thing. You're gonna mace me? Seriously, Jacqueline?"

"Get out! Now! Or I call the police," Jacqueline said.

"Oh, or I call the police!" Genesis said, mocking Jacqueline's shaking voice. "Well, what're the police gonna say about this?" Genesis fumbled to expose her breast, pointing to the bruise and cut. It looked bad, Jacqueline realized, but nothing like her own injuries.

"I can only be alone!" Jacqueline screamed, raising the pepper spray.

"Fine!" Genesis yelled back, but recoiling a little, swaying and throwing the canvas aside, the wet paint smearing the wall. "Where the fuck you want me to go? Gonna have to drive drunk, won't I, Jacqueline?

Gonna be your fault if anything happens! Blood on your hands!"

"I don't care about you at all," Jacqueline said. "Call your fucking mother. Catch a bus. I don't care. But you don't stay here."

"What about all my shit?" Genesis said, blinking, her lips pouting.

"Your shit will be outside. Get it tomorrow before it goes out with the trash," Jacqueline says.

"Baby, I love you, why are you doing this?" Genesis asked, moving towards her.

"No! I am alone!" Jacqueline screamed, backing up and pointing the pepper spray at Genesis.

"Well, fuck you, then!" Genesis yelled. "Get the fuck out of my way!"

Jacqueline backed out and down the hall, never turning her back as Genesis stuffed random belongings into a trash bag. When the bag was full, Genesis grabbed the vodka bottle, and extended her middle finger towards Jacqueline.

"Careful what you wish for!" Genesis barked at her she plunged out through the door, staggering out to her vehicle. She threw her bag in the back, started the car, and threw an empty bottle at the house. Genesis stomped on the gas, spraying a rooster tail of gravel, and clipping the mailbox as she peeled out.

Jacqueline watched, shaking. Again, she thought about calling the police, but again, rejected the idea. Out there was the outside world. They could arrest her for driving drunk, or not, but that was their concern, not Jacqueline's. Jacqueline had her own business to tend to, and the first order consisted of changing the locks.

But the locks did not keep away the police the next day. Jacqueline didn't know what to say at first. The news of the recovery of Genesis's body shoved a giant fist into Jacqueline's belly. When she did speak, she held back very little, sobbing and spitting out the details of the last days into the brains and notes of the officers, until both she and they were exhausted.

Jacqueline wondered if she would be blamed, but after a few days, she found that everyone was quite ready to wipe her off the record of Genesis's existence. Lacking a clear statement of suicide or any foul play, the police closed the case as an accidental, alcohol-related drowning. Genesis's relatives picked up her belongings from the front walkway, where Jacqueline had set them out. They exchanged no words, besides a terse phone call from Genesis's mother, who told Jacqueline not to come to the funeral service.

For Jacqueline, it felt as if Fate had written her decree across Jacqueline's life. She would be alone, and any violation of that condition would result in tragedy. Someone would die, Jacqueline reasoned. Genesis might have lived, had Jacqueline not pulled her into her world. Jacqueline would have to hate someone to love them, to want to destroy them, the way she had destroyed Genesis. Genesis was vulnerable, she was an alcoholic, and Jacqueline had taken advantage of her weakness, keeping her in the prison of Jacqueline's world, buying her caged bird vodka to prevent flight.

Jacqueline berated herself. Had Genesis died after crashing her car into a tree, Jacqueline still would have felt guilt, but could have considered it accidental. There was nothing accidental about Genesis walking into the ocean, an act obviously performed to blame Jacqueline. In her self-condemnation, Jacqueline chose to forget the violence she experienced from her lover. Genesis had been sick, she reasoned, even disabled, and Jacqueline had placed her in a position of destruction.

No. It could not happen again, she thought. No more humans. She would be solitary, alone but for her one surviving love, the Mistress of the Depths, The Lady of the Sea. Now was the time to go beyond pictures. Now was the time to seek a more direct communion. Now was the time to go to the ocean. Now was the time to go home.

Sitting on the beach now, on the anniversary of Genesis's death, Jacqueline found herself halfway through the flask bottle. The cheap vodka burned her mouth numb enough to not mind it so much now. She looked at her watch. It'd been two hours since she dropped her bait. She would wait a few more minutes, and then reel in, re-bait, and run the baited hooks out again. In the distance, the lights of a boat grew closer. Jacqueline turned on her flashlight and pointed it towards the boat, just to let them know someone was fishing in the spot. She didn't want them messing up her spot, as much trouble as it was to get set up.

Jacqueline sighed and stood, awkwardly, wiggling her hips, taking a wide stance, and adjusting the belt in order to adjust the toy inside her body. It was time to reel in. She wasn't disappointed, since she'd resigned herself to the fact shark-fishing may take many hours before a catch. For a big shark, it could take many months, especially considering Jacqueline's lack of experience. She picked up the close rod first, the one with the bait two hundred yards out, and reeled it in. The baitfish looked slightly mauled by crabs, but otherwise largely untouched.

When she picked up the farther rod, the one with the bait out four hundred yards, she turned the crank five times before the rod bent and the vibrator popped into life. Jacqueline squealed, both at the surprise of the vibration and the realization of having caught something huge. She almost regretting the vibe now, as the pull on the rod made her dig her feet into the sand to keep from falling over. She expected a fight, but not this much, and now wondered if she could handle it. She moaned, trying to release some of the feeling the vibe was pulsing through her pussy. It felt incredibly good, the sensation mixing with the adrenalin and alcohol for a potent high. But she now faced the prospect of an imminent orgasm while her arms burned, trying to lever in the beast at the end of the line.

Focus, focus, focus, Jacqueline told herself. *Remember what you read. Don't let it pull straight out, walk it down the beach.*

"Oh, fuck!" Jacqueline grunted, coming as she moved sideways, moving almost in a crabwalk. The rod took every ounce of her strength to hold, even with the butt jammed firmly into the fighting belt. How long could she keep this up? She groaned with the effort, pulling the rod in different directions, to try to save the strength in different muscles. She wanted to reach down and turn off the vibe, but the idea of freeing one of her hands seemed impossible. She sweated heavily inside her wetsuit. She had to pee, but there was nothing to do about it. Jacqueline couldn't stand the distraction of fighting one more thing in her body, so she released her bladder, pissing herself inside the wetsuit. The relief gave her just a bit more ground to hold onto.

Jacqueline wanted to look at her watch, but had no means of turning on the light. How long would this go on? How long could she go on? Her arms were beginning to grow numb. She had to resolve the fight somehow, before her muscles went out. In the absolute worst case, she could detach the rod and let it go, but the thought sickened her. Many times, she heard the catch of a shark this big could be a once in a lifetime event. This could be her one chance of physical communion with the most perfect creature in nature. Through the pain and discomfort, she realized she was as close as she could ever get to contact with the creature, the emissary of the one who hunted her dreams.

This was it, this was happening, and Jacqueline looked at the moon and sobbed with joy. Her muscles hurt and she didn't know how long she could hold out, but the vibe brought her to the crest of another orgasm and she cried out, victorious, letting the rod dip to push the toy deeper inside. They were connected now, she and the creature, a union brought forth by an act of will. Jacqueline worked the rod up and down, letting the beast fuck her with its power. Nothing could ever be the same again.

And then she fell backwards, the vibe moving painfully inside her as she landed on her ass. The tension was gone from the rod, the line slack. The line had broken or had been cut by the shark's teeth. Jacqueline reached behind the plate of the fighting harness and turned off the vibe, trying to collect her thoughts.

She had to get baited hooks out there, the manic urge to relive the experience riding her now. Jacqueline did not stop to remove the harness or the vibrator, but left it in place, ignoring the discomfort, overwhelmed by the desire to paddle out freshly baited hooks. She hastily attached a new rig, re-baited both hooks, and was soon paddling out.

The breakers were small, but annoying in that they slowed her down. Jacqueline panted, sweating, as she worked the paddles, left, right, left. She checked the GPS. Only fifty yards. Frustrated, she chopped the water with the paddles. She felt weak, but couldn't let herself stop, not now. The same shark was unlikely to bite again, but there could be more. She couldn't lose her chance, especially not with that fucking boat lurking nearby, threatening to disturb the waters. One hundred yards, she paddled harder, sucking in air. Two hundred yards, finally, halfway there, she dropped the first baited hook. Three hundred yards. It was taking forever. And what if the shark took the first bait before she returned. The bail of the reel was open so she wouldn't lose the rod and reel, but she would lose an opportunity she might never see again.

Three hundred fifty yards. Just another fifty yards to go, she thought when it felt like a log slammed into the kayak, and then she was in the water. She pulled the pin on her suspenders, and the devices hissed full of carbon dioxide. The kayak had hit something, or could it be possible? Could a shark have capsized the kayak? The moon seemed to shine impossibly bright.

Get back onto the kayak, she told herself. *You need to be afraid now.*

She saw the kayak, and it seemed not so far away, so she swam two, three, four strokes, and then something clamped her leg and she sucked water down her throat. She thrashed underwater, unable to breathe as something pulled her by the legs, and then she popped to the surface again.

Jacqueline gasped for air. The vibrator had switched on again, and her brain struggled to absorb what was happening to her. She tried to kick her legs, but the movement and control felt very much wrong. *It was a shark. This is real. You need to get to the kayak. Now.*

She pumped her arms and as much as she could, her legs, gasping for air and making slow progress towards the kayak. It all felt like a dream.

And she was underwater again, her body snapping back and forth. The force gripping her legs could not be fought, the power elemental, ancient. She was moving through water faster than she ever experienced, spinning, her chest aching, worse than even the day with Genesis. Genesis's face flashed in her mind, or had she seen it in the water before her, wearing the shark jaws, tearing her flesh. And there was no pain, only the orgasm exploding through her body. The moon blazed brightly, illuminating the sea around her like daylight. As she spun, she saw glimpses of something huge moving towards her, and Jacqueline knew it was Her before she could clearly see.

She swam towards her, infinitely graceful, but larger than any whale. Jacqueline wept at Her perfection. She would lead Jacqueline now to her new home, her true home. She swam above Jacqueline now as the woman twisted and writhed in the grip of the smaller shark, and Jacqueline fought now, clawing at this pretender. The Mistress blotted out the moonlight as She passed over, and when the light returned, Jacqueline felt herself rushing to the surface against her will. She tried to cry out but had no voice.

The surface air shocked her. Her flotation device had pulled her to the surface, and she coughed, racked with pain as her lungs sucked in air. She tried to pull off the suspender, but her limbs had no strength, and refused to move. She heard the sound of an engine and a bright light blinded her. Hands grasped at her, but she could not fight them. She heard men shouting.

Hands pulled her up and out of the water. Her back scraped across something and she felt herself laying on something solid, the deck of a boat she realized. Four faces surrounded her, shouting.

"Tie it off! Tie it off! Tie it off!"

"Jesus Christ!"

"Oh, fuck. Oh, fucking God..."

A haze hung in the air before her eyes, making everything foggy, but the strap of her glasses had held the entire time. Jacqueline looked down at herself. The men were tying ropes around her limbs, just as Genesis had tied straps, she thought. The plate of the fighting belt hung by one strap, the vibrator sticking up in the air, still buzzing. The other harness straps were a twisted mass, constricting tightly around her upper thighs, but little of her lower thighs remained. She wondered why her feet hurt, even though her legs now ended above the knees, ending in shreds of flesh and bone. She imagined herself as one of the pictures arranged on her bed. One hand remained, and she used it to point to the remains of her body.

"What?" one of the man asked, his face contorted.

"Take! Pictures!" Jacqueline hissed.

If you enjoyed this story, you can sign up for a free membership at
ForbiddenFiction and discuss it with other readers
and the author at the *All Consuming* story page
at http://forbiddenfiction.com/story/KH1-1.000177.

FORBIDDENFICTION
SHORT STORY

LOT'S SIN
KONRAD HARTMANN

Lot's Sin

Chapter 1
Insurrection

Lot swallowed the scream before it could escape his lips. The ground hardened his feet, sent tendrils of stone up his legs, rooted him to the spot where he peered over the boulder in front of the cave, hiding in the shadows of the night.

Punish them. Punish them, now! he told himself.

Within the cave, illuminated in orange from the fire, two naked forms writhed together on the makeshift bed. His younger daughter, Thamma, lay on the bed, naked with legs spread shamelessly, the fingers of one hand moving against her vagina. Sitting on Thamma's face, her back turned to Lot, Pheine quivered, lustrous black curls hanging down her bare back. Her full buttocks clenched and unclenched as she rhythmically rode her sister's face. The women glistened with sweat, reflecting the firelight. Thamma's slender body contrasted with Pheine's more voluptuous form.

Lot tried to speak, but no voice found its way from him. Was this a vision? Was this his wife, committing this sin with another woman? Was this Ado? The fine curve of the back, the narrow waist, and the perfect moons of the rear looked exactly like Ado; at least, how Ado looked when she was young.

No, he reminded himself, *that is Pheine, and she is shaming herself with her sister.* Lot suspected this, but the shock of seeing it overwhelmed him. His head throbbed and sweat appeared on his brow as his erection grew.

He touched his curved penis, knowing he shouldn't. Pulling his coarse robe aside, he stroked his erection. *What is happening?* He'd become impotent in the last years before fleeing Sodom, before Ado met her end.

And now this? Now? He realized he was pumping his fist up and down, unable to stop, watching as Pheine wriggled her hips. When she moved, he saw Thamma's tongue wiggling like a little snake against her sister's twat. Or was it in fact a small viper now, its diamond-banded scales wet with spit and slit-slime? The viper shot into Pheine and she moaned.

The surge shot through Lot's cock and he watched the seed spatter on the stone before him. Thick and viscous, the fluid slowly trickled into a narrow crack in the rock. He wondered how deep the fissure traveled. He shuddered, feeling linked to the spot now, his shame irretrievably embedded. He imagined a reptilian beast far below in a hollow space, catching his semen as it trickled down. What would it do with the fluid?

Burn, Lot, he heard a voice say, and he trembled, for it was the voice of an angel.

But still he watched Thamma fingering herself. Soon she stopped her licking and turned her face. She cried out, arching her back. As she relaxed, Pheine turned Thamma's face back to her vagina, easing herself down again on the smaller woman's face. Thamma held Pheine's ass cheeks, kneading them as she licked, until the older sister mewled and dropped forward, exposing asshole and cunt to Lot. The orifices seemed to stare mockingly at him.

His fluid spent, hot indignation now flooded his cheeks. Pulling his robe into place, he stormed into the cave, the ceiling just high enough for him to stand. He grabbed a switch from where it lay propped against the wall. He found himself using it more and more on his daughters, and, occasionally, on himself.

"Sinners!" he barked, charging the girls. He held the switch high, scraping the ceiling, a thunderbolt ready to fall.

Pheine and Thamma disentangled from each other and cowered against the wall of the cave, each women awkwardly trying to find a space between the stones. Pheine covered her full breasts with her hands, but Thamma squatted and held onto the wall behind her, too full of fear to cover her long-nippled teats.

"What I will now give you is only mercy! Did you learn nothing from Sodom? Lie on your bellies like the serpents you are!"

The girls scrambled to lay on their stomachs, both of them tucking their arms underneath their bodies and staring down at the bed.

"Not on the bed! You've soiled that enough with your sin! On the floor!" he shouted.

The girls slithered off the soft sheepskins and onto the cold stone of the floor. Lot watched as goose bumps broke out on their thighs and bottoms. He was grateful that his daughters could not see him, for he was already aroused again.

"Keep your brows pressed to the floor, or it will be worse!" he yelled. *What is happening to me?* Why, now, after all that happened in Sodom, should this monstrous urge rack him?

Without warning, Lot brought the switch down, the rod whistling through the air, then landing with a crackling sound across Thamma's ass. The girl yelped and shook, the branch leaving a neat red stripe across her buttocks, the cheeks clenching with the stroke. He would scourge this sin away from his daughters, and then he would punish himself with the lash. He brought the switch down on the tuck of her buttocks and she recoiled, as if to push herself through the floor. Again Lot lashed her. The sin had to be purged. He gritted his teeth and raised his arm high.

With the fourth stroke, Thamma broke and lurched to her feet. She turned to look at her father, crouching like a whipped dog. Her large, dark eyes fell on the bulge of his groin. Her lips quivered, as though about to ask the question, *Why?* Tears of humiliation stung Lot's eyes, though his penis remained erect under his robe.

"Pheine! Hold her down!" Lot yelled.

Pheine grabbed her sister by the arms and tried to pull her down. Thamma squealed and pulled toward the far end of the cave. Pheine was larger, but Lot knew Thamma had a wiry strength. He wanted Pheine to subdue not only Thamma's body, but also the unspoken accusation on the younger sister's face.

"Now, Pheine! Or you will take both yours and your sister's share!" Lot said, grabbing Pheine's hand and thrusting the switch into it.

Pheine glanced at him, a flicker of confusion in her eyes as they too passed over Lot's unabated swelling. But she did not hesitate, grabbing a fistful of Thamma's hair and pushing her younger sister face down on the floor. Pheine straddled Thamma to restrain her, and the position reminded Lot once again of the scene he witnessed. Facing Thamma's ass, Pheine placed one knee into her sister's back. Pheine braced herself with the other leg, leaving her legs open, her hairy vulva exposed to Lot's view.

Again and again, Pheine striped the pale flesh of Thamma's rounded bottom. It was smaller than Pheine's, Lot noticed, but no less shapely. Perhaps if he went to the entrance, he wondered, he could touch himself again and watch in concealment. *No!* he told himself.

Urine ran from beneath Thamma's legs, flowing across the uneven stone floor. A trickle ran towards the fire, as though seeking the flame, the fire sputtering on contact with the liquid. Lot stared at the flames reflected in the puddle, and saw a conflagration within that liquid mirror, people burning, screaming. He smelled the smoke of death, the acrid taste of burning human flesh in his mouth. Other things moved within the fire, things that were not people. He saw Ado, transformed in her final moment into that shape–

"Now, you lay on the floor, Pheine!" Lot gasped, stifling a scream as a fever burned in his brain.

Shaking, Pheine rolled off Thamma and lay face down on the floor, her forehead resting on the back of one hand. Thamma rose, her legs wobbling. Pee ran down her smooth thighs and tears streaked the dust on her face. Shame and humiliation darkened her face. Was there something else? Anger? *She wouldn't dare defy me again,* Lot thought.

"Punish your sister!" Lot said, and pointed to the switch still clutched in Pheine's hand.

Sobbing, Thamma grabbed the switch and began lashing Pheine's plump bottom. The younger sister swung the stick like a warrior in battle, her teeth clenched. *Perhaps that is also sin, if she enjoys this,* Lot thought. *As I enjoy this. No! I must not give in. Pain will cleanse. I will scourge myself tonight.* Thamma's hair whipped around as she punished her sister, her firm breasts swinging as she moved.

Lot collapsed on the bed, noting the scent of the womens' juices on the bedding. He had to find something to deaden the longing, for what he wanted brought tears to his eyes. He grabbed the large wine jug by the bed and drank deeply.

Lot heard Pheine screaming. He looked to see Thamma, her face contorted, landing a frenzy of strokes across her sister's thighs and ass. She looked inhuman, a mad look in her eyes, sweat plastering hair to her face. Blood beaded on the welts and Lot suddenly feared Thamma.

"Enough!" he shouted. "Cover yourselves now!"

Thamma staggered to her part of the cave and pulled on a short shift. The fabric covered her buttocks, but left the red welts on her slender thighs exposed.

Pheine slowly pulled herself to her feet, eyes vacant as she silently cried. Thamma helped Pheine slip on a long white shift. Lines of blood soaked through the linen that covered the swell of her ass.

Lot swallowed the wine as fast as he could. *It is shameful to drink in this way, but the sin is less than that which it restrains,* he reasoned. *God gives us the wine so we may subdue the beast within. The fire must not come here. It must not. I will stop it from coming here. We shall not turn into — what Ado became. I told the girls she turned into a pillar of salt. It was not salt. I cannot think of that now. Drink.*

The girls cowered against the wall, silent, not looking up. The fire burned lower now, allowing shadows to creep over the sisters. Their hair hung forward, obscuring their faces. *They do not even pull back their hair, but let it hang like whores do,* Lot thought. *What have they become? What have I let happen?*

By the time Lot set down the empty jug, he saw double. The girls now sat closer to him, and he did not like the way they stared at him. He would beat them in a moment, only now he felt so tired. He would rest his eyes for just a moment, and then he would find his switch.

"You cannot hide. We descend from the Heavenly Father Himself," he man said, grinning. "Would you have Zoar destroyed as well?" Taller than Lot by at least a foot, the man stared down at him from a face worthy of the finest sculptor. Lot recognized him immediately as a Nephilim, the bastard offspring of an angel and a woman.

Lot turned away from him. He was in Zoar again, the town spared from God's annihilation. Surrounded by a now scorched plain, the city suffered from its isolation. Lot tried to keep his daughters and himself inconspicuous, but every day, he found himself stared at more often, the citizens sneering, whispering, spitting on the ground. But now, he feared something worse than scorn.

"How much more will our Creator scorch, just to end our bloodline?" the man called out, following Lot.

He is not a man, Lot thought. *He is an abomination, a living violation of the Almighty's will.* Lot walked on through the twisting corridors which Zoar called streets.

"How long before he judges you and your people as unclean?" the thing continued behind Lot. "How long before you fail Him, and He commands your destruction? Your life has been a series of atrocities in the name of good. How will it feel when our Father tires of the sport you offer?"

"My God will stop you and your perverted race from poisoning the Earth," Lot shouted, spinning on his heel and shaking his fists at the Nephilim. "By whatever means necessary!" Lot shouted.

"Our Father may send flood after flood, firestorm after firestorm," the Nephilim said. "But He will never eradicate us. He may thin our ranks, but somewhere, in some part of the Earth, we will survive. And we will be fruitful and multiply."

"Abomination!" Lot shouted.

"Abomination? Perhaps we should look at what forms the Almighty chooses to create," the Nephilim said, pointing behind Lot. "Would you like to see the necessity of your wife's new form? Look at Ado, and explain to her the wisdom of Jehovah!"

Lot watched as a shadow loomed next to his on the dusty ground before him, a black bulk with writhing forms. He wanted to run, but his limbs could not move.

"Tell her, Lot, why you remained human and she did not!" the Nephilim said, laughing.

Lot screamed, then sobbed with relief as he woke from the dream to see the rough ceiling of the cave.

But something pulled against his wrist. He tried to pull away but the grip was too strong, and now it held his other wrist as well. The room spun as he screamed again, hoping to awaken from this new dream. He tried to get to his feet, but something gripped his ankles. If Ado came here, he would not be able to look or run away.

He cried out and willed the cave to stop spinning. Bound. His hands and wrists were bound with leather thongs, which were tied to ropes that wound around the heavy boulders in the cave. It was no dream.

And now his daughters stood before him, impudent, smiling. Lot couldn't stop shaking.

"Father," Pheine said, stepping up to stand over him, her hands on her hips. "Why do you scream so? Would you suffer your daughters to live to the end of their days in this cave? We will grow old and gray. No bees will visit these blossoms, and our wombs will bear no fruit."

"Untie me! Untie me or I will punish you in ways you've not imagined! We will not bring the fire here!" Lot howled, feeling his face grow purple. *Is there no escape from torment?* He asked himself.

"Punish us?" Thamma moved to stand on his other side. She ran the delicate toes of her bare foot along his thigh, but the touch only stoked his rage. "Is it not punishment to live year after year without love? We shall grow old, Father, and grow barren, never knowing the touch of a man. Stealing furtive pleasures from each other's tongues when you are gone, my own sister as my only lover. Is this the fate you wish for us?"

Lot listened, too angry to speak, too furious to form words.

"Would you have your line end now, Father?" Pheine asked. "Do you wish no offspring should come forth from us? That Lot should have no descendants to speak his name? Do you wish to simply become an old man, ending his life in a bleak cave, forgotten by the world?" She tucked her hair behind one ear, and let the shoulder of her garment fall low, exposing her neck and shoulder.

"How dare you question me!" Lot said. "What is God's will is His! He did not destroy us in Sodom because He did not wish it so. But to live in filth is to die in flames! It is not for me to question Him on the fate of my offspring, corrupted as they may be!"

"But Father," Thamma said, frowning. "We must question you, for you seem to defy the Almighty. God did not allow us to be soiled by the Sodomites, though *you* were willing for it to be so. But it was not us the people wanted, but the angels. And the angels did not desire the Sodomites. They desired us, Pheine and I!"

"Silence!" Lot screamed. He could not bear her voice, her words making real all that he refused to recall.

"And we desired them, Father," Pheine said. "As all desire to know the angels, the very Children of God himself."

"God would cleanse the Earth of the blasphemies produced by such union!" Lot shouted, his voice hoarse. "Be it with flood, or be it with flame!"

"But was it not you who brought the fire to Sodom, Father?" Thamma asked. "The angels came, and asked us to join with them of our own free will. You refused it, and Sodom burned. You sacrificed a city, only for the sake of denying our union with the Children of Heaven."

"Lies! Lies!" Lot shouted. "It is forbidden! It cannot be done! I will not allow you to create evil spawn this way, no matter how many sinners must perish!"

"Why do you hate the Nephilim so, Father?" Pheine asked.

"Speak not of them!" Lot screamed.

"Was Mother as evil as the Sodomites?" Thamma asked.

Lot choked on his response, clenching his fists, imagining choking a daughter with each hand.

"We fled to Zoar," Pheine said, "but that was not safe enough for you, Father. Who do you fear will come for us? What weight bears on your soul? Where will we hide next? A hole in the ground?"

"Perhaps our destiny is written," Thamma said. "You did not object to the Sodomites violating us; yea, you even offered us to them. Yet it was not God's will that it should happen. He would allow our bloodline to be pure. The angels sought to know us. It was not your will that it should happen, though the angels could have taken us at any moment. And so, it was God's will to allow you your choice, as he allowed the Sodomites to choose. And now, all paths are closed to us but one. No one remains to give us children, except for one man. God's choice clearly lies before us. He has chosen for Pheine and I. And He has chosen for you."

"What blasphemy do you speak of, sinner?" Lot gasped.

"Father," Pheine said, "was it blasphemy when you conceived us with our mother? Your wife? When you put your seed into her womb, was it wrong? Would it be wrong to love us the way you loved Mother? Give us children, Father, children of the purest blood."

"We must not!" Lot hissed. "I shall not join your transgressions, harlot!"

Pheine grabbed the hem of her shift and slowly lifted it, exposing the dark curls of her pubic hair. A tuck formed between her pubic mound and her thigh, her skin soft and creamy. Lot longed to touch her, to taste her.

"Does my sex look so different from that of our mother, Ado?" Pheine asked. She stood over him, one foot on either side of his head. "We are our mother, and we are you. What sin would you commit with us? We are of Ado, and we are not so different from your wife. Tell me. Do you not feel the same urges Mother once brought you? Do you not long to put your root inside of us?"

Lot stared up at her as she spread her labia, the moisture glistening in the fire light. Pheine slipped her shift off and threw it aside, standing naked above him now, the swell of her breasts jutting out beneath her face. She stood above him, a statue of sculpted flesh.

"I must shut my eyes! I must not look," Lot muttered to himself, but he could no more force himself to turn away than he could break his bonds, no more than he could save the cities as they burned. *Hopeless. Helpless. I fail you now, God. As Ado failed you. As Sodom and Gomorrah failed you. We all turn to ash before your burning splendor.*

He watched as the labia parted, but now they did so without Pheine touching them, and he heard a wet sucking sound. The sound became speech, the lips moving like a mouth speaking,

"Would you save us again, Lot? Would you build our tribe? We are in you. Ado was impure, but you are of the flesh, and you are our flesh, and you must come into this flesh so we may continue to live, Lot. God has only burned the dross. Come into me, Lot, that I may swallow your seed, and with it create life. With it, I will create a new people, a people of strength and virtue, purified by flame and destruction. We have been burned clean. Cleansed, untainted by forbidden unions. Come into me, and we shall live forever."

Lot felt his robe being lifted as the voice stopped. He looked down to see Thamma pushing the garment up over his stomach. Her soft hand caressed his scrotum, lifting it, rolling it gently as his penis swelled with blood, becoming almost painfully rigid. *The flesh of my body betrays me,* Lot thought. *And my offspring betray their father. I can-*

not resist what happens next, anymore than I could resist what happened in Sodom. Could I have done differently? Could I have permitted the angels to know my daughters? The Sodomites knew the angels often, without calamity, until I rebelled against the act in my own house. I have lived as a pious man, but have I ever had a choice? Perhaps I have, only to fail. This is my punishment, to succumb to my own flesh and blood.

Chapter 2
The Plot Betrayed

"This is how we see your member more often, Father," Thamma said. "Long and hard, like we saw on the men of Sodom. We are virgins between our legs, Father, but not in the back."

"What do you mean?" Lot sputtered.

"Sometimes," Thamma said, kneeling beside him, "the men would take their cocks, hard and be-veined like yours, and they would thrust them into our rear." She wrapped one hand around his shaft and slowly stroked him, cupping his scrotum with the other hand. "They would fuck us in the anus, Father." Thamma lifted her hips, slowly wiggling her bottom in the air.

Lot's cock grew even harder. He stared at Thamma as Pheine stroked her hair.

"But we don't want that with you," Pheine said. She gently pushed Thamma's head down, until Thamma's lips wrapped around Lot's purple cock, slobbering. Her sucking mouth pulled and pulled at him, her tongue rubbing against the underside of his shaft. Thamma's hand gripped the base of his root, pumping him as she worked. Lot thought of the little viper again. He imagined it inside Thamma's mouth, wrapping around his penis, probing the hole. The pressure built inside, his head grew light—

And then he lost himself, feeling nothing but the pure energy of his sperm squirting into Thamma's mouth. He looked down to see her frowning, her lips locked tight around the head of his cock. When the last drop of come had coursed out, Thamma sat up, not opening her mouth. She took her hand, then, and let the white slime flow out of her mouth and into her cupped palm.

"Quickly, help me, Pheine," Thamma said, laying on her back and spreading her legs.

Lot stared, puzzled.

Pheine knelt down between her sister's legs and spread the smooth petals of Thamma's cunt lips. Carefully, Thamma trickled the sperm from her hand into her vagina.

Thamma cried out as Pheine quickly thrust her fingers into her, pushing the seed in as far as she could reach. The younger sister clenched her teeth and gripped the sheepskin as, Lot realized, she lost her maidenhead to her sister's hand. But as Lot watched, Thamma's labia quivered, mouth-like, as though sucking at the fingers. He half expected the vagina to devour Pheine's hand, pulling her into her sister. Lot heard wet sounds, like a beast feeding.

He closed his eyes, afraid to open them again for a long moment. When he did, he saw the girls reclining. It was done now, he realized. They had crossed a boundary, and could never return.

The girls rested for a moment, and then Pheine held a wineskin to Lot's lips, letting him drink. Thamma crawled on top of him and laid her slender body on top of him, gently fondling his flaccid penis. Lot despised how good her body felt, and stared at the ceiling. That they physically forced him to carnal actions enraged him. But the fact that his inner being so badly desired this congress sickened him. There could be no redemption for his soul's collaboration with this plot.

"Show me," Thamma whispered in his ear, "how you licked Mother." Thamma slid herself up Lot's sweaty body and climbed up, sitting on his face.

Thamma's pubic hair pressed into his nose, her curly hairs wet. She rubbed her cunt against his lips. Her musky scent made something rage inside himself, and Lot stuck out his tongue, tasting pussy juice, blood, and his own seed in Thamma's slit. He could no more resist the act, than could a starving man turn away from food.

Thamma moaned and ground down, taking his tongue inside her pussy as his nostrils filled with her aroma. She slid back and forth, fucking herself with his tongue. How long had it been since he last enjoyed the silken taste of a woman? Lot wondered. Thamma wiggled back, using her fingers to expose the bump of her clitoris. Lot's tongue darted against the bump, remembering the taste of Ado so long ago.

He sucked hard at her clit, angry that it was not his wife. Thamma clutched his head as she yelped and came, shivering and trickling juices into his beard.

"Now, Thamma," he heard Pheine say. Thamma lifted herself and slid down his body, straddling his hips and rubbing her oozing cunt against his cock. As his member swelled again, he realized with a shock his daughter was about to mount him. *The sucking hole will take my seed directly*, he thought.

Pheine knelt between Lot's legs and grasped his penis, pressing the crown between Thamma's labia. Lot grunted at the tight resistance of Thamma's cunt as she slowly moved her hips, whimpering as the rigid shaft forced its way into her flesh. She rested her cheek on his shoulder, gently rolling her hips and taking him in and out of her slit. He wanted to be repulsed, but could not resist the pleasure, the terrible hunger for release, gnawing at his innards.

"Come inside me, Father," Thamma whispered into his ear. "Come inside me." More words spilled out of her mouth, and these words Lot did not recognize. As she whispered her voice changed, becoming strange, and the voice of another whispered in his ear,

"All of the tribe lies within the wombs of the daughters of Lot. Feed your people with the screams and the blood of the outsiders. Let this cunt be an engine of war, destroying the enemies of your children with its power," the voice said.

As her muscles loosened slightly, she held onto his shoulders and fucked him harder, smacking her bottom against his hips.

"I feel you deep inside me!" Thamma grunted. "Let it come, Father, do not resist."

Lot thrust to meet her rhythm. Nothing mattered then, not that it was Thamma, not that it was sin. There was only the ecstasy of the flesh, the perfect feel of her pussy sliding up and down on his cock. He wanted this now and forever, even if it destroyed him.

Thamma moved as she had moved when whipping Pheine, driven, pumping up and down hard enough to hurt Lot's hips. Her face shone, livid, leering. Lot cried out as his fluid erupted, his daughter suddenly still, holding him. She stared into his eyes as she took his come. When Lot no longer twitched, and his member softened, she rolled off of him.

Lot stared at the ceiling of the cave and wept.

Thamma watched her father wake the next morning, groaning as he tested the restraints. She wondered if they should unbind him, but she knew he was still too wrathful. Moreover, Pheine had yet to lift her share of the burden.

"Wine," was the only word Lot spoke, not even looking at her or at Pheine. Thamma tended to him that day, massaging his sore body, feeding him, and helping him to relieve himself. Lot accepted her help in silence. And she gave him wine, not too much, but more as the day faded.

"Sister, I dreamed of Sodom and Gomorrah last night," Pheine said to Thamma, as dusk approached. Pheine had grown pensive and quiet.

"And?" Thamma said, glancing up from her chores.

"I saw the people burning. I saw the things that moved through the streets and the desert. I saw angels," Pheine said. "And they reminded me what happens to those who anger our God."

"And what, my sister, does that portend?" Thamma asked, stopping and staring at Pheine. Pheine worried the edge of her shift, averting her eyes from her sister's gaze. *Look at me, damn it,* Thamma thought. Thamma continued her work, staring at her sister.

"Perhaps we need to stop what we are doing. Perhaps we should not force this sin upon our father," Pheine said.

"Strange," Thamma said, her face growing hot. "Very strange they would speak to you last night, and not the night before. Do they think that perhaps it suffices that your younger sister should bear the guilt? That your younger sister should bear the offspring of our father while you remain a virgin for your husband?" Thamma swore a silent oath such would never happen.

"I can only tell you of what I dream," Pheine said, her face placid.

"Do you think God is not guiding us now? What we do is holy, my sister. Remember that," Thamma said. "That which is chosen cannot

121

be unchosen." *You will not leave me alone with this,* Thamma thought.
Pheine stared blankly and returned to her chores.

That night, Thamma fed her father much wine. Lot accepted the drink
passively, and reflected on how much Pheine resembled Ado. Pheine
would not tend to him — only Thamma. And Pheine — was this truly
his daughter? How could it be his daughter when she looked exactly
like Ado? He listened to them talk.

"Pheine. My sister. Dusk has fallen. It seems it is your turn with
Father tonight," Thamma said.

"But, Thamma, what of my dream? Dare I ignore it? Dare *we* ignore it?" Pheine answered, her voice grown high-pitched.

"Whatever sin has occurred has already stained you, my older
sister, who I might have depended on for guidance from the very beginning," Thamma said. Lot watched her fists clench as she spoke.

"I am sorry, my sister. I can only follow the wisdom granted me
by God," Pheine said, turning away. Pheine? Or was it Ado, afflicted
with some kind of madness? She must be Ado, Lot thought.

Lot felt fingers moving against his wrist, and looked up to see
Thamma untying the bonds. She stood, walking toward Ado.

Lot did not understand why his wife was not tending to him.
Why did Ado stand with her back turned toward him? Why should
it fall upon his very daughter to rescue him? His hand was free now,
though. Pain shot through it as the blood flow resumed. He glanced
at the woman Thamma had her arm around — was it really Ado? Had
she not been turned into a pillar of salt? She must have survived. But
what was she doing? *She did not live, Lot. She is salt. She is gone. She was
not worth saving,* he heard the voice say.

"But she was good," Lot spit the words out. "What did you make
her into? You made her into a monster. And you let her live still out
in the desert!"

Quickly he untied his other hand. The young woman turned
around, and recoiled as she faced him.

This was not Ado! Lot was stung, infuriated. Thamma grabbed
Pheine, as Lot growled and untied the bonds around his ankles.

Thamma stepped behind Pheine and hooked her arms under her older sister's shoulders. The younger woman let herself fall backward onto the bed, grunting as Pheine's weight fell upon her. Still, Thamma maintained her grip, and wrapped her legs around to trap Pheine's soft limbs.

"You!" Lot roared, pointing at Pheine, "You who would pretend to be my daughter, and then pretend to be my wife! You will *serve* as my wife now!"

His penis pointed at the girl like an angry spear. Pheine kicked and writhed, trying to free herself from Thamma, but the younger one only tightened her grip.

Lot pushed himself between the grappling legs of the girls. He clutched Pheine's shift with both hands and tore it open. Her full breasts swayed and moved in the struggle. *This will be magnificent. Mine to enjoy. Mine to punish for her insult,* he thought. He mashed her breasts in his hands, relishing the soft warmth. He grasped her dark nipples, pinching them, watching her squirm as they hardened against her will.

"So, you would be my wife, would you?" Lot said, taking his cock in hand, pressing against the fleshy folds of Pheine's cunt. "Then so be it!" He felt her wetness on his glans, the moisture only confirming in his mind the sinfulness of this deceiver.

Lot thrust forward, pushing into the girl's hole. He wanted it to hurt. Pheine gasped and arched her back.

"You call this suffering?" Lot asked. He savored the warmth and tightness of Pheine's cunt, sinking his shaft deeper and deeper into her, holding onto her breasts as he thrust into her tender hole. There was nothing else as he pounded into her, just the gripping flesh and the pleasure. They were one and he was three. Why should his wife be salt and he be alive? Why should this harlot bite her lip and grimace at him so? What wrong was there in putting his seed into the girls? Were they not almost the same as his wife? Were they not his wife? Was it not his right and duty? God would punish him, as he punished all, and how should he defy the will of the almighty? He would sin now, and invite the inevitability of destruction, as God desired, as it must be written.

The false-Ado, the fight fading from her, quit her struggle as she lay trapped between Lot and Thamma. Lot listened to the younger one cooing in the pretender's ear. She relaxed her grip on the woman and reached around, sliding her hand in to rub her captive's fleshy clitoris while Lot pounded into her.

"We must do this, sister," he heard Thamma whispering into the False-Ado's ear. "We must build the tribe."

Lot's anger dissipated as Pheine moved beneath him, moaning, the skin of her chest and face blushing. He felt her cunt tightening around his shaft, and she cried out, shaking.

"Who is this woman who maddens my flesh so?" Lot whispered.

"You do not recognize your daughter?" Thamma asked, smiling at him. She slid her fingers along the woman's slit, touching Lot's thrusting penis for a moment before reaching to slide two fingers into Lot's mouth. He sucked them, tasting the woman's juices. "Do you not recognize Pheine?"

The woman blinked at him. Lot gasped, recognizing Pheine, but unwilling to stop, the pleasure irresistible.

"Come inside her, Father," Thamma said. "Plant your seed in her womb."

"No!" Pheine said, her eyes widening. She pushed at Lot's chest.

"Now, Father!" Thamma cried out. Her arm locked around Pheine's throat, holding her in place. "Do what you must!"

The pressure inside overwhelmed Lot and he let himself go, sinking deeper and deeper inside the writhing Pheine. A warm rush crashed in his ears and the clutched Pheine as tight as he could, spending himself inside of her. He saw Pheine's wincing face next to the laughing visage of Thamma.

The world spun before his eyes. He saw Ado and his daughters and the angels, as the city of Sodom sought them out. The crowd screamed and writhed before him, and he smelled fire and choked on smoke and heard the screams. When he could see again, the girls were staring at the mouth of the cave. *The people of Sodom and Gomorrah were evil and God destroyed them. But God did not destroy me,* Lot thought. *What I do cannot be evil. But what of Ado? Was she evil? She did not obey God, so she was transformed. And yet, I fornicate with my daughters, and I live.*

Lot looked at the mouth of the cave. They were there. Not Nephilim, no hybrid spawn these, but the angels from Sodom. They stood, gleaming against the ink-black night. Lot recognized them in his heart, though they no longer wore the guise of man. Their skin rippled and changed, sometimes the palest white, sometimes the color of smoke, but always flickered over their hides what looked like threads of lightning to Lot. Their faces looked only vaguely human, skin stretched tight over wolf-like, hairless heads. Their bodies surpassed any warrior Lot ever saw, muscles flexing asymmetrically on their limbs, enormous turgid members jutting into the air. The air tasted like a massive storm approached. Lot heard his daughters weeping. A hum filled the air like the buzzing of bees.

The flesh of one angel unfolded at its stomach, the skin opening like a box. Long white worms wriggled within the cavity. The worms lifted themselves and stretched forward, their heads expanding into round knobs, the round knobs of glistening tissue opening to form mouths.

And the mouths spoke as one, and they sang songs to Lot in words that he did not understand, but the sounds touched him inside his skull. White liquid dribbled from the mouth of each worm as it spoke.

We speak the seed of the tribe, Lot. Your daughters will know us tonight. We are the tribe and the tribe is you, and we shall all dwell together forever.

Behind the angels, a shadowy mass lurched into the mouth of the cave. Lot refused to look at it, and let the angels hold his gaze.

"Ado," he wept.

If you enjoyed this story, you can sign up for a free membership at ForbiddenFiction and discuss it with other readers and the author at the *Lot's Sin* story page at http://forbiddenfiction.com/story/KH1-1.000178.

Frogger Says

Chapter 1
Growing Up Is Hard To Do

"This is Jerry," Hannah said, holding up a pink rabbit.

"And this is Rhonda," she said, holding up—maybe it was a green dragon, Andy thought.

"This is Frogger." She held up a frog with googley eyes.

"This is Big Tony," she said, hefting a big, brown bear. "I guess you know why I call him that!"

"Because... he's a bear?" Andy asked, looking at Haley out of the corner of his eye.

Hannah giggled. Ponytails shot out from either side of her head in bunches of straight black hair, held together with hair bands adorned with plastic balls that looked like big red hard candy. Her pale blue eyes shined like polished stones, almost artificial. She wore neon-green footie pajamas, but Andy couldn't remember ever seeing them on anyone taller than a few feet, let alone—what was Hannah? Five-foot-six? Five-foot-eight?

Hannah hopped off the couch and skipped back to her bedroom.

She's nineteen? Andy mouthed the words to Haley.

Haley nodded, her eyes half-closed.

"So, where the hell did Tracy find Hannah?" Andy asked, sipping his coffee.

Haley sighed and glanced around the diner.

"Hannah is a friend of Kay who is a friend of Tracy. Yeah, I've got a couple things to talk about with Tracy. She's like, 'Oh, yeah,

Hannah's a sweetheart. You'll love her.' She didn't tell me my room-mate would be wearing footie pajamas and singing along to cartoons. I mean—she's really fucking odd," Haley said.

"Yeah, but, you met her before she moved in. I mean, couldn't you tell—" Andy said.

"Well, okay," Haley interrupted, holding up her hands. "Okay. She seemed a little weird. I mean, yeah. If I had more time to get a roommate, sure. But the girls I talked to before her—well, first of all, they both smoked. And they wanted to be able to smoke in the apart-ment, so right there, that wasn't working.

The first one had some kind of thing where, like, she wouldn't be able to pay the first month's rent but she would 'catch up with me,' whatever the fuck that means. The other one was, we're sitting there and—swear to God—she takes out this list of rules that would have to, that *I* would have to follow. No TV or taking showers after ten and all these special rules because she has trouble sleeping. No. It would've been crazy. I mean, in a different way from Hannah."

"So," Andy said, "did Hannah show up with a stuffed animal and a big lollipop and all? When I talked to you, you seemed pretty okay with her. You didn't say anything, you know…"

"Yeah! No, I mean, she seemed a little, I don't know, childish, but, I don't know. She seemed alright. I didn't really think. I wasn't think-ing of asking people if they had conversations with stuffed animals or if they had a list of animated movies they watch every week and have fucking memorized. You know what? Yesterday, I came home and I'm pretty sure she had a fucking tea party with her stuffed animals!"

Andy laughed.

"What?!" he said.

"Yeah! I don't know…" Haley said as the waitress refilled her coffee. "I mean, I guess there are worse things. She's clean. She puts things away. She's always nice. It's just…"

"Creepy?" Andy asked.

"Yeah! It kinda is…"

Andy pounded into Haley. Despite the air conditioning, sweat dripped from his forehead. Haley wrapped her arms around his shoulders and bumped her hips to meet him. He fucked her hard, feeling the wet flex of her cunt around his cock as he pulled out all the way to the crown and plunged deep. She had already come once, maybe twice; Andy noticed her tiring, losing interest, wanting him to finish.

And once he knew she wanted him to finish, it made it that much harder to finish. It felt good, the wet slide of Haley's pussy, the mash of her breasts in his hands, but every time he came close to coming, it felt like a switch turned off and he was back to zero.

And then there was the singing. He could hear Hannah singing in the other room, in her bedroom, just faintly, but it was enough to distract him. Her weird sing-song tune seeped through the wall.

Andy thrust harder. Faster. He held both of her breasts, moving in and out as fast as he could, until the blood pounded in his ears. He stopped and rolled off of her, panting, moisture cooling on the condom as his penis pointed up into the air.

"Relax," Haley said, "Don't try to come. It's like, paradoxical intention."

"What?" Andy asked.

Haley laid her head on his stomach so her ear was against his navel, facing away from him so her silky chestnut hair spilled across his belly. He felt her hand cup his balls.

"If you try too hard, you won't be able to," she said. "So try not to."

"Try not to think about it?"

"No, try not to come," she said. He felt her rolling the condom off, felt her warm mouth envelop his glans. She sucked him gently, rolling his balls in her hand as she took her time taking him in and out of her mouth.

He told himself not to come. He would refuse to come. Instead he would listen to Hannah's strange voice from the other room. He let it crawl into his ear and dance up and down in his brain, a tiny deranged rabbit leading a strange parade of notes into his ears. He smiled.

Pressure moved through him like a wave. He held onto Haley's hair and felt the juice surge out and into her mouth. Haley sucked harder then, swallowing until his energy was gone. She rolled off and lay next to him.

"Is she... *singing*?" Haley asked. "Jesus."

She rolled over, her ass a white moon as she crawled over to grab the remote for the small stereo. Guitars drowned out the faint voice of Hannah.

"Get us a drink, would you?" Haley said, curling up and pulling the sheet over until only her head stuck out.

Andy pulled on a t-shirt and a pair of shorts. He walked into the hallway and glanced towards Hannah's room. The door was open just a crack, but no light was on and he could hear no singing. He walked into the kitchenette and grabbed two bottles of seltzer from the refrigerator. When he turned and entered the hallway, Hannah's door slowly shut.

"Somebody was loud last night." Andy heard the words whispered from the other side of the library shelf.

"What?" he asked. He tried to peer through the racks, but saw no one. A piece of yellow construction paper lay on top of the books. Andy picked it up.

Red crayon scrawled out the words, "Somebody was naughty last night!" There was a picture of two stick figures; it took Andy a moment to realize they were laying down, one figure fellating the other's oversized erection.

Andy looked down the aisle. At the far end of the shelves, he saw Hannah's head peer around the corner and then disappear. Andy walked down the aisle, clutching the paper in his hand. He searched row by row, but did not see Hannah.

He walked outside and dug the phone out of his pocket, still frowning at the construction paper. He selected Haley, but a hand grabbed onto his wrist. He jumped, dropping the paper. It was Hannah, wearing a short dress, big shoes, and giant black sunglasses. A red belt circled her waist, a matching red scarf was tied around her neck, and red lipstick gleamed on her lips. Her hair was down, framing her chin.

Andy bent down to pick up the paper. Hannah squatted down next to him. Her perfume smelled sweet and made him think of summer vacation afternoons and cherry water ice. Her arm brushed his, darted forward, and snatched the paper. She stepped backwards and stuffed it into her purse in a crumple.

"I'm sorry, Andy," Hannah said.

"Why did you—"

"I thought it would be funny," she said. "I'm sorry. It wasn't funny."

"No," Andy said. "No, it was—it was pretty weird."

"You told Haley?" A tear trickled down from beneath her sunglasses.

"Well, no, but, I think I should," he said.

"Do you have to? It was just—you know. Just a joke." Hannah started to sniffle.

"It wasn't funny, Hannah."

"I know. I know. But if you tell Haley, I'm gonna have to, have to move."

"Well... why would you think that was funny?"

"I don't know. Just—sometimes I don't know what other people think is funny. But I want people to like me. So I try. And sometimes they get mad. I shouldn't try. I won't try anymore. I promise. I guess you have to tell Haley. It's my own fault that I'll get in trouble. I just wanted you to like me." Hannah's voice broke down with the last few words and she turned and started walking away.

"Hannah," Andy said.

She stopped but did not turn around.

"Let's just... forget about it," he said.

She turned and lurched towards him. He tried to step back but she was too fast, throwing her arms around him. Her sweet perfume crawled into his nostrils, pulling in the smell of her hair, and a puff of her breath. Her small breasts pressed against him, her torso wiggling. He felt his cock growing while he looked around for Haley or her friends.

And then Hannah was gone and Andy walked towards the parking lot. He reached into his pocket for his keys and found a scrap of yellow construction paper with a number scribbled in red crayon.

Haley picked up a stuffed bird from the couch and threw it on Andy's lap, sitting down next to him.

"Here you go," she said. "I'm about sick to fucking death of these stuffed animals."

Andy nodded and looked at the TV.

"I mean, wouldn't you be?" she said, looking at him.

"Oh, yeah," he said.

"Like if Jeremy kept a bunch of stuffed animals laying around," she said.

"Yeah, that would be weird. You know, there's a way of avoiding all of this crap with roommates," Andy said.

"I know. I know. I'm just not..."

"Not ready to upset your parents," he said.

"Right."

"I mean, ever?"

"I don't know. Yes. I'll have to, we'll have to someday. Let me kinda test the waters while I'm home this weekend. But, right now, I mean, they're not gonna pay for my share of the rent if we move in together. Not gonna pay my car payments. My car insurance. And I can't work full-time and then take 18 credits. You can't either. And I'm just not ready for the fight that's gonna start," Haley said.

"Okay," Andy said, raising his hands palms outward.

"Oh, look," Haley said, picking up a piece of paper and handing it to him. Andy stared at the drawing with her.

"Is that what I think it is?" he asked.

"If you think it's a unicorn raping a frog, I guess it is," Haley said.

"Did I tell you your roommate is odd?" Andy said. "She drew..."

"What?" Haley said.

"She drew a unicorn fucking a frog," he said, shaking the paper. "Who does that?"

"Oh," Haley said. "I meant to tell you. This morning? She had this weird bruise around her neck."

"Like hickies?" Andy said.

"No. No, it was like... more like a line," Haley said, motioning with her hands on her throat.

"Did you ask her? Ask her what it was?"

"Yeah! She said it was from her dresser. That she fell down and hit her throat on an open dresser drawer."

"That doesn't sound right," Andy said.

"Yeah, I know. She kinda sounded like she was making it up. She put on a scarf before she left."

"Um, hi," Andy said. A haze of smoke hung in the air of his apartment. Jeremy's glass bong sat on the table. Jeremy sat in one chair, his strawberry-cheesecake-bloodshot eyes darting back and forth between Andy and the girl sitting in the other chair, Hannah. Hannah wore a green shoulderless dress and a big smile, her eyes only slightly less red than Jeremy's. A green scarf covered her neck and green balls adorned her pigtail bands.

"Hey, what's up, Andy. Um... this is Hannah. Oh, wait, you guys know each other already," Jeremy chuckled. "Haley's roommate. Right." He waved his hand and smiled.

Andy nodded. He walked into the kitchen and stared at the floor, his hand on the refrigerator door. Jeremy appeared in the doorway.

"Uh, hey. I'm sorry. I would have saved you some but I didn't know you were home. Coming home," Jeremy said.

"No, no. That's cool. I'm just gonna head back to my room," Andy said.

Girl pop suddenly blared on the sound system in the other room. Andy smothered a smirk and turned to grab a beer before Jeremy saw his face. When he turned around, Hannah stood in the doorway, holding the hem of her dress with her fingertips.

"C'mon! Dance!" Hannah said, grabbing Andy and Jeremy by the wrists and pulling them out to the living room.

"No no no," Andy said, laughing. "I gotta, gotta go work on something."

Hannah hopped over to her purse and pulled out a stuffed frog, holding it towards him.

"Frogger says dance!" Hannah said in a rough voice.

"That's... um... not convincing me," Andy said, backing away.

"Good night, kids." He turned to walk back to his room.

Hannah slipped past and stepped in front of him. She leaned against him, pushing her ass back into him, wiggling it a little. He put his hands on her back to push her away but she grabbed them and slid them down her flanks, resting them on her hips. She ground her ass against him, making blood flow into his prick. The smell of her hair and perfume crawled into his brain again.

I need to go. Now! he thought. He looked back over his shoulder at Jeremy, who danced badly and shrugged at him.

Hannah held onto Andy's hands and pushed backwards, guiding him back to the living room dance-floor. She flitted back and forth between the two men, keeping them close to her on either side.

When she ground her ass against Jeremy, he grinned and slid his hands up her belly, feeling her breasts. Hannah stared at Andy, smiled and tugged the front of her dress down. Her breasts stood up high, with long, thin nipples Jeremy's fingers rubbed like he was trying to remove them.

Andy's feet felt heavy, his legs suddenly hard to move. His mouth felt dry and he felt himself stepping backwards.

Go, dumb-ass, he told himself. *If you don't go now, you'll regret it.*

Hannah frowned and bent forward at the waist, one leg behind her and aside Jeremy's leg for balance. Her hands darted forward, gripping Andy's belt and pulling, drawing him close to her as she was sandwiched between the two men.

"Don't leave," she whispered hard into his ear, her sharp teeth nibbling at his earlobe. She grabbed his hands and put them on her breasts, making him squeeze them.

"Frogger says you have to hurt me," Hannah said.

"Wh—what? I have to—" Andy said. *Have to what?* She was rubbing his swollen penis through his pants. *Have to go—*

He glanced over his shoulder, down the hallway. It seemed to stretch and stretch and go on forever. But the living room grew smaller and smaller and Hannah's perfume crawled right up his nose and put needles in his brain.

"He says you have to hurt me," she said. Andy glanced at Jeremy to see his reaction. Jeremy was looking down, pushing Hannah's dress up in the back and fondling her.

"Like, hurt you how?" Andy said. "Like this?" He squeezed her nipple and she sighed. He squeezed it a little harder, feeling it, like a rubber eraser between his fingertips. He felt like he was stepping off a cliff.

Andy felt Hannah's body stiffen a second before her open palm smacked hard against his face with a crack. He saw Jeremy staring open-mouthed at him behind Hannah. Andy started to back up but Hannah grabbed fistfuls of his shirt, her nails scratching him as she grabbed.

"Like how you want to have to want to," she said, her eyes boring into him, the pupils contracting and dilating. She reached down and rubbed his erection through his pants, the fabric of his underwear abrading his skin with the friction. She took his hand in her other hand, lifted it to her lips and bit.

Andy felt something detaching and coming loose inside. He felt afraid then, as if he knew what happened in the next minutes would change everything.

Andy hissed through his teeth as she nipped the webbing of his hand. Reflexively, he grabbed Hannah's face with his free hand and squeezed at the joint of her jaw. Harder than he had to. Longer than he had to. When he let go, she was grinding against him, her hands behind her, holding onto Jeremy's belt, Jeremy's face a mixture of horniness and confusion.

A pulse thudded in Andy's ears, out of sync with the pop music pumping out of the stereo. He thought of Haley and wondered what she was doing. He leaned down and grabbed Hannah's breasts, squeezing them hard, pinching her nipples until she squealed. He took one in his mouth, sucking it hard, harder, nipping it hard, harder with his teeth, stopping for fear he would want to bite through it, circling it, biting with his eye-tooth until the faint taste of copper told him to slow down. Her hands gripped his shoulder and he felt the energy flowing from him into Hannah's nerves, into her hands, and back into himself. The music, so insane a minute ago, took on a strange purpose now.

The room, dark around them, now just felt like a space surrounding them. Andy was in this space with Hannah, and Jeremy just happened to be there too, almost just an image in Andy's vision. Andy registered a faint annoyance at Jeremy, whose presence reminded him an outside world existed.

Andy had to be closer to Hannah, had to be *inside* Hannah. Without thinking about it, he felt his hands go to his belt, felt himself unbuckling it. His prick throbbed as he huffed the girl's perfume.

Hannah grinned at him, her wolfish eyes piercing him, and she yanked his shirt open to stare at the erection throbbing towards her.

Chapter 2
An Understanding Between Friends

Andy straightened up and unbuckled his pants, letting them fall around his knees, his cock pushing the fabric of his shirt out. Hannah grabbed the shirt and pulled it open, scattering buttons into the air. She looked down at his prick and smiled, licking her white teeth with a pink tongue. Andy didn't like undressing in front of other guys in a locker room, and he vaguely registered the thought as he stood within a foot of his roommate, his penis erect.

Hannah punched him in the chest, her small fist knuckling him hard.

"You gonna fuck me with that? Hunh? Gonna fuck me? Gonna fuck me?" Hannah asked, punctuating every other word by hitting him.

"Hold her," Andy said. "No—like—a full nelson. Yeah. That's it."

Jeremy hooked his arms underneath her shoulders.

Andy pulled up Hannah's dress. She wore green panties decorated with little skull-and-crossbones wearing pink ribbons. He hooked his fingers and pulled them down, his head feeling hot, and pulled, until her legs were horizontal and she was suspended in the air.

And then they were off and her feet slapped against the hardwood floor as they fell. Andy looked at her pussy, the delicate hairless folds around her vagina, her mound shaved bald.

Andy hooked his arms under her legs and lifted them up, reaching under and struggling for a moment to work his penis into her slit, until the glans slid past the slick, tulip petals of flesh and she squealed as he pushed himself all the way inside her.

Jeremy staggered backwards, still holding Hannah but pushed

until his back hit the wall. Andy pounded into her, feeling the pressure of her tight cunt around him, pressing down at the top. Hannah made little wailing sounds.

"Choke me," she said in Andy's ear.

"What?" he asked.

"*Choke me!*"

"Jeremy, hold her. Under the legs," Andy said.

"Uh, OK," Jeremy said, struggling for a moment but eventually hooking hands and forearms under Hannah's legs, just like he did with the arms. Sweat trickled down his forehead.

Andy looked at her neck. How should he do it? With her scarf? He tried it, his fingers fumbling unsure of how to do it. How hard to do it. He stopped when the scarf bunched up into a thick cord. Hannah's fingers flittered at the knot and the scarf fell free. She grabbed his hand and wrapped it around her throat, so the webbing lay across her windpipe. She pressed down on his thumb and index finger.

Hannah shut her eyes and a flush of red blossomed across her pale face. Her mouth hung open. Andy fucked her hard, his hips slapping against her thighs. Purple spread across her face.

"Dude, is she...? Are you...?" Jeremy said, but Andy heard his voice like it was far away. The wet clench of the girl's cunt held him, pulled him in deeper with every thrust. And as he thrust into her, she seemed to relax, everything except her vagina, and her nails digging into his shoulders.

"Andy! Hey! Let go!" he heard Jeremy say, and then the pressure spurted through his shaft and Hannah was pulling away from him. He let go of her throat. His cock slid out, still pulsing, shooting a jet of pearl across her green dress.

Jeremy was lowering Hannah so she sat on the floor, gasping for breath. She looked down at the fluid running down her dress, trailing her fingertips through the white.

"Ya—," Hannah coughed, clearing her throat. "Yay!" she said, her voice rough. "You did it, Andy!"

Andy tried to smile. He avoided eye contact with Jeremy, and sensed Jeremy was doing the same. He started pulling his pants up. Hannah reached for her purse.

"Frogger says, 'Leave them off! You ain't done, yet!'" Hannah said, holding up the frog stuffed animal again.

"Now, you know, you sound like a frog. Sort of. I mean, your voice is hoarse," Jeremy said to her. Hannah rose to her knees and held the frog in front of her face.

"I don't know if I want to," Hannah said.

"You have to," Frogger's voice said. She shook him when she made him talk.

"I have to... to suck...?" she said.

"That's right, bitch. Suck his dick!" Frogger said.

And now Andy and Jeremy did make eye contact. Andy saw a glimmer of panic light up in Jeremy's eyes, but then Jeremy shrugged, a tiny movement that seemed to chase the panic away.

Hannah was unbuckling Jeremy's pants now, and Andy realized he was undressing himself. Hannah set Frogger on the floor next to them.

"Frogger likes to watch," Hannah said. She unzipped her dress and threw it aside on the floor, glancing back and smiling at Andy. She was one of the palest girls he had ever seen, ghostlike as she knelt down in front of Jeremy's prick, her head bobbing back and forth.

Andy grew hard again. He saw Jeremy trail his fingers along Hannah's hairline. She took his hands and pressed them firmly against the back of her head. Andy heard a slurping sound.

"Frogger wants you to do it like this," she said.

Moments later, Hannah repeated the motion, impatiently pressing Jeremy's hands down so he would pull her closer.

Andy wasn't sure why he did it, but he found himself kneeling on the floor behind Hannah, holding her by the ponytails, pushing her back and forth, using Hannah's mouth to fuck Jeremy's cock. The idea repelled him as much as it excited him, a queasy exuberance bringing drops of sweat to his forehead. He heard her gag sometimes, but still he worked her head, rocking it back and forth until Jeremy groaned and grabbed onto Hannah's head.

Jeremy backed away, his cock already sagging. Andy pushed Hannah forward, relieved when she put her hands out to stop her face-forward fall. He felt relief, but also vague alarm he had almost driven her face-first into the hardwood floor.

He gripped her bubbly ass-cheeks, bent down, and bit the firm flesh. Hannah squealed and arched her back. Andy slid between her legs, pushing his penis between her fuck-swollen labia and driving into her before pulling out again.

"What chew gonna do with that?" he heard Frogger say. Hannah held the frog so it looked over her shoulder. "You gonna fuck her in the ass? Or are you afraid?"

"No! Don't!" Hannah said, starting to belly crawl away from Andy. Andy realized he was holding onto her hips.

Palming each ass cheek, Andy spread her butt open with his thumbs, looking at her sphincter before she clenched her cheeks shut again.

"Do it! Buttfuck her!" Frogger croaked.

"No! Please — I don't wanna!" Hannah squealed, wriggling on the floor and trying to get away, though she still held Frogger over her shoulder.

"Uh... maybe — maybe you shouldn't, uh —," Jeremy said, but Andy trailed a long line of spit into Hannah's crack, working it into her tight hole with his finger.

"Oh! Oh, no! Stop!" Hannah cried out, but soon Andy had a second finger inside of her, the muscle fighting him at first, then gradually relaxing.

"C'mon, already! Fuck her butt!" Frogger rasped.

Andy lay down on top of Hannah, pinning her with his weight as he pressed his glans against the hole, pushing, pushing. He had only done this with one other person. Miranda. His cousin. The shame mixed with longing and he pushed more.

"Ah! Oh, no! No! Ow!" Hannah squealed as the head popped inside the ring.

"Make her shut up!" Frogger said. Andy cupped his hand over her mouth and pressed, trapping her squeals in his palm. And still he slid deeper, gripped by the tight ring.

Though she cried and slapped the floor with her free hand, Hannah pushed the stuffed frog underneath of herself now, under her pussy. As he sodomized her, Hannah ground against Frogger, moaning, pushing her mouth against Andy's hand. He reached with his other hand, groping her breast and crushing her nipple as he pounded into her.

Her breathing took on a hard, erratic rhythm, increasing, and then Andy clamped his hand down over her mouth and pinched her nose shut.

Hannah's whole body seemed to convulse, her anus squeezing so hard, almost painfully tight. And as he rode on top of her spasming body, he felt the jolt of power flow from his feet into his cock and he thrust farther as he came, hearing Hannah gasp for breath as he let go, white heat burning in his vision.

He lay still for a minute as the blood pounded in his ears, his erection softening inside of Hannah until it slid out. She was whispering something, but he couldn't make out the words. He heard her, but the words sounded like nonsense.

"What... what are you saying?" Andy asked. He climbed off of her and she stopped talking. Hannah rose to her knees, then onto the balls of her feet, softly farting as she squatted. She stood up and dressed without a word, all three people avoiding eye contact. When she was done, she turned to face Andy, the come a dark splotch on her green dress, her make-up runny and smeared, her hair disheveled.

"I'm sorry," Hannah said to Andy, and she smiled a sad smile before she turned and walked out the door.

Andy watched the door close behind her. He looked down at the drops of come on the floor. He looked over at Jeremy. Jeremy looked away and turned on the Nintendo.

Andy dressed, walked over, and sat down in front of the TV. He cleared his throat and watched the game on the screen for a few minutes.

"Um... listen... I don't want to talk about this, but—," he said.

"Oh, no, it's cool. We—you know. No discussion necessary," Jeremy interrupted, not looking at Andy as he played his game.

"Right, but, how about no discussion with anyone about this? Like, don't mention it to anyone. Okay?"

"Oh, yeah, no, no, I'm—who would I want to tell about it?" Jeremy said. "No. It's cool."

Andy sweated and looked at his phone. His fourth and last call to

Haley was an hour ago. He had no calls and no texts from her today. He both wanted her to call and wanted not to speak to her.

Not even Jeremy was returning his messages; he knew something went wrong. Had Hannah said she was raped? Andy pictured the police at his door and tried to imagine what he would say, and what he would say when he called his parents. Was she raped? Was it rape? What would Jeremy say?

But the police would have already come for him over the weekend. Probably. It was five PM on Monday. They could have found him at his classes. And he *saw* Hannah on campus, walking around and chatting with people, though he did not approach her and she did not appear to see him.

He wanted someone — be it Haley, Hannah, or Jeremy — to approach him and talk to him as though nothing happened. The dead silence communicated *something happened.*

He tried to call Jeremy again. No answer. He needed to talk to him. They needed to be on the same page. What was he doing? What was he saying or not saying? *Fucking Jeremy. You ran your mouth. What did you say? Who did you tell?*

Andy leaped from the couch when his phone buzzed, his heart pounding. It was Haley. His hand hovered over the phone, and then he grabbed it.

"Hello?" he said quickly. *Too fast. Slow down.*

There was silence, except for the barely audible sound of breathing. Connection ended. He stared at the phone until it buzzed again, and he jumped just like the first time. Haley.

"Haley?" Andy said.

Again, only the breathing at first.

"You fucking *asshole!*" Haley yelled. "You motherfuckingpieceofshitfuckingasshole! How could you fucking do this to me??! Why?"

"Do... what?" Andy tried, feeling stupid for playing stupid, feeling the confidence running down the leg of his pants onto the floor. The room shook in the corners of his vision

"Do — not—fucking—what—me! You — *know!*" Haley yelled, the syllables punctuated with sobs and sniffs.

"What—okay—what are we talking about? What did you hear?" Andy said, his voice sticking in his throat. The room started to spin.

"No! No! Why don't *you* fucking tell *me*? Why don't *you* tell *me* what you and your little friend Jeremy did Friday night? You know, like, when I was driving to my parents'? When I was driving up, thinking about," sobbing choked off her voice. "Thinking about our *future* together?"

"We," Andy cleared his throat. "We got high. I know, I told you I wasn't gonna smoke anymore, I just, I don't know. It was, just, you know, there, and Jeremy had offered it to me — I know it was stupid. Maybe I have a problem."

"Oh. Oh is that all? 'Cause I'm just upset about you getting high." Haley asked, mock calm. "So it was just you and Jeremy? Like — there wasn't anyone else there?"

"Yeah," Andy said, losing his voice. Pain stabbed into his belly. He wanted to cry. It was done now. He had lied and felt himself step over the edge.

"I'm sorry, I couldn't quite hear you," she said.

"I said, 'Yeah.'"

"So there was no one else there that night? *No one else,* Andy?"

"No," Andy said, his voice hitching. His finger found a hole in the couch and pulled. Tearing. Digging.

"Really? Hunh," Andy heard her voice cracking, trying to stay even as she cried while she spoke. "Well, that — that's really weird, Andy. Because *Katie* saw Jeremy going into your building with Hannah. You know? My roommate? Of all people? So, *then?* Saturday night? Jeremy hangs out with Corey. Jeremy tells Corey, while they're all fucked up. You know. He tells Corey that *you* and *him* had sex — no, I'm sorry, had *anal* sex with Hannah. And Corey told Katie. And Katie. Told. Me.

"So, I wonder," Haley continued, her voice barely audible through mucus and tears, "I wonder why Jeremy would tell such a horrible fucking story. You know, like, after you talked about us moving in together."

"Haley, listen—" Andy tried to stop her.

"Hold on. Hold on. Before you fucking lie to me *one* more time, let me finish. So. I confronted, no, I *asked* Hannah about it. And you know what? At least she didn't lie to me about it. She told me everything. More than I wanted to know. About—how—you guys — made her a bubble bath—massaged her. How—you—told her that—that you loved her. Called her your little princess. Is *Hannah* your little princess, Andy?"

"I did not! I didn't tell her that—"

"Oh, no, Andy? What *did* you do with her, then?"

"Oh, God, I'm—I'm so sorry. We messed around but, I—I never told her that I loved her or—"

"Andy. Andy. Shut the fuck up. We. Are. Done. You fucked that, that retard. I am not speaking with you *ever* again after I hang up this phone. I don't. Want. To. Talk. To you. Or see you. *Ever again.* Don't come up and talk to me if you see me on campus. Don't talk to my friends. I'm moving back in with my parents. You can have your *retard.*" When Haley said *retard*, she pronounced it like *retart*, and something cold twitched in Andy's chest.

Haley hung up.

Andy held the phone for a long time and stared at the floor. He felt hot, felt himself sweat. He heard the door open.

"Hey. What's goin' on?" he heard Jeremy say.

Jeremy sat down. Andy looked at him. Jeremy's face stiffened and Andy thought he could see the possible excuses running through his brain. Jeremy's brows knitted and he squinted. Then his face went slack, his shoulders sagging, and Andy knew he gave up trying to come up with something.

"Corey," Jeremy said. "Oh. Motherfucker. I am... Who did he tell?"

"Katie," Andy said.

"And she told, what, she told Haley. Right? Yeah? Fucking cunt. I mean, Katie. And Corey. He's a cunt, too. Fuck. Dude, I am so sorry." Jeremy pushed his hair back and scratched his head like he wanted it to bleed.

Andy's phone buzzed. He took the yellow paper from his pocket and compared the numbers.

"I mean, fuck, I'm just, I apologize. If I can make it up to you, just tell me," Jeremy said, rambling, pacing.

Andy heard Haley saying *retart* in his head. He looked at the phone, picked it up and looked at it, turning it over and over.

"You know what? Don't worry about it," Andy said.

"I mean, you're not pissed at me? 'Cause you have every right. I mean, are we cool?"

"Yep," Andy said.

Phone in hand, Andy walked out the door, then walked back and set the phone down on the coffee table. He nodded at Jeremy and walked back out the door.

"I'm sorry."

Andy heard the voice coming from the bottom of the staircase as he climbed the steps, walking to his Anthropology class. He paused a step, not looking back, and continued climbing.

"I'm sorry." The voice was louder now. He stopped and turned around. At the foot of the stairs stood Hannah. Students walked past her, bumped into Andy, and sometimes looked at him or Hannah as they walked.

Hannah wore a red-and-white checkered dress, tight like wrapping paper, with matching checkered-fabric heels, a red bow in her hair and a red scarf about her neck. And it seemed to match her face, because her eyes and cheeks were red. Red-nailed, white fingers shook as they clutched a cherry red bag.

"Please?" Hannah's mouth silently formed the word.

Andy's limbs felt stiff. He descended, making a conscious effort to put his foot down on each step, until he stood before her. She smelled like cherries and her eyes glistened wet.

"What?" Andy asked.

"Please?" she asked, audibly this time.

"What do you want?"

"To talk to you," she whispered, a tear trickling down her cheek.

"What did you tell her, Hannah?" Andy asked.

Hannah shook her head no.

"Not here. At home. My apartment. *Please.*"

"Is—" Andy started.

Hannah shook her head again.

"She's gone," she said.

Andy nodded, not looking at her.

"Let's go," he said. "I have nothing to lose now."
Hannah stopped and her eyes grew wide.
"*I* do," she said.

Chapter 3
Saving the Princess

"What did you tell her, Hannah?" Andy asked. He sat on a worn easy chair. The couch, other furniture, and half of the decorations were conspicuously absent from Hannah's apartment.

Hannah sat on the floor, her legs bent beneath her, the lower legs splayed out.

"I told her... what happened," she said, shrugging.

"Haley said that we — ," Andy moved his hands slowly in the air in front of himself, his eye falling upon Frogger who sat in one corner of the room. Andy shook his head.

"She said that you said, that we, like, bathed and massaged you and called you princess and said — ,"

"That you said," Hannah said.

Andy shook his head.

"That I said what?" he asked.

"You know...," Hannah said, looking down and blushing.

"What? No. I never said that I loved you or that you were my princess or any of that crap," Andy said.

"Yeah! She's a dirty liar!" Hannah said in the Frogger voice.

"No, I'm not!" Hannah said, looking at Frogger.

Andy stood up.

"Whoa. No. No, stop. We're not doing the fucking... the Frogger crazy voice... whatever," Andy said.

"I told you he wouldn't understand," Hannah said in a high-pitched voice.

"Ah, whadda you know, Jerry," Frogger voice said. "He understands just fine. He came here to fuck her again. Came here to fuck all her little holes."

Andy glanced around and saw the stuffed rabbit sitting on a kitchen chair. Jerry.

"Okay, look. I'm going. This is—Yeah..." Andy said, walking towards the door.

"He doesn't have friends like us," Jerry voice said.

"Ah, who you kidding, buddy?" Frogger asked. "You gonna go call up that dumb girlfriend of yours with the big head? I'm sorry. I mean, ex-girlfriend with the big head. What were you gonna marry her? Go to her dummy church with her dummy family? Or you gonna get a new girlfriend? Don't worry. Hannah will get rid of her, too."

"Shut up, Frogger! You're ruining everything!" Jerry voice said.

"Andy, I'm sorry! I can't help what they say!" Hannah said.

"Hannah! You know what to do and you better do it," a darker voice crept out of Hannah's mouth. Andy looked around, trying to locate the voice among the stuffed animals.

"Which one is that?" Andy said, his voice cracking. "Never mind."

"*Okay, okay,* I'll do it," Hannah said.

"Do what?!" Andy said.

"I'll do..." Hannah walked towards him, staring into his eyes. "I'll do whatever you want. Have to." She walked closer to him. The scent of cherries rooted him to the spot. She put her hands on his hips. "Are you mad at me?" she asked, pressing herself against him.

"I think you need help. Lots," Andy said.

"Do I? Do you need help?" one fingernail stabbed into his chest, finding his nipple and jamming into it. Andy grabbed her wrists, but she had both sets of nails out now, gripping his flesh. "Do you need help? You know, coming? Did you come that fast when you were with Haley? No? Had trouble? Oh, yeah, paradoxical intention, right?" Hannah laughed as she spoke.

"What, you two talked about that?" Andy asked, his grip loosening as he thought about what she said.

Hannah's crazy wolf-eyes glittered and she said, "Tchacolik hin Mikka."

Her hands went under his shirt and her nails raked his sides. Pressure surged in his head and he pushed Hannah away. Hard.

Hannah did not fall but only danced back a few steps until she stood in the doorway of her bedroom. Andy felt his skin crawling on top of his flesh. She should have fallen. She braced herself in the doorway and started to climb up it, pressing against the frame with feet and hands until her head touched the top. Her tight dress rode up her white thighs, revealing white panties. Andy could smell her. He could smell her sex, could almost hear it pulsing.

"What the fuck did you just say?!" Andy yelled.

"Hmm?" Hannah giggled. "Oh, um, *paradoxical intention*. Now, you didn't have trouble coming with Miranda now, did you?"

"You gonna take that from her?" Frogger said.

"Shut the fuck up!" Andy said, and then realized he was yelling at the stuffed frog and not Hannah. "*Miranda*? What the fuck are you talking about?!" he said to Hannah.

"Mi—*ran*—da," she said, bracing herself in place effortlessly in the door-frame. "Your *cou*-sin. Who you *fucked*. In. The. *Butt*."

He felt himself walking towards Hannah. Putting his hands on her soft white throat.

Her limbs wrapped around him like a trap, arms around arms, legs around hips. Andy never stopped walking, carrying her to her bed by her neck as she held on, her face turning red.

He threw her down on the bed, plush animals scattering as if they fled to avoid the violence. As Andy unfastened his belt and pulled it from the loops, Hannah rolled backwards and rose to her feet. She stood on her bed, her back to the wall. Her eyes were wide, staring at the belt.

"That's it! Whip her ass! Show her who's boss!" Frogger said.

"Tchacolik hin Krikka!" Hannah said.

"What—the fuck—are you saying?" Andy said, climbing onto the bed. He didn't understand why he felt so angry. Still, it wasn't fair Hannah should act like this.

Hannah recoiled as he approached, stomping on stuffed bears and birds and turtles. She cringed and he pushed her so she faced the wall. He grabbed the back of her dress and pulled and tore, breaking the zipper apart, yanked the ruined garment down around her knees. Her cotton panties rode down, revealing the top of her ass cleft. Andy grabbed them and pulled them down as well. The bruise of a bite

149

mark remained on one cheek.

"Whip her!" Frogger said.

"Punish her!" Jerry said.

"Beat her!" another voice said.

A succession of different voices flew from Hannah's mouth, almost seeming to overlap, and the belt leather felt limber and warm in Andy's hand as he doubled it up. He pinned her to the wall with one hand pressing into her back, holding her bra strap like a handle.

No art or technique informed his hand as he struck, the hot crackle of leather on skin stiffening his cock. He struck again and again, each time making her jerk and splay her hands out against the wall. Andy swung again and again, his arm a machine, working to punish the white spheres of Hannah's ass, bringing the blood out. He swung like he wanted to peel the skin from her hide, and by the time the whole of her bottom and thighs pulsed red and drew thin lines of blood, she crumpled, sliding down the wall.

Andy stood over her, shaking, sweating, his knees weak.

"Go ahead. Do whatever you want with her," Frogger said.

Andy pulled his clothes off and threw them aside. He knelt on one knee above Hannah, his erection casting a shadow over her face. She looked up at him, her face tear-drenched, and shook her head.

"No," she mouthed silently.

Andy straddled her face, fish-hooking her mouth open as he shoved his penis inside. Fresh tears streamed from her eyes and he heard words.

"Tchacolik hin Brekka."

But they were words in his head and there was a quiet chuckling but that was in his head and it was this girl, this crazy fucking Hannah that was making him crazy, enraging him, and he slapped her face one, twice, three times as he thrust into her mouth, pushing it deep, deep into her throat, her hands slapping at his thighs, weaker and weaker as he fucked her throat. It felt good so good, gripping her head as he pumped.

Andy felt cold in his chest and pulled out, watching Hannah gasp like a fish and cough slimy spit onto her chin. When her coughing subsided, her lip curled and she spat into Andy's face.

Andy flipped her over on the bed, unhooking her bra, pulling it off, and reaching around to crush her breasts in his hand. He reached down and pulled her dress and panties from around her ankles, then pulled her arms behind her back, wrapping the bra around her wrists and tying it around them. He sat down and stretched his legs under and between hers, pulling her on top so she straddled him, facing away from him, the wet slit of her pussy on top of his cock.

He wrapped the belt around her neck and held it in one hand. With the other, he guided his penis, pressing upward.

"Fuck it," Andy hissed.

Hannah lowered herself, taking him quickly inside of the dripping grip of her cunt. She lifted her hips slowly, haltingly at first, then building to a rhythm, her reddened ass slapping down against him. He tightened the belt around her neck.

"That's it! Let's see if you can make him come before he chokes the living shit out of you!" he heard Frogger's voice, in his head now as clear as if he were in the room. No, she was saying it. No, he was choking her. No...

Andy had the belt in both hands now, bucking his hips and pulling tighter. Tighter. Hannah writhed, jerked. Her pussy felt tight and tighter as he pulled the leather. She crumbled, her head bumping the wall as she fell to the side, Andy's cock sliding out. He let go of the belt.

Shaking he climbed onto her as she lay on her side, limp. He slid the head of his penis in between her wet pussy lips and jammed in, thrust, and came in seconds, the hot gush surging through his shaft, out his hole, making him grunt, drool hanging from his lip. His body convulsed as he pumped fluid inside of her, staring at her scarlet face.

He held onto her still form, listening to her shallow breathing. The belt lay loose around her neck like a decoration. Her face was red, her neck a purplish bruise.

Andy pulled out. Hannah lay still, unconscious. He spread her ass cheeks and watched the thick come trickle from her swollen labia, white on red.

He lay down behind her, cradling her in his arms. He smelled cherries again and sniffed her hair and closed his eyes. He thought he heard whispering but he covered his ears with a pillow and felt

Hannah's breathing against his chest.

It was dark except for the slice of light coming from the hallway, the door slightly open. It took Andy a moment to realize where he was: Hannah's room. Right next to Haley's room. What used to be Haley's room.

Something pinched at his neck and he reached up, something sharp hurt his finger.

"Don't move," the words growled into his ear and he felt something cold and hard and sharp pressed against his throat.

"You belong here now," the voice continued. Was it female? It sounded like gravel rubbed against smooth marble.

"You will do what I say, just like Hannah does. Or it will go badly for you. You will leave when I tell you to leave. You will come when I tell you to come. Do you understand me?" The knife shifted against his neck.

"You will love Hannah because I tell you to love her. You will call her your princess. You will marry her, and she will be your queen. Do you understand?"

"Yes," Andy whispered.

"Do you agree to what I said?" the knife moved slightly.

"Yes."

"She owns you now, and I own her," the voice rasped, louder now.

Andy felt the knife move away from his throat. Something moved behind him on the bed, about the size of a cat. It walked over his legs and he heard it drop onto the floor. He stared, not daring to move, until it stepped into the light.

A tiny old, woman, not a foot tall, stepped into the shaft of light and walked towards the door. She turned and looked back at him, her face shriveled and wrinkled, unrecognizable as a face except for the gaping hole of a mouth that leered at him and the tiny, shiny black eyes that glinted in the light.

Andy clenched his eyes shut and buried his face in the pillow. When he dared to look again, the thing was gone and the door was open a bit wider.

Tears welled up in his eyes and he began to cry, quietly at first, but soon heavy sobs racked his body. He tried to stop them, tried to contain them, but they poured out of him now. Hannah stirred and a light snapped on beside the bed, a purple plastic unicorn whose horn lit up.

"What's wrong, baby?" Hannah asked, stroking his shoulder.

As Andy reached for her, he saw the knife laying on the sheet. It was either his knife or one identical to it, but he kept his knife in a dresser drawer in his apartment. He picked up the knife and stared at Hannah.

"Did she hurt you, baby?" Hannah said, gently touching his neck.

Andy looked at his hand. It wasn't a bad cut, but a fair amount of dried blood now stained the sheets and lay in dried rivulets on his skin. Hannah took a corner of the sheet and dabbed at his cheeks, mopping up his tears as he spilled them. She took the knife from his hand.

Andy stared as she squeezed one of her breasts and, holding the knife by the flat of the blade, began to prick a circle of tiny cuts around her nipple. She smiled and set the knife on the dresser, then lay on her side and pulled Andy's head to her breast.

Andy suckled, tasting the salt and copper tang, scrubbing the wounds with his tongue, sucking the nipple to the roof of his mouth. Hannah held the back of his head and stroked his hair. He imagined he could taste something else, something sweeter, and the tears soon left him.

Daylight streamed through the window. Hannah looked down at him. She wore tight pajamas decorated with stars and moons. She kissed him on the forehead, and then the lips.

"Where does — she come from?" Andy asked.

Hannah's eyes grew wide and she put a finger to his lips and shook her head back and forth. A light bruise covered one cheek and one side of her lower lip swelled. She wore a purple collar of bruising around her neck.

Andy looked around the room. All of the stuffed animals sat neatly arranged on the bed, on the dresser, and along the wall and shelf. Posters of children's TV shows and movies, many of them forgotten by Andy until then, covered the walls.

"Let's... why don't we go for a walk this morning?" Andy heard himself ask, regretting it.

"Umm...," Hannah said, looking at the washcloth. "Well, maybe after my shows are over!" She looked up and smiled at him. She leaned closer to him. She smelled like peaches that day. "Don't leave, yet," Hannah said, her lips brushing his earlobe. "I want to play with you today. Masavala pi krikkli." Andy smiled and kissed her.

"What did you just say?" he asked.

"I said," Hannah said, cuddling close to him, "I want you to stay here and play with me. You like me, don't you?"

"Yes," Andy said.

"Just like me?" she asked, looking out the window.

"I," the words stuck in Andy's throat. A sad look crossed Hannah's face and then vanished with a smile.

"That's OK. You don't have to say it, yet. Let's eat breffix!" she said, hopping up and pulling him by the hand. Andy stood up, naked.

"OK, sure. Um, I just need to use the bathroom," he said as they walked.

"Number one or number two?" Hannah said, giggling.

"Um, number one," Andy laughed.

"Me too!" Hannah said and walked him into the bathroom.

"What!?" Andy asked. Hannah began fondling him, rubbing his cock and balls. "No, seriously, I need to go," he said.

She squatted and stuck her tongue out, flicking it against his penis and making it harden. Andy recoiled as she tongued the tip, poking his slit. His bladder felt painfully swollen.

"Put her in the tub!" a voice said with Hannah's mouth.

Andy looked around at the collection of rubber ducks and sharks and dolphins in the bathroom, wondering which one this was supposed to be.

"She's a potty mouth!" another said.

"I am not!" Hannah yapped.

"You better say the words before she comes!" another voice said.

"No! It will be gross!" Hannah said.

"But it will be worse if you don't—"

"Tchacolik hin Sakka. Mol breander fol chek!" Hannah yelled, shaking her head.

Andy felt the rage rise up from the soles of his feet, up to his throbbing erection, up his belly. He did not fight it this time, but let it come as it rose through his chest, up his neck, into his head. He felt electricity pulsing in his veins and fire in his bladder.

He grabbed Hannah by the arms and dragged her into the bathtub. He yanked the pajama top from her and forced her to her knees. He held her jaw open with one hand and pushed his penis into her mouth. Hannah winced, squinting. Andy relaxed his bladder and let the urine flow into Hannah's mouth.

"Swallow... swallow," Andy said, holding fistfuls of hair.

Hannah grimaced in evident distaste, but her mouth formed a seal around his shaft and she gulped obediently. Andy sighed as he felt the warm buzzing flow leave his cock, felt the girl's mouth convulsing as she swallowed over and over again. She held onto his thighs, her arms rigid.

"Stand up!" he said when he was finished, pulling Hannah by her hair to her feet. He saw the tiny scabs circling one of her nipples.

He pulled down her pajama bottoms and white panties, and she stepped out of them. He threw the bottoms onto the tile floor but held onto the panties. He felt himself sweating, his hands shaking. Part of him wanted to stop, wanted to leave.

"I want to stop," he whispered.

"You can't!" a voice mewled from Hannah's lips. "We can't stop. None of us can. Just do it. Do what you have to want to have to."

Andy pushed Hannah until her back hit the tile wall, bumping her head and making her wince. Tears ran down her cheeks. Andy reached between her legs, his fingers seeking her peehole, probing, poking. He took the panties and pressed them against her vagina, stuffing part of them inside her.

"Do it," he hissed in her face.

"I don't—I don't want to," she sobbed.

Andy placed the flat of his palm against her abdomen and pushed. Hannah grunted. He pushed again. Hannah squealed. Hot urine flowed over Andy's other hand, soaking the panties and running down to patter on the tub. Once started, it gushed for a long moment, and then quickly stopped.

"Hands and knees. Now!" Andy said, pulling her down until she crouched on all fours facing the faucet. Red stripes covered her ass and the backs of her thighs. The bite bruise had yellowed.

Andy closed the drain and turned on the water. Quivering, he worked his turgid prick into her piss-wet vagina, parting the lips with his thumb and prying his way inside.

As he pressed into her, she felt swollen and the muscles seemed to push back. He felt a fever burning in his brain and he listened to the water flowing, trying to hold onto something, trying to focus on it as he fucked Hannah hard. The girl put her hands in front of herself, bracing herself so as to not get pushed into the wall.

Andy reached around and stuffed the pee-soaked panties into Hannah's face, pinching her nose shut.

The water rose to their thighs. He felt her pussy slicken, loosen. He took the panties away long enough to let her catch her breath, and then he smothered her again. Her vagina clenched him and a red flush filled in the gaps between the stripes on her lower back. Andy dropped the panties.

He grabbed a bottle from the edge of the tub and squeezed a clear gel into the crack of Hannah's ass, working it into her sphincter. He pulled out of her cunt and pressed his cock into her anus, pulling her back by the hips, impaling her deeply.

Hannah moaned like she had been hit in the stomach. Andy grabbed her by the hair, pushing her head underwater. She kicked and struggled, hands slapping against the wet tiles, water sloshing from the tub.

Andy felt come surge like fire through him and he held her under as long as the sweet flame burned him, pulsing into her bowels. When he finished, he let go and Hannah gasped and spluttered for air.

She climbed out and stumbled, dripping, out of the bathroom. Andy sat in the tub, staring, until the water grew cold.

Andy waited until he felt the cold steel on his neck. It was a different knife, he knew, because he held the first one. He counted to three in his head and then twisted away, using a pillow to protect his hand as he swept the small figure from the bed. The knife cut him, but not badly enough to stop him.

The thing, a tiny and grizzled woman, fell to the floor with a thud. Andy pounced, covering her with the pillow as he stabbed. Stabbed. Stabbed. Stabbed until feathers stained with black blood spilled onto the floor and still he stabbed, hearing Hannah screaming in the background behind the sound of blood rushing through his ears.

When the frenzy left him, he lifted the slashed pillow and looked at the mutilated remains. He cut away at it, until he was satisfied that no life remained. And then he covered it with the pillow again, thrusting the knife in and pressing down until the point stuck in the floor.

"Oh, baby, come here!" Hannah cried.

Andy turned and climbed onto the bed. Hannah kissed him all over his face and pulled him on top of her. She smelled like wine. Andy wanted to cry.

Hannah rubbed against him. She pulled her pajamas down, rubbing his cock to forced erectness, squirming beneath him, pushing him inside of her wetness.

"You saved us, Andy," she whispered, bucking her hips against him, erratically. Her voice sounded hard, metallic. "You saved us all from her. Do you love me?"

"Yes," Andy whispered.

"Am I your princess?" she asked. She was slipping something over his head, and he did not resist when he felt the leather band encircle his neck.

"Yes," he said, his tears falling on her face.

"Will you marry me?"

"Yes," he said, feeling the belt tighten around his neck. He grabbed her wrists but could not move them. Her arms felt like iron as his grew weaker and weaker. His lungs convulsed, empty of oxygen. His ears rang louder and louder and he felt the orgasm like a shock as he lost more strength with every drop of liquid. Something broke between his ears and fell like shattered glass.

"Masaval pi yirri." Andy heard the words from a distance as he watched Hannah's pale blue eyes vanish in the dark.

If you enjoyed this story, you can sign up for a free membership at ForbiddenFiction and discuss it with other readers and the author at the *Frogger Says* story page at http://forbiddenfiction.com/story/KH1-1.000036.

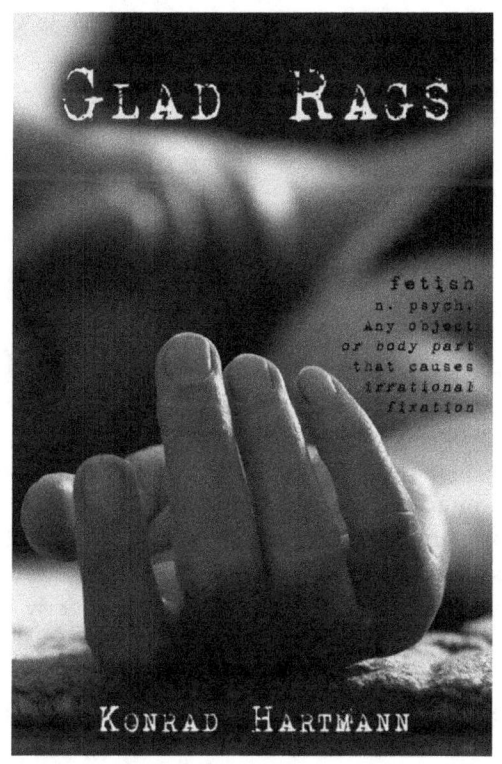

Glad Rags

Glad Rags

Sheldon thought of his desire this way: that a woman be utterly and completely receptive. That he should have all of the time in the world to explore her body, to enjoy her however he wished, that he should not have to please her or wonder if she liked what he was doing — this was his ideal scenario.

He did not want to talk or be talked to. He did not want to hear her moan or comment or give praise or criticism. He wanted nothing to interfere with the ultimate enjoyment of her body and her form. He wanted the magnificent adventure of the flesh to be shared with no one.

That a dead partner should arouse him, Sheldon would have completely and utterly denied. It was aberrant, perverse. Were he to answer honestly, he would say that he simply wanted a completely unresponsive partner that showed as little sign of life as possible.

And so Sheldon first realized he yearned for something unusual when a nervous young woman drank to the point of passing out. Her name was Marissa. Marissa would never know she would be one of the first steps on Sheldon's path to realizing his fantasy. Before her, his desire had just remained a fantasy. After Marissa, he knew it could be real.

When Marissa crumpled into the pillows on Sheldon's sofa, her form took on a yielding softness that awakened something dark in the back of Sheldon's mind. As she lay still, her little purple dress riding up, her limbs akimbo on the couch, he felt his cock immediately stiffen.

It wasn't just the opportunity for sex. Sheldon had little trouble with finding that, especially the kind of sex that did not interest him. It wasn't that she was helpless either, or that he had power over her that excited him.

Two thoughts, mainly, came to mind. The first was she would have no realization he was there or what he would be doing to her. The second thought was more troublesome for him, and it was one he tried to push down into dark waters, as though it were a slimy eel trying to climb out. It was that she looked dead.

Ten years earlier, Sheldon witnessed the aftermath of a fatal fall from an apartment balcony. In the two seconds he saw the dead woman crumpled in the bushes next to the building — just the brief glance he saw before the body was covered — the image took root in his memory. He masturbated furiously that night, thinking of her.

And then he forgot. Sheldon forgot he had seen her, or at least, he did not remember. But now, looking at Marissa, he remembered. And now he prayed, for a few precious minutes, Marissa could be that woman.

Sheldon looked at Marissa where she sat half reclined on the couch, her legs hanging off the side. He quietly pulled the coffee table away from the couch. He crouched next to Marissa. He wanted to fuck her with a drive that was both hot and cold. But he only wanted her like this, like a limp rag doll. He did not want her if she woke up. Whether she woke up struggling and enraged, or aroused and horny — either outcome would equally disappoint him.

"Marissa," Sheldon whispered.

"Marissa." Louder this time.

"Marissa!" he called, not yelling, but loud enough to wake someone from a natural sleep. At this last call, she snorted lightly. The sound bothered Sheldon, but not enough to deter him.

He put his hand on her shoulder and shook her slightly. Her breathing changed, just a bit, but she did not stir.

And so Sheldon knelt down on the floor between her legs and said a prayer. Who he prayed to, Sheldon did not know, but he said it with passion all the same.

"Please," he said, feeling his lips quiver, building to a tremor that spread through his body. He stretched out his shaking hands, flexing the muscles and them clenching them into motionless fists. "Do not let her wake up until I am finished. Let me have this moment. Let me have it now."

Sheldon pushed Marissa's dress up past her waist. A small purple thong barely covered the bump of her pussy. He lifted the crotch of the panties, and found the fabric was light and sheer and narrow enough he could simply pull it to the side.

Marissa's cunt had not a hair on it, the skin smooth and silky. Sheldon touched it, enjoyed the soft, rubbery texture of her labia between his fingertips. Her slit was wet, and he took turns sliding each finger into its moisture. He leaned in and smelled the musky scent of her vagina.

He wanted to lick her and play with the hood of her clit, making it slide back and forth. Yet, though he planned to fuck her, he feared stimulating her to the point of waking. Likewise, he wanted to undress her and expose her small firm breasts to his attention, but he mainly wanted to fuck her and avoid the disturbance undressing her might make.

Gently, Sheldon pulled her hips closer to the edge of the couch and spread her legs further. He put a pillow under his knees to place himself at the right level, and unbuckled his pants. His cock throbbed as it pointed to Marissa's pussy. As he rolled his foreskin back, Sheldon worried he might cum too soon and miss out on his game.

He took a deep breath and rolled a condom onto his cock.

Sheldon thought of the dead woman as he parted Marissa's cunt lips with the head of his penis. His hand shook, making it hard to insert into her.

He would have cum faster, had he not worried so much about waking her. All the same, he treasured his aloneness in that moment— he didn't have to share Marissa's body with Marissa. And for a few minutes Sheldon saw her laying perfectly still and imagined her chest did not rise and fall as she breathed. He concentrated on the tightness of her pussy around his organ and the quiet of the room where the only sound was that barely audible sliding in and out.

Marissa's eyes opened slightly, as those of sleepers sometimes do, and in the self-honesty preceding orgasm, he knew she looked dead, and it was *this* that made him cum, made him cum hard with every muscle tensing up, his whole body rigid.

She stirred seconds after he came, or else he would have considered a second fucking, his arousal only slightly abated. He slid the crotch of her thong back in place, and covered her with a blanket.

Sheldon slept alone in his bed. When he woke up, Marissa was gone. They never spoke again.

The evening with Marissa haunted him. He tried to repeat the experience, cautiously, with other women, but never again were circumstances just right. Inexperienced drinkers typically became sick rather than passively unconscious, and experienced drinkers typically would not fall asleep. And when he suspected the women guessed his intentions, he felt ashamed.

But the desire became obsession, and Sheldon could not walk away from the chase. He did not himself use drugs, but he did know several dealers.

He considered slipping Restoril, Versed, or another type of drug to women in order to repeat, or even improve, the experience. But the realization he was simply becoming a rapist disturbed him. He did not consider himself much of a criminal, at least not a good one, and he was correct. He knew not how to go about things, to lie easily, and to not lie awake wondering if he would be arrested. Furthermore, the idea of overdosing the women frightened him, though he suppressed a certain thrill at the same time.

Sheldon thought about another option, and that was to simply offer drugs openly to the right women. He would not give them just any drug, only the ones that produced some variation of sedation. Perhaps he could repeat the Marissa experience. But he would not sell the drugs, only give them out. It would be a free choice for both parties. And when he pursued this option, a new world opened up for him.

Sheldon found that all roads generally led to heroin. When he wanted to find a partner willing to drug themselves into a deep nod without any questions asked of his intentions, this drug was the easy choice.

These were glorious days for Sheldon. Heroin was cheap, since he wasn't using it himself. In time, he found a semi-regular group of mostly attractive women who could achieve a deathlike stupor with some degree of predictability. This became even more predictable when Sheldon learned to cut heroin with a smidgen of Rohypnol.

And he appreciated the unspoken honesty of the encounter. Each party knew just what the other wanted and each walked away temporarily satisfied. At times he found it sad for the women, in a way, but after all, he thought, he didn't make them addicted to the drug. He only offered a mutually beneficial situation.

When Sheldon's dealer friend (now Sheldon's supplier) came upon a higher grade of heroin, he warned Sheldon to cut it down with filler.

"This isn't some bullshit, Sheldon," Jeff said, covering the bag on the table with his hand, as if to stop Sheldon from picking it up. "This is hard. Close to pure. Makes the other crap seem like *oxy*." The pointer finger of his other hand stabbed the table with each word. "You wanna cut the shit out of it with the quinine, just like I showed you. Don't give this out straight. Motherfucker's eyes'll roll back and *stay* rolled back," he said. "For real. I ain't fucking with you Sheldon, pay *attention*." Jeff nodded at Sheldon for a few seconds and then slowly took his hands away from the table and sat back.

Sheldon felt high himself driving home that night with the bag nestled against him in his jacket pocket. It felt like power, like it was an explosive. He thought about the words "close to pure." In his mind, he pictured women scattered all around his living room. In the fantasy, Sheldon was naked. He went to the first woman, a young woman, a brunette who looked much like Marissa, more like Marissa as he thought about her. She had on a pink, ruffled dress, a party dress.

Sheldon tugged it from her, roughly, no need to worry about her waking up, not with the strong stuff pumping through her veins. She lay on the couch in her pink bra and panties now, and he peeled them off like he was undressing a doll. He crouched next to her, shoving his hard penis into her slack mouth, poking it into her throat enough to make her gag reflexively.

Then he was on top of her, ramming his cock between her silky cunt lips, fucking her as hard as he could, her pussy very wet, soaking into the couch.

He hooked his arms under her legs and propped them on his

shoulders, sliding himself out of her vagina, placing the head against her asshole, and ramming it in all the way with the first stroke. He did not fuck the women like this outside of his fantasies, but this was his dream and this was his Marissa.

Her soft breath bothered him, though, and he wrapped his hands around her throat, just to make her hold her breath, but his grip tightened and tightened. As his hands tightened, so did Marissa's sphincter, and in a few minutes, there was no more breathing and she lay perfectly still and Sheldon forgot about the other women.

He climbed up and, sitting on her breasts, came a huge white streak across her blue face.

The image faded, replaced with red and blue police lights. Sheldon gripped the steering wheel and whimpered. But the car drove past and Sheldon realized he sat frozen in his own car and the crotch of his slacks was wet with semen.

He drove home sweating, and clutching the bag of heroin.

Her name was Stacy. She was blond in a color so pale as to match her skin, hair pulled back in little ponytails on either side of her head. Make-up almost covered the bruise under her eye and her long sleeves almost covered up her chicken pox arms.

Sheldon had been with Stacy before. A combination of features endeared her to him, and each time he saw her, he liked to make an inventory. The paleness of her skin. The variety of cuts and bruises. The way her ribs and hips jutted out. The way she would lay still, so deathly still.

They sat in his apartment, Stacy staring at him with half-closed eyes shrouded in the smoke of the cigarettes chained together. That was part of their unspoken contract, that Sheldon would have a carton of cigarettes on his coffee table when she arrived.

Sheldon put a small bag (not his big bag) on the table, along with a bottle of quinine. He learned early on not to try to sound cool or to pretend he knew the right words to say.

"I was told that you should cut this with this," he said, pointing to the bag and then the bottle.

"And why is that, Mr. Sheldon?" Stacy slurred.

"Well. Because it's so strong. Probably stronger than you're used to," he said.

Stacy laughed, her voice hoarse, a sandpaper throat.

"Wha'chu think, I'm a fuggin' lightweight, Sheldon?" she said. Her laugh sounded almost like a cough.

"Well. You would know about these things better than me," he said. Sheldon felt something pulling inside of himself. He pushed it down and told it to be still.

He had warned her. He couldn't be blamed if she didn't listen, but he did try again.

"I really wouldn't know," Sheldon continued. "So...as long...as... you think...you're...safe..."

Stacy no longer noticed him, her cloudy eyes clearing as they only did when drugs appeared. On the table lay the kit of a nightmare junkyard doctor. In seconds she had water and heroin in the spoon and Sheldon realized she hadn't cut it at all. He wondered what his dealer would say about that.

"You probably know better than most doctors," Sheldon said.

"Hunh?" Stacy asked. "Doctors? Yeah, I'm a fuggin' doctor, Sheldon. Sometimes you just go on and on, right?"

"Maybe...do you think...," he said. Stacy no longer appeared to hear him, or even notice he was there.

Already, she was unbuttoning her shirt and casting it off, her torso a canvas with bones threatening to poke through it. Sheldon noticed that she wore a new bra, one that fit and didn't look like it was falling off her small and firm breasts. Her body was malnourished but still had shape, still had life and beauty. He looked at her and thought of the bones underneath, her shoulder blade wings, her ribcage carved ivory. Sheldon thought of the white tulips in the vase on his kitchen table, past their peak and waiting to drop their petals. Some of the other girls were already shooting up in their foot. Stacy still had a few good veins in her arms.

"I guess there are risks in everything, right?" Sheldon said, his pulse quickening.

"Um. Yeah," Stacy said.

She sat on the couch and found an angry red hole on her arm to reuse, a little crimson cloud blossoming inside the barrel. Soon she tossed her empty rig onto the table where a drop of blood beaded on the wood.

Stacy's eyelids, already heavy, collapsed under their own weight and she sunk backwards into the couch. Sheldon's erection felt almost painful as he waited, giving it a minute. The word "priapism" scrolled across his brain.

Then he undressed as though his clothing burned him. An expectation, even a hope, tried to surface in his thoughts, but he pushed this thing aside until it climbed out and stood next to him, an almost palpable presence in the room.

Her chest rose slightly and fell quickly, having little distance to travel. He slipped his hands behind her and unhooked her bra, peeling it off. He cupped her breasts in his hands, and squeezed her nipples until they flattened between thumb and forefinger, making them hard, flicking them. Kneeling on the couch next to her, he sucked them, feeling her ragged breath as he laid his hand on her ribs.

Sheldon untied her shoes and tossed them across the room. He pushed her down on the couch and lifted her legs. Then he unbuttoned her jeans, pulling them down like he was skinning an animal. He paused at the sight of her panties. Were they made for an adult? he wondered. Even for her, they looked tiny, the image of a kitten stretched tight across her vulva.

He paused to look at her, to savor her. Stacy's breath seemed so light. A mild blankness crossed Sheldon's mind. Were her fingernails a bluish color? Were they always that color?

Sheldon hooked his thumbs under Stacy's panties and slid them down and off.

Her pubic hair was dark, almost black against her off-white skin. He pushed one leg aside until it dropped, boneless, alongside the couch. He examined the folds of her vagina, her dark labia like a puffy flower.

Sheldon reached under the couch and, for the first time, ignored the condoms there, only extracting the bottle of lubricant. He drizzled some into his palm, lubing his cock and then stuffing his fingers into Stacy's pussy, probing inside her, feeling every nuance of her flesh. Something buzzed in his brain and he wondered why the lips of her mouth looked so blue? Was it her lipstick or were they always that color?

"You'll be fine," he whispered.

His cock hurt, almost itching, and feeling like the skin would split. He climbed on top of her, punching his penis into her cunt, pinning her down, fucking and fucking. He heard no breathing as he touched his ear to her lips. Still pumping into her, he felt for a pulse on the side of her neck and found none. He was sweating now, sweating hard despite the cool air conditioning and cool skin.

Sheldon clutched the back of her neck and thrust as hard as he could into her. He felt weightless, only the smooth wet grip of Stacy's cunt around his shaft. And he had to know, had to know if it was happening. If this was real.

"You're dead. You're dead," Sheldon whispered. And he felt the pressure rise as he came. He grunted and wailed, letting his cum pulse into Stacy until he collapsed, laying his full weight on top of her.

"You're mine. You're mine. You chose this. You chose me," Sheldon whispered, stroking her hair.

As Stacy's form relaxed that night, Sheldon cleaned up after her. He washed and caressed her.

"We should buy you some new clothes," he said to her as she lay on his bed. "But we don't have much time, do we? You're already getting stiff. Still, we have some time."

Sheldon looked at her. The sheet was as white as her skin. He lifted one of her legs, lifted it all the way up until the knee touched her chest. He pushed the leg aside, her joints crackling. He lifted her arm, and tucked the leg behind it. He let go, and the leg stayed in place.

He did the same with the other leg, the joint popping even louder now, and it too, stayed in place.

Sheldon lubricated his hand, and one by one, slid all of his fingers into her pussy. Further and further he pushed, until his whole hand lay trapped in the tight embrace.

He looked up at her, at her half-open eyes, at her open mouth.

Sheldon climbed up next to her, his hand still inside her, turning it as he clambered on top of her, straddling her head and facing towards her feet. He felt inside of her mouth. It surprised him with its dryness, and so he poured more lubricant into it. He pointed his erection downwards and leaned forward as he pushed it into her mouth. Her lips and teeth brushed his cock. As he fisted her cunt, he felt the resistance of Stacy's closed throat. Still he pushed in, squeezing past the muscles that clenched him almost painfully.

His head spun and he pulled his hand out from between Stacy's legs, sucking at her clitoris as he pounded into her unyielding throat. A loud pop, and he saw a bulge under the skin of one of her hip joints. He clenched her head between his thighs and came, weeping into her vagina.

"I wish...," Sheldon said, stroking Stacy's skin, running his fingertips over her ribs, "I wish that you could stay here forever." Tears ran down his cheeks.

"I wish you could stay, but they'll come looking for you. Somebody will. The other girls will talk about me.

"And you'll never be more beautiful than you are now.

"We did our best at who we are. You couldn't help what happened. And what could I do? Accidents happen. But we will make a few — more — memories before you have to leave me."

Sheldon turned on the video camera and climbed onto the bed with Stacy.

Sheldon's course of travel took him from hardware store to hardware store. Plastic tarps at one store. A saw at another. Cleaning supplies at another. In between stops, he cried as he drove.

Sheldon tried to lift Stacy gently from the bed, but her rigid form only allowed him to grip her under her arms and drag her, her heels squeaking along the hardwood floor. He dragged her into the bathroom and, when he tried to set her carefully into the tub, she fell in so that her skull thudded against the enamel.

Though rigor mortis kept her limbs straight, her dislocated hip joints allowed her to bend, so that now her upper body rested inside the tub while her stiff legs propped her ass in the air.

Sheldon struggled out of his plastic coveralls and pulled his pants down. He grabbed a jar and threw the lid aside, slathering petroleum jelly into Stacy's rectum before pressing his penis into it. It slipped in easily, though the flesh was hardening. He grabbed her hips and fucked her as hard as he could without falling over, hearing her back crackle as he leaned into her. When he came, he pressed in deep, relishing the strange feel of her ass and knowing he would never have this experience again. But it was his moment, and he knew it would always be his and his alone.

Sheldon slid out of her and slowly lifted her legs into the tub. He dressed again in his plastic coveralls and picked up a saw.

He remembered a book written by a forensic anthropologist. When disposing of a body, the author said, many people labor to cut through rigid bone. Sheldon treasured that book when he was young, keeping it alongside an anatomy book featuring cadaver photos, the edges of certain pages worn from frequent handling. Sometimes, he would line the pages of pornographic magazines up next to the photos of bodies, creating a temporary collage of the two.

One of Sheldon's stops had been to a sporting goods store, where he picked up a book about deer hunting, including a chapter on dressing game. And so Sheldon knew to cut through the joints first.

Stacy bled slower than Sheldon had expected, but when she did it never seemed to stop, a steady flow of thick, dark blood. Soon her limbs lay neatly stacked at the upper end of the tub while he severed her head. Sweat soaked his clothes inside his coveralls.

He knew he was supposed to eviscerate her first, yet something stopped his hand from doing so until her torso lay separated from the rest of her. Using a razor and scissors, he cut carefully down her belly, and then cut a horizontal intersection.

Peeling back the flaps of skin, he felt himself grow hard once more as he plunged his gloved hands into the creamy coils of her small intestines. They seemed endless as he gently began lifting them out of her belly. Impossibly smooth, like wet silk, he lifted them and let them slide through his fingers. They were darker than he expected. He thought of the anatomy textbooks, with their eggshell-colored intestine illustrations. These were more the color of uncooked sausages.

Sheldon thought of Mrs. Grosch, his eighth-grade Health class teacher. For the first time in decades, he remembered her saying that the human body contains twenty feet of small intestines and five feet of large intestines.

Quivering, Sheldon picked up a knife and cut a foot-long section out of the small intestines. He washed it out thoroughly under the tub faucet and set it down upon Stacy's naked breast while he peeled his coveralls down around his knees and dropped his pants again.

Completely erect, he stretched and tugged the length of gut down over his cock like another foreskin. Though moist and slippery, he struggled for a moment to enter it, but soon it gripped him tightly and he closed his fist around it and pumped feverishly.

Hot tears flooded his eyes. It was a gift, a new way to be with Stacy, another way to still remain with Stacy, he thought. They were close now, closer than ever before. Sheldon felt himself blending into her, as there being such a small part of her body made it easier for her to be part of himself. He knelt on the edge of the tub as he came grunting into the tube, staring down at the pile of intestines spilling out of Stacy.

Dreaming, Sheldon stared at Stacy and Marissa, both girls lying with each other in one casket. A faint smile graced the lips of each. They lay entwined in each other's arms, their hair spilling into each other's faces. Mourners filed out of the funeral home and workers began wrapping the white sheet around both of the women.

As they lowered the lid, the funeral director approached Sheldon.

"You'll be taking them home, then?" he asked Sheldon.

Sheldon felt surprise and then embarrassment, followed by something he couldn't name. Why shouldn't he take them home? These precious forms; lifeless, beautiful things who — that — felt nothing now would be carted off, dissected, embalmed, stuffed in a metal box to liquefy in the earth within a concrete box.

"I'm not—uh—I'm not doing anything. Anything weird with them," Sheldon said.

The man nodded, frowning slightly, his lips pursed.

Sheldon stood outside now. He saw the beach in the distance. Men in coveralls loaded the casket into his car, which was now a large station wagon.

His heart pounding, Sheldon drove away quickly with the casket.

Sheldon woke, sweating, sitting up on the couch. His back ached, tired from the work of disposing of Stacy's remains and cleaning up the bathroom.

He walked quickly to the freezer and removed a plastic freezer bag from a stack of more bags. He pulled out the frozen contents and placed them in a bowl, and then put the bowl in the microwave. He pushed the defrost button.

When the intestine was thawed and warmed in the bowl, Sheldon carried it back into the living room. He turned on the DVD player, and watched as Stacy appeared on the screen, her lips slightly parted, her hands half-clenching at the empty air.

Sheldon worked his penis into the piece of intestine and stared at himself fucking Stacy on the screen. Fucking the gut in his fist, he whispered her name over and over.

Aubrey was young, just 18 when she agreed to play dead for Sheldon. She was not an addict, and she was not interested in passing out.

But for enough money, she was willing to feign death while Sheldon took his pleasure.

"On one condition," Aubrey told Sheldon. "I have a webcam set up and recording and saved online where a friend can view it. I mean, if anything weird should happen and I disappear, someone will know to look at this video. And you have to show me, *on the camera*, that you have a condom on. That's the only way I'll do this."

So for a time, the arrangement satisfied both parties, until Aubrey called him after an appointment.

"I just watched the video. What fucking kind of condom was that?!" Aubrey yelled into the phone. "Is that fucking homemade or something?!"

Sheldon swallowed hard.

"I got it from a friend," he said.

If you enjoyed this story, you can sign up for a free membership at ForbiddenFiction and discuss it with other readers and the author at the *Glad Rags* story page at http://forbiddenfiction.com/story/KH1-1.000029.

Arena Breed

Chapter 1
Dying Well

Avitus peered through an opening in the arena wall and watched the fighters circle each other. The larger one, Hadrianus, lumbered about and tried to keep the smaller, but muscular and much faster Blasius, at a distance. Normally, the loser would be granted *missio*, the grace of losing honorably, and allowed to live. But Avitus knew the men hated each other. In the training yard, each swore to kill the other. Each swore to not raise a finger in surrender.

Hadrianus fought in the *murmillo* style, wearing a broad-brimmed helmet adorned with the image of a fish on its crest. His sword arm was covered by a *manica* arm-guard, consisting of layers of linen strips wrapped and bound with leather thongs so as to form a thick but flexible protection for the limb, with a leather piece protecting the hand and a leather cap for the shoulder. Loose thongs and strips of the linen material now hung in shreds. Small greaves, pieces of curved armor, covered his shins. Leg wraps, now blood-stained, further protected his lower legs. He bore a tall, oblong shield and a *gladius*, a straight, double-edged short sword.

Blasius fought as a *thraex*, a style different than that of the murmillo, favoring speed, His helmet crest bore a griffin decoration, the symbol of Nemesis. He also wore a *manica* on his arm, now crimson with Hadrianus' blood. Quilted wraps made his legs look as thick as small tree trunks. He carried a small round shield and short *sica* sword, the blade angled to enable its wielder to reach around an opponent's shield and armored parts.

The helmets covered the faces of both men with a grill, but Avitus did not wonder what their expressions might be. The way they moved told him everything. Hadrianus staggered, too tired to stop Blasius from lunging around his shield and raking his back with the curved sword. With each strike, Blasius' *manica* mopped up more of Hadrianus' blood. Blasius' attacks made Hadrianus lower his shield, up and down, left and right, struggling to block. Avitus also knew crushing headaches had plagued Hadrianus in the last weeks, and his performance reflected this; meanwhile Blasius had only grown stronger and faster.

Avitus counted them both as his friends, but now he tried to dissolve any feelings of affection. As he watched, he allowed their helmets to obscure their identities. It was not Hadrianus. It was the *murmillo*. It was not Blasius. It was the *thraex*.

As a *secutor*, Avitus would never have to fight either one. He almost always fought against a *retiarius*, a net fighter, and he counted none of this group as friends. When equipped for the fight, a *secutor* wore a heavy helmet, decorated with only a small ridge on its crest, the helmet's only openings two small eyeholes. The *secutor* fought with a *gladius* and a *scutum*, a large curved shield. A *manica* covered his sword arm. If the day came when he had to fight a friend, he would think of their combat idiosyncrasies and not their names.

The fighters paused, facing each other several yards away. The senior referee slowly stepped closer, his long staff ready, and Avitus expected him to stop the fight for a break to refresh the fighters. But as the referee began to lower his staff, Blasius launched himself towards Hadrianus.

The *murmillo* staggered and Avitus smiled, immediately recognizing the feint. The *thraex* swung his sword around for a killing plunge into Hadrianus' back.

The *murmillo* pivoted and caught Blasius' sword arm on his big shield. Hadrianus' feet churned the sand as he rammed his shield into the *thraex*. Blasius fell on his back, and Hadrianus dropped his shield onto the smaller man, kneeling on it. The crowd cheered with the sound of a thunderclap.

Blasius' heels hammered the sand as he tried to get up, his *sica* still in hand, but his arm pinned under the shield. With his small shield on the other arm, he flailed at Hadrianus' neck. Avitus knew he was trying to break the *murmillo's* collarbone, instead of trying to trap the sword arm as he should have. The mistake indicated panic.

The *murmillo* ended him quickly, jamming the *gladius* into the *thraex's* chest from the side, under the armpit, almost to the hilt, then twisting it back and forth until Blasius lay still.

Hadrianus patted his opponent's chest and Avitus wondered if the crowd noticed the gesture, before the *murmillo* stood and raised his *gladius* to the roaring amphitheater. At his feet, Blasius' blood puddled around him and soaked into the sand.

Avitus sighed.

"You died well, friend," he said quietly. "May your spirit travel well."

As the bearers came into the arena to carry Blasius away, Avitus happened to glance at an opening in the opposite side of the arena wall. Though shadowed by the afternoon sun, he could still see the large dark eyes burning into his, the eyes of Faustina, the *retiarius*. The *retiarii* fought with net, trident, and dagger. Wearing little armor, the fast net fighters were almost always matched against *secutores*.

"Carnuntum will remember today for a long time," Avitus heard a voice at his side. It was Felix, his *doctor*, the trainer for the *secutores*.

"They haven't seen a gladiator die in months. And Blasius a veteran at that. A waste. He would have given many more good fights," Avitus said.

"Yes, a waste. But it reminds us of who we are, doesn't it? From time to time, Carnuntum needs it. And the two of them could no longer stand to breathe the same air. But I also mean, they will remember Faustina's fight. Not only a left-handed net-fighter, but a woman. Does that bother you?" Felix asked.

"No. I don't care about the crowd," Avitus said, smiling. He gazed out into the arena.

"Hmm," Felix said, stepping close to Avitus. "Well, that isn't what I asked you, is it?"

"If she fights well, I don't doubt she will receive *missio*," Avitus said. He watched as a man dressed as Mercury came out with litter bearers and carried Blasius away. Slaves darted in, raking the sand smooth and filling in holes.

"Ah. If she fights well. And you? Three *secutores* versus three *retiarii*. And one single duel. Either way, the odds of you facing her in the arena are fair. The other net-men?" Felix shook his head, scowling. "Well, it won't be much of a fight. But Faustina?" He chuckled, staring at Avitus. "The rumors about her are true, you know. She has fought before. Fought a great deal. They're giving you 4-to-1 odds tonight, but that's because they're lumping her in with the other *retiarii*. They don't know how to make book on her. She ruins the odds. Take care tonight, Avitus."

Felix began to walk away.

"And where did you lay your coin, Felix?" Avitus called after him.

"On the *murmillo*. That was a clear wager," he said, walking away. "Oh, no. Your fight? I wouldn't bet on your fight tonight. I like to have some idea of the outcome."

Avitus turned back to look through the aperture. The magistrate was handing Hadrianus the palm frond of victory, the big *murmillo's* helmet now off, revealing a pale but emotionless face. Behind them, Avitus saw Faustina's eyes still staring at him and a cool sweat broke out on his skin.

They trained you for two weeks, he thought, *and you fight tonight. Never have I seen someone come into the arena so quickly.*

Faustina arrived two weeks ago with two young men and one young woman, all four of them bearing a convict brand on the forehead, as did Avitus. Three of them bore the mark of "FUR," for *fure* or thief. But only Faustina bore that of false accuser, or *kalumniator*, the mark of "KAL" on her brow, as did Avitus.

On the same day Hadrianus killed Blasius, the three others would be en route to Rome for the midday executions at the Flavian amphitheater

But Faustina was sentenced to be a gladiator instead of being condemned. Avitus attributed this sentence to the fact that she was a woman, thus providing a large draw for the events. But for such a short training period? She must have fought before, unless this was simply a ruse meant to bring in spectators. And her brand looked no less fresh than that of the others.

But then they would have matched her with the other female convict, or even any convict, Avitus reasoned. Such a match would provide much more of a show. And why would they condemn Zari, the other convict woman, to death but spare Faustina? No. He would pay attention to Felix's warning.

It all felt odd. Carnuntum itself felt odd to Avitus of late. When he was a child, Rome seemed like a place that must be a day's travel away. Now it seemed as far away as Egypt.

And it felt odd that condemned convicts were left at the *ludus*, the school and housing for the gladiators. That night, when the *contubernium*, the unit of eight legionaries, dropped them off, a silence fell across the school. The gladiators, confined to their cells upon the arrival of the condemned convicts, heard the soldiers give quiet instructions to Crispus the *lanista*, the manager of the *ludus*.

While the men and the girl wore dingy white garments, Faustina wore a blue *palla*, the shawl-like garment covering her head. The *palla* draped over a red *stola*, an article resembling a sleeved long dress. Even these loose garments failed to cover her sumptuous curves. Dark eyes blazed within an almond-colored face, reflecting the torches and lamps illuminating the yard. Were it not for the chains and forehead brand, Avitus would never have taken her for a slave, let alone a convict. While the others stood with slumped shoulders, Faustina stood erect, her chin raised, defiant.

Avitus watched as they led her away, and a murmur broke out as the gladiators saw her taken to a cell in the *retiarius* section. Hoots and cat-calls rose from the cells, growing louder and louder until the lead guard struck an iron bell, and they fell back to a murmur.

The other three convicts were separated and led away at the same moment. The first man was taken to the *murmillo* section. The second man began to drag his feet, but the guards prodded him on towards the *thraex* section. Avitus swallowed the bitter memory of his own first night at the *ludus*, and knew what awaited the men.

When the guards walked the girl towards the *secutor* section, she stared at the ground. Avitus heard giddy laughter from the neighboring cells and rapping on the walls. Avitus' cellmate had recently been sent on to Rome, and as the only cell with one occupant, Avitus heart pounded as he heard the bolt slide in his door.

He stepped back and sat down on his bed. The door swung open and the guard removed the girl's manacles. She hesitated at the door and the guard placed his hand on her back, pushing her slowly inside. The door shut behind her and Avitus heard the heavy bolt shoot home. She stood with her back pressed against the door, her eyes wide and staring at Avitus in the light of a small lamp.

"You're Persian, I think," he said.

She nodded. Unlike the other female convict, she was slender and short. Her long hair hung in her face.

"You speak Latin, then?" he asked.

She nodded again.

"What is your name?" he asked.

"Nona," she said.

"That doesn't sound very Persian."

She looked down at the floor, shivering. *Shivering not only from the cold April night,* Avitus thought.

"Zari," she said, clutching her thin *stola* around her shoulders.

Avitus looked at the spot where his cellmate's bed had rested until last week. He looked back at Zari as he moved to the far end of the bed.

"Are you hungry?" He asked, motioning to the bread laying on the table next to the lamp.

Zari looked at him and slowly picked up the bread, taking one bite and then another, until she had soon devoured the small loaf. She picked up the pitcher of watered wine and drank deeply, all the time never sitting down.

Avitus stood up and undressed, unfastening his tunic and loincloth and hanging them on the wall. He looked over and saw Zari, her back pressed against the door again, again swaddling herself in her *stola*.

"If you want to sleep, I won't fuck you," he said, climbing under his thick blanket. The rapping against the wall resumed until he banged the base of his fist against it. "But what my comrades do tomorrow, I can't say."

Avitus did want her, wanted to feel her slender form beneath him and her sweet breath in his mouth. He wanted to be with her and fall asleep with her in his arms. But it was more pride that he could have other women in Carnuntum, that he did not need to rape a condemned convict. That was the sport of old men and weaklings, those who could no longer catch the eye of an interested spectator.

Zari extinguished the lamp and Avitus saw her as a ghostly form draped in white in the dark cell. The form moved closer, and he felt her lay next to him on the bed, still dressed. He felt his cock stiffen as her shoulder touched his arm. He laid still, listening to her soft breathing.

"When will I die?" she asked.

"A fortnight? A month? It all depends on when the caravan reaches Rome," Avitus said. "You are all *noxii?*" The *noxii* held no hope of survival, most of them perishing in the jaws of predators.

"I am. And the men. Not Faustina. She fights," Zari said. "So. In a fortnight, perhaps I die. How?"

"Is it easier to know?" Avitus asked. "There are a number of possibilities. Why spend time thinking about it?"

"You do not know who you will fight? Are you a *retiarius?*" she asked.

Avitus snorted.

"I am a *secutor,*" he said.

"Then you fight *retiarii.* You always know what you will face. Would you want to not know?"

"A lion, probably. Or it could be a bear. Or dogs. Leopards. Or, a bull. But it will probably be a lion. Maybe a few of them."

He heard her quietly sobbing next to him and he put his arm around her.

"Cry now," Avitus said. "But do not cry when they bring the beast into the arena. Run towards him and shout at him. It will anger him and he will strike you down quickly. If you run, he may play with you and slowly kill you."

Zari cried louder now, and Avitus held her tighter now, feeling her thigh press against his erection.

"Pray to Hercules. Or pray to Nemesis if you wish. How well you die is your only choice left," he said. He leaned down and kissed her on the forehead, feeling the raised letters of the scar on his lips.

He felt Zari's hand sliding down his body, lingering over his own scars in its descent, until her soft grip closed around his penis, stroking him. She lifted her face to his and he felt her tongue flicker over his lips before intertwining with his, and he tasted her tears as they ran.

Avitus reached between her legs and lifted up her garments. He pulled her leg to the side, sliding his calloused hand along her smooth inner thighs, up between her legs. He trailed his fingertips through the short curls along her labia, slipping between the folds and wetting them with the dew from her cunt before sliding them up to circle the nub of her clit. She breathed harder now, squeezing his prick in her hand.

He slid his middle finger inside of her, resting his thumb on her fleshy nub while he hooked his finger and rubbed back and forth. Zari sighed, her hips moving into a slow roll as Avitus slid in a second finger.

She held onto his hand, pressing it harder against herself and whimpering. She reached down, caressing herself, pressing her lips against his fingers. Her body stiffened and she tightened around his hand. He heard her gasping through clenched teeth, until her breathing slowed and she collapsed.

Avitus felt her limp body become rigid, and she jumped from the bed. He heard the table knocked to the floor and the pitcher shatter. He heard things being thrown, shattered, and spilled.

He jumped up and clutched the flailing white form. She reached back and clawed at him in the dark, her nails digging furrows into his neck and scalp. He grabbed her arms from behind as she kicked wildly. He twisted her arms up behind her back, hoping to subdue her with pain, but she only kicked harder, punting his belongings against the wall and across the floor, kicking his shins. He gripped both of her slender wrists with one hand while he grabbed a supple belt from the wall, wrapping it around them and fastening it tightly.

One hand in her hair and one on her wrists, he forced Zari face down on the bed, her knees on the floor. He pinned her with his weight, feeling her linen-covered bottom against his erection as he managed to light what little fuel remained in his cracked lamp.

Debris littered the floor. She had smashed, thrown, or kicked everything within her reach. Avitus found a leather thong and forced Zari's ankles together, binding them tightly. She hissed and spat and cursed at him, and he knew he had to be inside of her now. He felt his scalp and neck, and his hands came away bloody. Now, she was only an opponent to be subdued, defeated. He felt his body moving without thinking, without having to direct it.

He grabbed the hems of her *stola* and *palla* and wrenched them up over her back, revealing her soft clenched buttocks.

He knelt behind her, his penis like heated iron now as he slid back his foreskin, and pushed between her legs, the angry head of his cock prodding against her lips. Zari clenched every muscle, now pulling away from him, now twisting and pushing back to deny him entry.

His skull throbbing, Avitus smeared his fingers with oil from the floor and drove them into the cleft of her ass. Her anus clenched as he drove his finger into it, jabbing it in and out as she squealed in rage. *This kindness was more than I received my first night here*, he thought.

Avitus pulled out his finger and took her small ass cheeks in each hand, pulling them apart to reveal her sphincter. He took his erection and set his glans against the tiny hole, pressing slowly but never stopping, relishing the tightness, feeling the muscle twitch around his shaft as he went in further and further, gripping her by the shoulders now as she cried out and and the other *secutores* pounded on the walls. Soon he was all the way inside her, listening to her gasp, crushing her body beneath his, sliding all the way out only to plunge all the way home, again and again. His girth stretched her asshole into a tight band around his shaft, squeezing him, seeming to flutter at times. He smelled her fear and her rage and her pain and her sweat. The orgasm rose within him and roared, pulsing through him, shaking his body as he pounded into her, jetting his scum deep into her bowels.

He slid out and stood over her, dizzy, his cock erect and reddened. Zari laid perfectly still now. He watched a last drop of come fall from the tip of his penis onto the small of her back, trickling down into the cleft of her ass.

Zari lifted her head and slowly looked over her shoulder at him.

"I will die well," she said to him, grinning defiantly through tears.

Chapter 2
The Arena

Faustina inhaled deeply, held her breath, and exhaled slowly through her nose. Her *doctor*, Albus, checked the fastenings of the *manica* on her right arm and of the one piece of armor on her right shoulder. Albus massaged her neck and shoulders and then let her run in place as they stood in the corridor. Faustina honed the points of her trident one last time and did the same to her *quadrens*, a dagger consisting of four, foot-long spikes extending from the guard instead of the usual dagger blade. She tucked one of the prongs of the *quadrens* into her belt, adjusted her tunic, and checked the net-cord tied to her left wrist. Braids held her thick black hair tight and high on her head. Bouncing from one bare foot to the other, she stopped moving only long enough for Albus to give her water.

Faustina's stomach churned. She felt hot, though it was a cool evening. Everything on her skin felt prickly. She smelled her own sweat, pungent with anxiety. She made her face rigid and looked for any reaction from Albus.

Albus was the first good trainer Faustina ever had, she thought, wishing he had always been her doctor. As the *retiarii* wore no helmet, they could not hide their expressions from their opponent or from the crowd. Albus constantly reminded his fighters that as *retiarii* wore no helmet, they must wear no emotion, save that which they wished their opponents to see.

"Avitus is an actor," Albus whispered. "Remember that. If he looks tired or weak, it is just for show, just to bring you in for the *gladius*. You must be a new net-fighter, one he hasn't fought before. Being left-handed isn't enough. You must move like water. Make him react to you, always moving, always striking. Do not expect him to tire. Do not expect anything from him."

The horns of the musicians bellowed.

"Go now," Albus said. "And show Carnuntum how the East fights."

Faustina set her face and rounded the corner. As the *secutor* appeared in the hallway, she did not acknowledge him, nor did his stride change. His polished helmet covered his head completely, save for two small eye holes. Muscles rippled like river water over his body, and he carried his *gladius* and *scutum*, the curved and heavy rectangular shield painted with a roaring lion, almost carelessly.

So you are Avitus, she thought. *Did you even see me through your little eye-holes? How do you wear that bucket and even see?*

They walked side by side to the gate, Faustina peripherally observing the bulky form next to her. As always before a fight, she pushed down the urge to face him, to attack. His proximity quickened her pulse and tightened her muscles.

The guard at the arena gate smirked at them. Faustina stood still next to Avitus, waiting to be announced, her stomach twitching. When the guard opened his mouth as though to speak, Faustina stared at him, calculating how she could best punch her trident through his eye sockets. The guard closed his mouth again and slowly looked towards the arena, placing his hand on the door.

Faustina heard their names announced from the podium, the accented voice strange to her ears. The guard slammed the door open and Faustina felt herself walking out, propelled by her feet as though riding a horse. A mixture of cat-calls and cheers thundered down from the oval of the amphitheater as she raised the trident in her right hand, vaguely aware of Avitus doing the same with his *gladius*. They passed each other as they circled the arena, and then the horns blew again and she stopped to salute the magistrate serving as editor for the event. At the next sounding, she took her place opposite him and prayed quietly to Nemesis.

Nemesis, guide my hand and let me strike true.
Let me see my enemy's weakness. Let my enemy feel my strength.
Let me not falter, and if I fall, let me perish with weapon in hand.

Faustina felt a coolness over her body and felt the air warp around her. Despite the torchlight, she felt more than saw the stars and moon above her. She felt her body tighten like a bowstring as she stood, her right foot forward, net clenched in her left hand as it held the back of the trident, her right hand forward on the trident shaft. She held the trident pointed towards Avitus' feet.

Avitus faced her, the top of his *scutum* even with his eye-holes, his *gladius* held almost behind him.

Faustina felt herself moving as the horns blew, moving backwards as the *secutor* charged her. The man's feet churned the dirt. This was not a man, this was a bull. His speed surprised her as his blade lunged towards her lower abdomen. She swiveled, still moving backwards, and swept the *gladius* aside with her trident, then jabbing into his arm through the *manica*. Stepping to the right to break Avitus' forward momentum, she saw a moment when she was in his blind spot, beyond the eye holes of his helmet.

On Avitus' right-side, his sword-side, Faustina whipped her net, bundled together like a flail, using the weights to wrap it around the neck flange of his helmet. It was a trick that worked many times before. She would snag the neck flange, the *secutor* would lift his sword to cut the net cord, and she would stab him in the ribs, with a good chance of at least one prong penetrating the lung.

But Avitus made no attempt to cut himself free and Faustina now found herself tethered to him by the wrist cord. She choked up her grip on the trident, but the rope occupied her left hand, forcing her to wield the trident one-handed. The *secutor* lunged at her like a machine as she tried to block awkwardly with the trident. She felt a punch right above the crease of groin and thigh, and she knew she was now cut, the strike aimed at an artery.

Faustina now stabbed at his wrist and forearm, and knew she was striking the flesh beneath the linen of the *manica*, but he did not slow his attack. She felt another bite, this time at her waist. She pulled backwards, hoping to unbalance Avitus with the net, but he only leaned backward himself and left a line of fire across the top of her breasts with a horizontal slash.

Faustina felt herself falling backwards, but rolled to one knee. She was free of the cord now, but her body ached with the wounds and she dared not look down as she felt the blood wetting her tunic. Avitus paused and threw the net aside, apparently waiting for Faustina to raise a finger. Faustina grinned, though the arena tilted in her vision. She was not sure if the roar in her ears was the crowd or if she was passing out. But she stood and leaned on her trident, feigning a yawn of boredom, and now knew she heard the applause and laughter of the crowd.

She regretted her taunt as Avitus suddenly appeared before her. She felt hands pushing down on her shoulders from behind. She fell to her knees, regaining her sense in time to lift the trident. She held the prongs sideways and the tips slid past the *secutor's* shield, stabbing into his belly before he checked his charge. When he stepped backwards, Faustina realized the wounds were shallow. She cursed herself for not thrusting, but lurched to her feet and kept the trident in the space past the shield. If she would fall, she would fall plunging holes into the *secutor*. She stabbed into one pectoral, twisting and tearing the skin before he moved back. He knocked the trident down with his sword arm, but Faustina stabbed into his thigh.

As she stabbed, she saw Avitus' shield fall away, realizing too late he was now grabbing the trident shaft with his shield hand before she could back away. She felt the weapon wrenched from her hands and thrown aside. She blocked a *gladius* thrust with the *manica* on her right arm, but still felt the bite. With no time to run, Faustina pulled the *quadrens* from her belt, the hilt sticky with her blood, and thrust at the *secutor's* groin.

Avitus blocked the weapon, the blade of his *gladius* wedged between the prongs of the *quadrens*. He forced the weapon to the ground as Faustina held onto it. She watched as his bare foot stomped on her hand.

Hold onto it. You die if you let go, she told herself.

She freed the weapon, but saw all but one of the prongs were broken off. She launched her arm forward, striking, an animal in her death throes. Avitus staggered backwards, the hilt of the *quadrens* projecting sideways from the left eye hole of his helmet. The breath vapor pouring out from the holes made him look monstrous. Faustina could not tell if it was a mortal wound or if it was only lodged between helmet and face.

187

Faustina staggered over to her trident and picked it up, turning in time to see Avitus wrench the *quadrens* from his helmet and throw it aside. He bellowed, a voice of rage and pain resonating inside the helmet, and charged again. Faustina screamed, running towards him. She felt weak but he had no shield now. She had a chance if she could stay on her feet.

She felt something hit her chest and looked down to see the referee's staff restraining her. He was screaming at her, his face red, something about ignoring a command to halt. Looking over at Avitus, she saw him similarly restrained by the assistant referee. She set the butt of her trident on the ground and leaned on it, struggling to stand up, refusing to fall.

She saw everything else through a fog. The officials came out. *Missio. Missio.* She was being granted *missio.* But she hadn't yielded. Avitus was receiving *missio.* He hadn't yielded either. She was being cheated. She could have won, but it was being taken from her. She would not go as champion in her next fight. She dared to look down at her blood-soaked tunic. Dirt stuck to the rivulets of blood on her legs.

Will I die? she wondered. *Am I already dead?*

She looked at Avitus as he took off his helmet. The remnants of a ruined eye filled his right eye socket. He turned a pain-filled left eye to look at her, nodding to her. She stared back, and he did not look away until she nodded back. Somewhere, the crowd roared. The sound seemed to vibrate inside her skull. The arena spun for a moment, then she found herself laying in the sand. She had fallen. She stared up at the waning moon and let darkness overtake her.

Faustina writhed in the bed, opening her eyes to stare puzzled at the ceiling, then closing them again. In dream, she watched as the *secutor* charged. She felt hands pushing down on her shoulders again as she fell to one knee. She looked around. Both senior and junior referees stood nowhere near. The *secutor* stopped and backed away. She now lay on a bed in the middle of the arena, the sky dark. She looked up at the amphitheater and found the seats empty. The arena began to spin, or the amphitheater spun around her. Torches flared to life, lit by unseen hands, and she realized it was the bed that spun as the torches formed a ring of flame with the movement. The arena grew brighter and brighter.

Still on the spinning bed, Faustina found herself awakening in a strange room, ornately painted and decorated, and brilliantly lit by oil lamps and candles. It felt warm. No, hot. Very hot. Was it summer? No, it was still spring. The room slowed now, soon only shaking instead of spinning. She felt pain and looked down to see bandages on various parts of her body. She plucked at the one on her arm, trying to lift it and see the wound beneath. A soft hand grasped hers and she looked to see a doe-eyed young woman who smiled sadly and shook her head. The woman lifted a cup and trickled cold water into Faustina's mouth. Faustina swallowed and closed her eyes. *If only the room wasn't so hot. It feels like an oven,* she thought.

She felt a cord on her left wrist and realized she'd been sleeping. Someone was putting something in her right hand. Her trident. Was it time? A new match already? The fight with Avitus. She had not finished it. She must fight him again.

Faustina opened her eyes in time to see the *secutor* approach the bed. He wore the helmet, but he looked smaller now, carrying no shield and naked except for a broad belt, an erection and a *gladius* jutting towards her as he approached. A piece of uncut amber hung on a gold chain from his neck. There was a second *secutor*, as well, this one female, soft and full-breasted, and wearing only helmet, belt, and a necklace similar to the man's.

Faustina needed to get up, needed to fight, though she did not understand the reason why they were in a room and not the arena. She tried to rise, but fell back on the bed, dropping the trident and hearing it clatter on the floor. Her head throbbing, she reached for her *quadrens*, but it was gone and she was naked. She tried to gather up the net. She cast it at the male as he approached, but there were no weights on it and it fluttered to the floor.

The woman stooped and gathered up the net. Faustina tried to yank it away from her but the woman was too strong. The female *secutor* spread the net over Faustina, holding her down with it. Faustina struggled, but found the net only pulled tighter. She felt sweat drench her body and now the room felt cold.

Hands pulled her legs apart, and Faustina thought to kick too late. The male *secutor* knelt between her legs, his hand stroking her vulva, his finger penetrating her, his thumb rubbing her clit too hard. The pounding in her head felt better when she closed her eyes.

Pain forced her eyes open again. The bronze of the helmet rested against her face and she looked in to see two brown eyes staring back at her. *Not Avitus,* she realized. The weight of the helmet hurt her, but the coolness of the metal felt good. From inside, she heard the hollow echo of his breathing. The aching came from the *secutor's* weight resting upon her wounds. She grunted with pain and the *secutor* rubbed against them harder. Faustina gritted her teeth and realized his penis was thrusting in and out of her. She focused on the feel of his cock inside her. She had to keep sliding her concentration from her wounds back to the sensations inside her pussy. The net still covered her, but the man reached up and squeezed her breasts, and she welcomed the pinching of her nipples as a diversion. The wound above and to the side of her groin hurt worst of all. Faustina looked up to see the female *secutor* kneeling on the bed beside her, fingering herself as her breasts bounced.

A moan rang inside the man's helmet and Faustina felt him thrust deep into her. She felt his cock throb as it pulsed inside, and then he slid out and off of her. She gasped with relief. The net was pulled from her head, but she looked to see the woman's bottom as it descended to her face. Faustina growled with rage as she turned her face aside, trapped between two thighs. She felt the wet softness of the woman's sex on her cheek, rubbing on her.

For a moment, she clenched her teeth, ready to bite this woman. As a *gladiatrix*, slave, and convict, Faustina knew what it was to have her body used by others. This she accepted as a chore in most cases. Sometimes it gave her pleasure. Sometimes it disgusted her. But rare were the times when someone defiled her mouth.

"The *retiarius* does not submit, my love," Faustina heard the woman say, the voice muffled in her ears.

"No *missio!*" she heard the man cry out. Pain stabbed through the wound near her groin.

"Submit!" the woman yelled, her voice metallic in her helmet. She

bounced on top of Faustina's face. The pain in her wound grew ago-
nizing. She felt a finger probe it. Sweat poured anew from Faustina's
brow. She tried to push the woman off, but her arms felt like willows.
The female *secutor* twisted Faustina's hair, pulling her face into her
musky pudenda.

Faustina forced her tongue out, haltingly. It made contact with the
women's folds and she tasted the salty tang of her cunt. The woman
sighed and sank down, holding her labia open as she pressed down
against Faustina's mouth. The intense pain in her wound stopped,
leaving only a dull throb, pleasant in comparison.

Keep the pain away, Faustina told herself. She drove her tongue
deeper into the woman. *This is nothing. Only a game. There is nothing
but doing this and stopping the pain. The faster you pleasure her, the sooner
this ends. No! There is no 'her.' There is only this cunt. Connected to nothing. Only this. Lick it. Suck it. There is only this. Nothing else. This is not
you. This is not her. You enjoy this. You like this. This is someone doing it
to you.*

Faustina let the room, the bed, and the woman fall away as she
lapped. She flexed her tongue as far as it would go, deeper, sliding
out and sucking at the lips, and then plunging back in. The pussy
twitched and bounced on her mouth. It slid forward onto her chin,
and she wiggled the tip of her tongue against a puckered anus, tasting
and smelling dirt and sweat, buttocks enclosing her face. She heard
a woman moaning, the sound hollow. The cunt slid backward again
and her tongue slid into the wet slit. Faustina stabbed her tongue towards the inside front of it, probing its piss hole. The pussy mashed
down on her, suffocating her, her nose inside the wet slit, inhaling
her scent. It slid back further and Faustina sucked at the long, fat clit
resting on her lip. A woman cried out and hands squeezed Faustina's
breasts, nails digging into them.

The cunt lifted from her. Faustina looked up to see the female
secutor squatting over her face.

The helmeted head tilted down to look at her. A voice rang out
from within the helmet.

"Keep. Your precious mouth. Open."

Chapter 3
Joining the Stable

Avitus sat in his chair and watched as Paula squatted over Faustina's mouth. He set his face, aware that Paula's husband Gratianus was watching his reaction. The *secutor* helmet hid Gratianus' expression, but the man hopped from foot to foot, masturbating and cheering Paula on.

The exhibition sickened Avitus, mainly the mockery of the *secutore* and the *retiarii*. He wanted to kill Paula and Gratianus. But instead he could only watch, staring as a stream of golden piss squirted from Paula's cunt into the mouth of the *gladiatrix*. Faustina retched, spitting up some of the urine, but when she turned away Gratianus stepped forward and poked his finger into the wound above her groin. Faustina righted her face again and opened her mouth, swallowing the last trickles of urine pouring in. An involuntary quiver twitched through Avitus as he watched and he reminded himself this was wrong.

Gratianus clapped as Paula dismounted from Faustina's face. Paula made a mock bow before Avitus, and then Gratianus laughed and did the same. The pair took off their helmets. Gratianus grinned. Avitus realized the man's face was considered handsome, but it held the suggestion of a rat in expression.

Paula's red-dyed hair rested in a hairnet. Dispute his disgust, Avitus admired her form. She was soft without being flabby, like some of Carnuntum's best prostitutes, her breasts full without sagging. But in her expression, Avitus saw not a rat but a snake. The vaguely reptilian cast of her face alarmed him as much as it intrigued him. On the bed behind them, Avitus saw Faustina laying on the bed, defeated in her fever and too weak to clean herself of the piss soaking into her hair and pillow.

"You are not entertained?" Gratianus asked, sarcasm staining his voice.

"But we thought to amuse the gladiator himself for a change!" Paula said. "You who entertain others so well deserve to see a match from time to time."

"Your remaining eye still works, does it not?" Gratianus asked. "Why do you not clap? You still have two hands. I said, clap!"

Avitus raised his hands, mechanically, and beat his palms together. The couple laughed, gathering their *gladii* and walking out of the room.

It had been two days since Avitus learned he and Faustina would be sent to the villa. He dreaded the visit. He hated Gratianus, though he barely knew him. Rumors circulated wildly about him, including many stories of prostitutes and visitors never seen again. None of these stories involved the nobles, but for an actor or a servant, perhaps few would question their disappearance too closely. And maybe, Avitus thought, a gladiator still under sentence could simply be reported as a runaway.

"Sir, I wish to decline the invitation," Avitus said to Crispus, the *lanista*. Avitus stood in Crispus' office, while Crispus wrote at his table.

Crispus set down his pen and looked up at Avitus. Avitus saw the man's face soften for half a second before turning to stone.

"Decline?" Crispus said, his voice almost a whisper.

"Yes, sir," Avitus said.

Crispus stared at him without speaking or moving, then said,

"One of the most powerful and wealthy men in Carnuntum sends you a personal invitation to recover at his estate. And you wish to decline."

"Yes, sir," Avitus said. His thigh ached from the inflamed puncture wounds.

Crispus cleared his throat and folded his hands in front of him on his desk. He stood up and walked slowly to the door, opening it and looking casually left and right before closing it again. He stood next to

Avitus and spoke quietly, not facing him.

"My best fighter, no, my two best fighters have received invitations to recuperate at a most important man's home. I will speak frankly with you, Avitus. By turning down this invitation, you would insult Gratianus. Your insulting of Gratianus would be seen as my insulting Gratianus. There are persons of influence involved in this matter. The politics of hospitality often supersede one's own desires. That bears true for a gladiator. And it bears true for a *lanista*.

"You belong to this school, and the school, and I, belong to Rome. The Emperor's Rome. Faustina has already been sent to Gratianus. I cannot emphasize enough how ill-advised a refusal of Gratianus' hospitality would be at this time. The only help I can render you is this advice. Reconsider long and hard your choice to decline. That is my final word on the subject."

Crispus walked to his table without another look at Avitus. He sat down and began writing.

"You may go. And have your bandages changed," Crispus said, his voice strained.

"Yes, sir," Avitus said. His hand shook as he opened and closed the door on the way out. He walked away from Crispus' office, blood pounding in his ears. He was still adjusting to seeing with only one eye, and he felt dizzy as he stomped along the way. He didn't know where he wanted to go, but he walked toward the sound of the drill yard, towards the sound of Felix's rasping voice barking out commands.

Avitus rounded a corner and saw Felix holding something too flexible to be a rod, and too rigid to be a whip. Rows of *secutores*, each wearing an extra heavy training helmet, sprinted back and forth between two lines on the ground about ten yards apart. The men threw themselves along as Felix screamed at them to charge. Those too slow, or who fell, Felix stepped forward and struck with his whip rod. Most of the men bore at least one fresh red stripe on their sweating, dirty bodies.

Felix looked over at Avitus, and whistled to an assistant doctor, who ran to Felix's side. Felix handed the man the whip rod and pointed to the *secutores*. The assistant took over the sprint drills as Felix walked up to Avitus.

"You look like dogshit, boy," Felix said. "Change your bandages before you turn green."

"How long will they keep me at Gratianus' villa?" Avitus asked.

Felix looked away and shrugged.

"I don't know," he said.

"Well, has this happened before? That gladiators had to recover there?" Avitus asked.

"A couple years ago," Felix said. "A few gladiators were guests for a week. No one still at the *ludus*."

"What did they say?" Avitus asked. "I've heard what the whores say about Gratianus. And Paula."

"Well, then you've already heard it," Felix said, rubbing the back of his neck. "What can I say? They are a pair of rich fucking degenerates. Have fun. Fuck. Make the best of it."

"Crispus warned me not to decline the invitation," Avitus said.

"Decline, eh? Avitus. Gratianus is a friend of Diocletian, or at least a friend of an important friend. You and Faustina, you're a favor. Do you think Crispus has any say in this?" Felix shook his head and laughed without humor, and spat in the dirt. "No. Gratianus did something for somebody in Rome. What, I don't know."

Felix stared off in the distance. He smiled suddenly, his face a mask but for the toothy grin forced onto it. He slapped Avitus on the shoulder. "You're looking at it all wrong. You'll go there, probably hump his wife raw, and come back to the arena fresh as springtime. See you in a few weeks, Avitus." He grabbed Avitus' hand, squeezed it, and walked away, his back stiff.

"And change your fucking bandages!" he called back over his shoulder.

Avitus watched as Felix took the whip rod, dismissed the assistant, and resumed screaming at the *secutores*.

Now into his third day at the villa, Avitus waited in his room, laying on the bed. The humiliation of Faustina the other day had confirmed his fears. From different prostitutes, Avitus heard stories about the house he hoped were exaggerations. He never expected to be sent there, didn't know he *could* be sent there. True, as a successful fighter, he received and accepted many invitations for dinners and parties. He'd even been a party guest at this villa. The luxury impressed him but the quality of the hosts did not. Gratianus behaved like most of the retired officers, one with an undistinguished career, owing his fortune to intrigue and birth more than achievement.

And now Avitus found himself a prisoner through virtue of politics. Though so far he had suffered little but boredom, he dreaded the days to come and looked forward to returning to the amphitheater. He saw little of his hosts. He wondered if Faustina still lived. His hand strayed towards the bandage covering his right eye socket.

He was down to one eye. Fighting as a *secutor*, his helmet impaired his line of sight even with two eyes. What would happen next? This changed everything. He would need to retrain entirely. Perhaps he should train in a new style, he thought. And what? Begin as a novice *murmillo* with one eye? If he would fight with this limitation, would it not be better to use the style he knew and excelled in?

The door opened and Paula stepped inside, her red hair pinned up, her *palla* gleaming white. The amber chunk hanging from her necklace caught the light and cast orange rays across her bosom. An enormous hound stood at her side, its short fur black and shining in the sunlight streaming in through the window. The dog's shoulder reached Paula's hip, its muscles rippling under its slightly loose skin. Avitus thought of the girl Zari and wondered what became of her. The dog ignored him and sniffed around the room. Avitus recognized the breed as one similar to a type used by the army. He'd been told the breed was sometimes used in the Flavian amphitheater in Rome. The head of the massive beast seemed larger than Avitus' head.

"You look well, Avitus," Paula said, approaching him and checking his bandages. "You must forgive us for being such poor hosts. But we have been extremely busy. I hope the servants have treated you well?"

Avitus nodded. Paula's lip curled.

"This must be quite a change for you. Not training. Not fighting. Doing nothing but lounging and eating. You must be bored," she asked. The dog exhaled loudly and sat next to Paula. She stroked his head without having to bend over.

"No, ma'am," Avitus said. Admitting boredom seemed unwise to him.

"Good. All the same, I thought I might impose on your reverie by asking you to visit the garden with me."

"Of course," Avitus said, standing up.

"Come then. Gratianus is already waiting for us."

Avitus walked next to the dog, who walked next to Paula. They walked down several halls toward the rear of the building. Though having learned almost nothing of art, Avitus marveled at the paintings and mosaics on the walls. Scenes of gladiators gave way to sylvan scenes. As they went further, human figures reappeared, the scenes beginning as erotic and becoming increasingly bizarre. Centaurs and satyrs impaled women on their gargantuan penises. Pairs of women pleasured themselves with the opposite ends of snakes.

The last hallway emptied onto a tiled circle outside, surrounded by trees. Gratianus sat on a chair, while a naked young woman knelt on the tiles to both his left and right, while a third knelt on the tiles before him. Unlike the dogs, each girl wore a collar and leash, the lanyard ends of the latter casually hung from the wrist of Gratianus. Next to him sat an empty chair. The center of the area was untiled, green grass growing in a circle of about two yards in diameter. Two more dogs, similar to the first, paced aimlessly about the area, casually approaching their comrade as he arrived with Paula.

Paula walked over and sat in the empty chair. One of the dogs sniffed Avitus loudly, slowly circling him. He extended his hand, letting the dog smell it, but when he tried to pet her, she pulled her head back and growled, her sound deep and resonant. Avitus placed his hands on his hips and ignored her after that.

Gratianus and Paula spoke to each other quietly, occasionally glancing at Avitus and giggling. None of the slave girls, as he assumed them to be, met his eyes, and instead stared at the ground, shifting uncomfortably on the tiles. Avitus let himself start to shut down. In times of imprisonment, he learned to still his mind. It took years of practice, to think of nothing, no feelings, no reaction, but to remain alert to danger. He looked up at the sky, watching the clouds move.

"Avitus!" he snapped back into the moment when he heard Gratianus call his name. "Avitus, come here, will you? Instead of standing like a tree waiting to drop its leaves. Come here."

Avitus approached and stood rigidly before the couple.

"Avitus, I don't suppose you know anything of animal husbandry, do you? Now I don't mean to speak of a man marrying his horse, you see," Gratianus said as Paula tittered. "I mean, the breeding of animals."

"No, sir," Avitus answered. "I don't suppose I know anything about the topic."

"You weren't a farmer before you were a gladiator? What did you do?"

"I...," Avitus started to speak.

"Never mind. I don't actually care," Gratianus said, waving his hand. "But you know nothing of animal husbandry. And I admit, I know little of it myself. But, my dear Paula here knows a bit. She actually knows a great deal about breeding livestock." He lifted one foot and set his sandal in the middle of the girl's back before him. She flinched, her brown hair spilling over her face, but she remained still, except for the rocking motion as Gratianus jiggled his foot.

The girl suddenly lifted her green eyes and stared at Avitus. He met her gaze but did not hold it for long, not wanting Gratianus and Paula to witness the contact. In her eyes, he saw she was taking a chance and knew she only did so because her back was turned to her masters. He wondered if those who never knew slavery understood how to speak this way, to talk with nothing but the eyes. He realized Gratianus was still speaking.

"Horses and dogs, mostly. She's skilled enough that the Legion even buys breeding stock from her. Yes, indeed. But she does, from time to time, experiment with other species, don't you, dear?"

"I do, I do," Paula said, reaching down to pet the chestnut hair of the girl next to her. This one also flinched at her touch.

Avitus tried to take everything in, how the girls reacted, what the masters said, and more importantly, the sound of their voice, the way they moved, and the look on their faces. Avitus tried to feign boredom and recognized the couple doing the same thing. But where Avitus tried to mask alarm, the couple masked excitement. A tang of anticipation wafted through the air. He smelled it there in the garden, the same way he smelled it surging from the crowd in the amphitheater.

"You see, Avitus," Paula said, standing up and taking the green-eyed girl's leash from Gratianus. "As I breed the finest dogs in Carnuntum, if not all of Petronell, I intend to breed the finest gladiators. The next generation of fighters will not be broken miners and crippled prisoners. They will be beautiful beasts of combat, like my lovely hounds. Like my handsome Avitus. Come." Paula walked the girl over to the grassy circle in the center of the area, the girl walking on hands and feet. She looked too comfortable doing it, Avitus thought, as though she had been trained, her shapely bottom thrust high in the air. "Fours," Paula said as they reached the grass, and the girl got on hands and knees, facing the chairs. "I think you know what to do, Avitus."

Avitus stared at the scene before him. The girl's beauty stunned him. She looked like she came from one of the tribes north of Carnuntum, her movements feral, her limbs well-formed. A cord of smooth muscle ran down either side of her spine, her back narrowing sharply to a wasp-waist. Her firm buttocks swelled and parted, revealing the fleshy lips of her pussy seeming to sprout from the soft frame of chestnut-colored hair.

Yet his audience unnerved him. Paula and Gratianus leered at him from their chairs as the two girls cast furtive glances.

"Go on," Paula said, motioning Avitus toward the girl with a gesture and a look, her eyebrows raised. When Avitus hesitated, Paula jumped to her feet and stamped her foot. She grabbed the two other leashes from her husband and walked quickly towards Avitus, a leash looped over each wrist. Neither of the girls were as nimble as the green-eyed one, and they struggled to keep up. Paula's eyes blazed as she grabbed Avitus' tunic and yanked it upwards.

Avitus took hold of the garment and pulled it off, less humiliated by stripping than being stripped. He felt cold iron against his belly and froze. Paula smirked, a small dagger now in her hand, and cut the loincloth from him. The proximity of the blade to his genitals did little to engorge his cock as it hung flaccidly. Paula grabbed his organ with her free hand, squeezing it.

"Do tell me you find this attractive," she said motioning to the green-eyed girl's ass.

"Is our little gladiator not up to the challenge?" Gratianus called out, tittering.

"No fear, my love. These beasts just need a little help from time to time," Paula said. The blade disappeared again under her *palla* and she grabbed the curly locks of the nearest girl, lifting her to kneel before Avitus. "Suck!" she said, and the girl docilely opened her mouth, her eyes closed, and dipped her head to take his soft prick inside.

Avitus tried to ignore Gratianus and Paula, as would ignore the spectators in the amphitheater. The girl's cheeks sucked in and out as she pulled at him with her mouth, her cheekbones high and delicate. He felt himself begin to stiffen. Paula grabbed the girl's hair again and forced her head back and forward roughly. The girl grabbed onto Avitus' thighs, trying not to fall over. He felt her tongue scrubbing his shaft and concentrated on the pleasure, trying to ignore Paula's barking voice. His face stung as an open palm smacked against it, and felt his dick sliding out of the warm mouth.

"I said fuck! Now!" Paula yelled in his face, pointing at the crouching girl on the grass. Avitus stepped forward and knelt behind her. The girl twitched her hips. His head felt hot as he parted her lips with his fingers, the flesh warm and slippery. He eased the head of his cock between them and the girl cooed softly as he penetrated her. He focused on the warm grip of her cunt around his shaft as he sank deeper, trying to ignore the pain of the puncture wounds on his thigh. He gripped her hips, pumping harder and faster. Sliding his hands down to her ass, he held onto her cheeks now, listening to her groans. He leaned forward, setting his knuckles on the ground, then reached up with one hand to feel her firm breasts as they swayed. As he stroked one nipple, she whimpered. He slid his hand down her belly, into the soft patch of curls between her legs.

"Breeding, not pleasure, Avitus," Paula said, squatting next to them. She grabbed his arm and pulled it until his now clenched fist rested on the ground again.

Avitus stared forward, pumping into the girl, feeling her push back against him, her pussy wet and tight. In the corner of his vision, he saw Paula touch one of the other girls, and in a moment, a slippery finger slid between his buttocks and rested on his perineum, massaging him. Another finger pressed against his rectum until it slid inside.

He felt himself coming without warning. He lifted himself up again, clenching the girl's ass in his hands as he pulled himself deep into her, grunting, letting all the pain dissolve into the white heat of the orgasm flashing through his brain.

"Good boy!" he heard Paula say, and the girl was suddenly pulled away from him. Avitus saw the delicate girl thrust to the ground before him. "On your back," Paula said. The new girl lay down on her back, her dark eyes wide, frowning as her legs were pulled open by her mistress. Her curly locks haloed around her head.

Paula clenched Avitus' wet cock as it started to soften, pumping vigorously and forcing it rigid once more. Avitus felt himself sweating as Paula pulled him by it. She spit on the girl's vagina, rubbing her saliva into it as she pulled Avitus down and pressed his prick against it. He lay down on top of the girl, working himself into her slit. She felt almost too tight, and he wondered what was wrong. He felt a foot on his ass, pushing down.

Trying to penetrate, he suddenly realized the girl was a virgin. The thought bothered him, for he had never been with a virgin. But he did remember his own first unwelcome penetration. He remembered the pain and in that moment, he realized all of his life had been spent giving and receiving pain. There was no avoiding giving and receiving it. One could only bear it well. One could only deal it well. Running from it only made it last longer.

Avitus plunged his cock into the girl in a slow, steady push, closing his eyes as he heard the girl mewl beneath him. He fucked her with neither sadism nor callousness, but accepted her pain. Right now it was her agony, but perhaps tomorrow it would be his. Better to grasp it, embrace it. He held her small breasts as his flesh slapped against hers, listening to her grunt with each thrust. She held onto his wounded arm, but he welcomed the ache of her fingers pressing against the unhealed gouge, feeling somehow closer to her for it. In his ear, one of the dogs sniffed him.

"What a good boy," he heard Paula say, not knowing whether she was talking to the dog or to him.

Chapter 4
The Amber Road

Faustina felt the wine spread a pleasant numbness through her mind. In the string of bad days spent at the villa, it had been an exceptionally bad day. Now she found herself, along with Avitus, guests of honor presented at the dinner party of Gratianus and Paula. Three musicians played their strings in the corner, ignored and frequently drowned out by the guests. Granted the privilege of place on one of the couches around the table, Faustina gazed back coolly at the hard looks of those seated on simple chairs. In their faces, she saw jealousy mixed with contempt. Three of Paula's dogs wandered about the room, eating bones and scraps from the floor.

Faustina gazed across the dining room table from her couch and found Avitus staring back at her. Like her, he rested belly down, his chest propped by the cushion. He now wore an eye patch over his right socket, and a wide leather bracer over each wrist. To his right, a middle-aged man spoke loudly to Gratianus, who lay on the center couch in the horseshoe arrangement of couches. The man gestured towards Avitus and slapped him on the shoulder from time to time between plucking dormice from the dish before him. He seemed to inhale the flesh and cast the bones on the floor in one movement.

On the other side of Avitus rested a small and young fair-haired woman named Iulia. It took Faustina a moment to realize Iulia was speaking to Avitus, her lips barely moving. Her ribboned garment resembled that of the other women in the room, but her copious amber jewelry spoke of exotic and distinctly un-Roman elements. Faustina watched as Avitus inclined his head, apparently listening to her. Iulia sometimes punctuated her speech by touching Avitus' hands.

When Faustina saw her walk earlier in the evening, she noticed the girl possessed a slight limp, a feature that neither slowed Iulia's gait nor failed to impart a strange charm to her mannerisms.

Faustina felt her stomach twitch, a small pain in her side. She drained her cup and refilled it. Faustina watched as Paula, seated on the center couch, darted glances at the pair. But whereas Paula's face seemed otherwise calm and happy, Gratianus looked visibly distracted, answering the loud man who sought his attention, but frowning at Iulia. One of the black dogs paced around Paula's couch.

"You met my daughter earlier this evening, yes?" the amber merchant, Aelius, said to Faustina from his place next to her on the couch, on her left. Faustina stared at him in surprise, for he spoke in fluent Persian. He smiled behind his long gray beard, his weathered skin crinkling. His eyes looked mad, pupils dilated. Like his daughter, he wore an excessive amount of amber jewelry. Faustina noticed, in contrast, neither Gratianus nor Paula wore their usual amber pendants.

"Your Persian is excellent," Faustina replied in the same language. She glanced across the room as she heard Avitus guffaw.

"Thank you. I hoped you would understand it, and your master and mistress over there trying to read our lips would not."

Faustina laughed and nodded. She could feel the couple's eyes upon her now.

"Without looking down," Aelius said, reaching for a thrush from a platter on the table, "you will find a tiny shard under your cushion."

Faustina fidgeted in her place and slid her hand under the cushion. She felt a sliver of something hard but not metallic, and needle-sharp, less than an inch long. She watched Aelius curiously as he ate the thrush. He spoke between bites.

"Keep it near you always. When the time comes, slide it into your skin, like a splinter."

"When what time comes?" Faustina asked, tucking it inside her leather bracer and reaching for her cup. Paula had given her the bracers earlier that day. They covered the rope-burns on her wrists.

"A time of desperation. When you absolutely must slay one who needs slaying. You will know the time. Laugh now," he said.

"What?" Faustina asked.

"Laugh as if I told you a very funny joke," Aelius said, draining his cup.

Faustina forced a laugh.

"Good enough," Aelius said. "And when your enemy is finished, run towards the Pole star. You will find us there. Now act as if I just told you something ridiculous."

Faustina sighed and shook her head, chuckling.

"Perhaps you did," she said. She realized she was slurring her words.

"Perhaps I did," he said. "Or perhaps not. Drink less wine in the days to come."

"Why?" Faustina asked. She had been drinking more wine in the past few days, nursing her wounds between her hosts' increasingly taxing demands.

"Because it is making you weak and foolish. And you need to see clearly. You need your strength. Suffering is not new to you. You've always known it. It's made you stronger. Faster. Smarter. But this luxury?" Aelius said, holding up a snail, plucking it from its shell and eating it. "This luxury you haven't known. And it will kill you. It tricks you. It tells you to avoid facing the pain with one more drink. One more concoction. One more nap on silk pillows. But the drink fades and you wake up from your slumber. And the suffering returns. And you experience it the same way you did the first time. Over and over again. No. Endure instead, Faustina. Your time will come."

Faustina drained her cup and sneered at Aelius. She felt the hand of the man to her right sliding his hand up her thigh, stopping at the tuck of her buttock.

"Endure?" Faustina said, still speaking Persian. "Ah. I shall endure. Tell me, Aelius, have you ever drank piss? Ever had an eel inserted into your body?" She was speaking louder now, and those around them were becoming quieter. "Ever felt a stallion come in your face? No? Never? Well I could tell you more about these things. More than I wish I could. And do you know why? Do you know why I get to experience these lovely experiences, Aelius? Well, it's because I am an honored guest! An honored guest of Diocletian's most honored shit-heel in all of Carnuntum!"

"Ah, Faustina!" she heard Gratianus say. "Would you grace us with your speech in a civilized tongue?"

"Would you have it so, sir?" Faustina hissed in Latin.

"I would," Gratianus said, raising one eyebrow and crossing his arms. "Especially your thoughts on our beloved emperor, since you appear to be on that subject." Silence hung in the room, the guests staring and the musicians pretending to adjust their instruments.

"I've nothing to say about the emperor," Faustina said, checking herself but gritting her teeth. "Only about you," she said, rising to her knees and pointing at Gratianus. "And you," she said, pointing at Paula. "Tell me, Gratianus, when last did you see combat? Did you ever watch it from a hill, perhaps? Did your soft hand ever shake that of a soldier? Did you listen to his stories, remembering them in detail so you could claim them as your own during these soft dinner parties?" Gratianus glared at her, fists shaking, clenched. "And you, Paula? How many senators have you sucked to attain your current position of Queen to the King of Sycophants? Were the two of you the only rotten fish left in the bottom of Carnuntum's aristocratic barrel?" Paula's face reddened and she stared at her husband, her burning eyes demanding retribution.

"Ah, these Persians and wine," Gratianus said, pressing his face into a grimace and presenting it as a smile. "They mix poorly. And unlike my wife's hounds, they forget how to conduct themselves in public. I'm afraid your face gives you away." Gratianus ran his fingers over his forehead, smiling in mockery of her brand. "You're simply a lying slut with a net, misusing her short-lived fame." Faustina now saw the villa's guards appearing in the doorways, silently filtering into the room in surprising numbers.

Faustina let herself fall forward onto the table as her hand grabbed a knife. She rose and threw it in one motion. The room tilted in her vision, and she cursed the wine now as the knife passed over Gratianus' head, clattering against the marble wall. She saw movement towards her from the corner of her eye, and drove her elbow backwards, feeling teeth break as a guard stumbled backwards, cursing and spitting blood.

The dogs were almost upon her now.

"Hold!" she heard Paula call out. Only for hearing this word did Faustina pause. Had Paula given no command, she assumed the dogs would have attacked to kill. And no sooner had she paused than hands gripped her arms. She felt her legs kicked out from beneath her, until they too were held. As the guards carried her from the room, she watched the scene upside down as her head hung. Aelius and Iulia were gone. Avitus watched, his chin in his hand, with no expression. When she passed the sneering face of Paula, Faustina spat, the projectile landing in the woman's hair. Stars crackled in Faustina's vision.

Faustina became conscious as she felt her *palla* pulled from her, and when she felt her undergarments being unwrapped, she tried to kick. Her body arched with the movement, but the hands held her leg firmly. She looked around at the circle of guards holding her, leering over her. By the torches in the undecorated walls, she knew this was what the house called the Inner Room.

She felt herself spinning, turned, and lowered face-down to lay naked on her belly. The cool stone felt good at first, as Faustina pressed her throbbing forehead against its surface. But almost immediately, it chilled her. She felt her limbs jerked, manacles clamping down on wrists and ankles. Her bracers mercifully protected her wrists from further damage, but the iron bit into her ankles. Chains connected to four of the dozens of rings bolted into the floor pulled her limbs out, forcing her body into an X.

It would be worse now, she thought. Whatever relief from her situation vanished when she threw the knife at Gratianus. She'd humiliated him in public, and was overheard speaking about Diocletian shortly before her outburst. Maybe, she would be sent to Rome to fight with no weapons against animals. Or maybe she would be made to disappear as a runaway. She would have been wise to remain silent as Avitus, she thought. He understood the wretched people of Carnuntum.

What had Aelius given her? A poison needle of sorts? She tried to reach it but could not bend her wrist enough. She would use it. It was time for an end. If she couldn't die in the arena, she would at least claim this last measure of control. It was time to use every moment, every opportunity.

Faustina raised her head, testing her range of motion. Above her, the guards leered. She lowered her head and paused to collect her strength. Flexing her neck, she whipped her head up and slammed her forehead into the floor. Faustina crumbled, unconscious, to the floor.

She awoke and tasted metal. Something pulled at each corner of her mouth, forcing her to grimace. Touching the pieces with her tongue, they felt like dull hooks, not piercing the flesh but pulling her lips back. There was something bound around her head, the binding running from the mouth hooks around to the back of her head. Someone crouched before her and she looked up to see Gratianus grinning down at her. He had one hand behind her head, clutching the binding. When he tugged it, the hooks pulled painfully at her mouth. He reached with his other hand and touched her forehead, then held up his hand. It was bloody. As she looked at his hand, she saw Paula now stood behind her husband.

"There," he said. "You see. We had to take measures to prevent you from hurting yourself. These," Gratianus said, making Faustina wince as he pulled and the hooks tugged her mouth. "These are to keep you from beating your brains out on the floor. And this room is to keep you from getting in trouble with friends of the Emperor. I do, after all, have a responsibility to you as my guest. As a man of influence, I am here to help."

Chapter 5
Wolfmarked

Faustina tried to take in every detail. If he came close enough to her jaws, she would allow her cheeks to be torn if it meant getting her teeth into him. If he tried to use her mouth she would bite off anything she could.

"You look like one of the wolves we sometimes trap. Right before we allow Paula's hounds to tear them apart. But listen. I cannot hold your harness all day. So I have another means of keeping your head up." Gratianus reached around with his free hand and showed her a thin chain, apparently running to her head harness. At the end of the chain was fastened an almost circular bronze hook, perhaps three inches in diameter. "We have this," Gratianus said. "I'll admit it isn't sharp, but you'll notice it's fairly thin and hammered flat. Trust me when I say this will hurt you if you pull against this. Your asshole will start at your waist if you don't keep still." Paula tittered behind him.

Faustina's mind teetered, half of it testing every limb, every restraint, quickly searching for a way out. The other half of her mind began to shut down, began to view her body as a thing separate from herself. The hooks yanked her mouth back, the metal hard against her gums. She felt herself tilting her head back to avoid the flesh tearing.

She felt something wrap around each knee, something that felt like leather bands. She watched as two guards each ran a rope across the floor, each running their rope through a ring in the floor. Then she winced as she felt someone's knee pressed into each of her calves.

"Faustina!" Gratianus hissed. And no sooner were the knees lifted from her calves than the ropes were pulled tight, dragged her knees up under her. The irons remained on her ankles, but there was no tension on them. She tried to kick but the hands were on her legs again, forcing them into a frog-like position, splaying out to the sides. Unable to turn and look, Faustina felt her knees and ankles secured to floor rings in this position.

The hooks tugged at the corners of her mouth again, but now she also felt a cold metal point poking into her rectum. She sucked in her breath.

The greatest pain now rested in Faustina's neck as she strained to keep her head back. She tested the hooks, stopping before they tore. She realized she had the tiniest movement available, in order to relieve the tension in her neck. She began to abstract the pain, letting it happen to her body, watching it happen to her body. She focused on sounds and smells in the room. She focused on the smell of coals burning. Her head throbbed, and she thought of the day she had received the KAL brand on her forehead.

"Look, Gratianus, she's already used to it. These Persians know their place if only you keep them properly," Paula said. She loomed over Faustina, and Faustina sucked in air as she felt the hooks pull at her mouth and anus. Rage welled up within her, but she pushed it down, letting it turn to cold liquid inside herself. *Feel nothing. Show nothing.* "Is it ready, yet?" Paula asked.

"Yes, I believe so. Not white, but orange will do, won't it?" Gratianus said.

"Quite so," Paula said. "Bring it here."

Faustina's eyes scanned the room, her heart pounding harder. The smell of smoke increased as guards carried a brazier and set it on a table against the wall. Above the table, a long, funnel-shaped copper shaft extended to the wall, apparently covering a window. One guard methodically worked a lever back and forth, and the wisps of smoke began traveling up into the funnel. Faustina felt herself breathing harder now. Behind the smoke, she smelled her own sweat, pungent with fear. She worked her wrist back and forth, hoping to drive the shard into her skin.

Paula approached and squatted in front of her, a set of iron rods in her hands. Each iron ended in a letter.

"Can you read, Faustina? Yes? Maybe you can tell me what this spells?" Paula's eyes sparkled and a small twitch moved her cheek.

"P.A.U.L.A. I think you know how this works," Paula said, tracing letters on her own forehead. "Well, let's start with P." Paula stood up and handed the irons to a guard. "You've done this, before, I know, but it's a novelty to me."

Faustina felt herself going numb as she remembered the day of her own conviction. Already a slave, she had told of the murders committed by her owner. She remembered the way the sky spun in her vision when the brand touched her face. It had been one brand with all three letters that time.

And now her body cartwheeled through pain. She spasmed at the burning in her back, lurched back at the pain in her mouth and anus. Her body twitched and shook beyond her control. She heard someone shrieking and smelled burning flesh, but she focused only on moving her way through her dance of agony. She shut out everything else, accepting the pain and pulling it outside, only to welcome it back again, over and over again. Darkness fell like a curtain in her vision, only to be wrenched free by pain. The faces of Paula and Gratianus danced in her vision, grinning, leering, spitting.

And then she lay face down on the floor. The tension was gone between her asshole and mouth. Her back throbbed with the pain of a burn, making the pain in her orifices feel almost insignificant. She lay on the floor, gasping as though washed up and thrown from a violent surf. The room became black.

When Faustina opened her eyes again, there was light, confusing her since the torches were gone. She looked up to see two fine-boned white feet walking towards her, the figure limping slightly. The person squatted down in front of her. Iulia. Iulia touched her wrists and Faustina realized the manacles were gone now. Iulia held the tiny shard between thumb and forefinger, and held it before Faustina's eyes.

"They will find this when they take off your bracers. Hide it in your teeth. Open your mouth," Iulia said, gently tapping Faustina's swollen lips.

"Poison?" Faustina asked.

Iulia cocked her head and squinted.

"No," she said. She held out the shard, and Faustina opened her mouth. The girl slid her fingers in, and Faustina felt her pressing the shard in between her back teeth. When she finished, the shard rested somehow molded into place. Iulia smiled with her white teeth and stroked Faustina's cheek. She sat down cross-legged before Faustina and reached for her arms.

Faustina crawled forward, every muscle quivering in pain. Her back burned with fire. Iulia guided her, until Faustina lay draped across the smaller woman's lap.

"Not much longer now," Iulia whispered in her ear. She stroked Faustina's hair. Faustina felt the pain rise up inside, every branding, every beating, every unwelcome penetration of her life, welling up and spilling over. She wept with loud jagged sobs as Iulia held her, rocking back and forth. She flinched as Iulia touched her back, but where the soft fingers touched her, the fire in her skin cooled and faded.

Iulia held her tightly and stood, carrying her in her arms. It seemed absurd to be carried by such a small woman, Faustina thought. But Iulia seemed to have no trouble doing so, though she walked with her familiar limp. Iulia carried her towards the wall, but instead of feeling the hard marble, they passed through it into the cool night air. Faustina looked down and saw they no longer walked on the ground, but above it. As Iulia walked they moved faster and faster, ascending into the sky. Faustina laughed, euphoric to be free from the villa, the night whipping past her in a blur.

They descended, finally, in the hills north of Carnuntum, before a huge oak tree, massive in the light of the waning crescent moon. A gray-bearded man stood before it, crouching to strike sparks to a small pile of wood. Iulia set Faustina down, standing next to her as the sticks kindled into flame. Aelius smiled and sat down on a stone. He motioned for Faustina to come closer, to sit next to him.

"Not much longer now," Aelius said as Faustina sat down on the stone.

"What?" Faustina asked.

Aelius produced a bundle of cloth and unwrapped it, revealing a thin sheet of lead.

"Do you wish for justice, Faustina?" he asked.

"I do," she said.

Aelius pulled an iron, stylus-like tool from his sleeve. Picking up a small wooden tablet, he flattened out the lead sheet on it. Faustina felt a hand on her hand and turned to see Iulia. The girl smiled as she flattened out Faustina's hand, as though studying the lines on her palms. Iulia's hand fluttered, and Faustina saw blood running from her own palm. Iulia then grasped her father's wrist, and Faustina now saw the small blade in her hand as Iulia made a cut on the man's forearm. Dazed, Faustina examined the fine cut on her palm, but then Iulia took her wrist and placed her palm against the wound on her father.

"Hold tight. Do not let go," Iulia whispered in her ear. "Think of justice. Think of vengeance." Faustina felt an urge to please Iulia, and she gripped the man's arm. Faustina thought of Nemesis, and remembered the feel of hands on her shoulders, guiding her to avoid a death blow from Avitus. She thought of Nemesis flying above her now, sword and scourge in hand, soaring towards the villa. For the first time in weeks, Faustina felt strong again, felt glad to be alive.

Aelius stared into the fire, his face slack. His hand dragged the stylus across the lead sheet, and soon the image of Nemesis took shape, wings outspread like a bird of prey, sword and scourge raised high. He now scrawled words on the sheets, a strange mixture of Latin, Greek, Persian, and other languages Faustina did not know. Aelius spoke, and his words were a mixture of the languages, the word sometimes spoken in a language different than that written,

"Honor to the divine Nemesis. I complain to you winged justice-bringer that we have suffered grievously at the hands of Gratianus and Paula. The pair have inflicted countless sufferings upon Faustina and another, Avitus. Gratianus and Paula have stolen the burning stones from my order and broken oath with us. I would ask the genius of your divinity that the guilty pair suffer a doom wrought by their own perversions. I would ask that you provide vengeance to us, the aggrieved, and that you would guide this retribution past the couple's own safeguards, and that their evil be their own undoing. With fervent prayers, I ask your divinity that our petition may bring satisfaction to us by your righteousness.

"Give me your palm, Faustina."

Faustina released his arm. Aelius guided her palm to the surface of the lead sheet and smeared their mixed blood across it. He then folded the sheet three times. He produced a nail, and with this he pierced the folded sheet nine times. He moved a stone, revealing a hole just small enough for the folded tablet to pass as he dropped it inside. Faustina could not see how deep the hole was before Aelius covered it again with the stone. He turned and smiled at her, and she felt herself lifted again.

Faustina turned to look at Iulia as they ascended, Aelius and the tiny fire disappearing below them. With a shock, Faustina realized they were traveling towards the villa again. She squirmed in Iulia's arms, kicking free only to feel herself free-falling through the night air. As the ground rushed up towards her, it grew darker and darker, until, looking up, she could no longer see the stars.

She blinked, and seeing torchlight, realized she was awake. She felt the restraints again on her limbs and the cold floor, but her back no longer burned. She looked at her palm, and the dried blood smeared over a thin cut.

Chapter 6
Camilla

Avitus' confinement began with his first thoughts of freedom. For the first weeks at the villa, he complied with the wishes of Paula and Gratianus and accepted his role of stud in their stable. Focusing only on the flesh of the women, he concentrated on the pleasure of the experience. He became a dull thing, a machine powering a collection of nerves. The girls were also things to him, they had to be, because if they were something else, he would have to realize he spent every day coercing his seed into the wombs of unwilling women, rape after rape, interspersed with an occasional willing female. But aside from the few noblewomen seeking novelty, were any of them willing, or only acting to please their masters? Only one convinced Avitus of her enthusiasm without doubt, and that was Camilla, the green-eyed girl he met in the beginning of his visit.

He thought of her often, and he was pleased by Paula's enthusiasm for him to breed with Camilla, for it meant she would be the first brought to him each day. They found each other in the evening, and spoke whenever they could. She was indeed from the north, and spoke often of her tribe. Avitus found himself worrying about her in a way he knew to be unwise. Yet he also wondered about his own well-being, for he had not seen Faustina in the week since her ill-advised dinner party outburst. He assumed her to be dead.

"Have you seen Faustina?" Avitus whispered to Camilla one night as they sat in an alcove. Camilla looked both ways down the hallway.

"No," she whispered. "She may be dead. Or she may be..."

"May be what?" Avitus asked.

"She may be in the cellar with the others. That's where Paula keeps them, you know."

"The girls?" Avitus asked.

Camilla nodded.

"Stalls. Like animals," she said.

"But you have a room on this floor," Avitus said.

"Aye. That I do," she said, a sad smile on her face. "It appears I have favored pet status with our master and mistress." She looked away.

"How long have you been here?" he asked.

"A week longer than you. Long enough to know I don't want to go to the cellar."

"Let's run," Avitus said, hearing the words tumble from his mouth. He felt giddy, hearing himself.

"Where?" Camilla said, half-smiling, half-frowning.

"To your people," Avitus said.

"My people sold me, and would sell me again," she said, quietly laughing. "We have nowhere to go, Avitus. Where would you go that Gratianus wouldn't have you looked for?"

"We could go to one of the other tribes," Avitus said.

"You've never lived outside of Rome's reach, Avitus. You don't understand," Camilla said, taking his hand. "They would kill you and fuck me to death. If you're not one of them, you don't stand a chance. You have no tribe. Neither do I anymore. Stop struggling. This is what we have. Accept it. Believe me, it could be much worse in Carnuntum. Or in this house. Don't be a fool like Faustina. I love you. I want you to survive."

Avitus felt the little sphere of amber, tucked away in a hidden pocket he had sewn into his tunic. He stared at Camilla for a moment. Could he trust her, he wondered? He reached into the pocket and pulled it out, holding it in his open palm. In the light from the hallway lamps, something dark seemed to move about inside the sphere, but when Avitus held it up before his eyes, it became clear. He looked at Camilla. Her eyes narrowed.

"Iulia gave this to me," Avitus said, whispering quietly. "Do you know what it is?"

Camilla's face looked slack. She shook her head, no.

"She gave this to me, and she told me something strange. She told me that one day, I would need to kill someone. And when that time comes, I am to swallow this. And when the deed is done, I am to run to the Pole star, and meet her and her father."

Camilla stared at him, her lip quivering. She grabbed his hand and closed it around the amber ball.

"Do *not* let them find this on you," she said, barely audible, her hand shaking.

"But you will come with me?" Avitus said.

Camilla stood up and stared at him, as though wavering. She reached down and took the amber piece from his hand.

"Open your mouth," she whispered. "Hide it like this." She reached into his mouth and pressed the sphere against his back teeth. Avitus felt the amber soften and mold itself into his teeth.

"I cannot come with you," Camilla said. She turned and sprinted down the hallway, the balls of her feet padding softly on the marble floor.

Avitus did not sleep that night. He lay in bed, wondering about Camilla and her reaction to what he told her. He wondered what happened to Faustina. The woman nearly killed him in the arena, and perhaps destroyed his career, but now? She was plucked from Carnuntum before she could reap the rewards of fame. She was magnificent, tiger-like in her movements. Her eyes blazed like black fire. And now perhaps, that fire had been snuffed out in the plush expanses of the villa. They were nothing now, lions stuffed into cages, deprived of even the dignity of a death in the arena.

And what of Camilla? Was she loyal to Gratianus and Paula after all? Would she betray him? Would she tell them of the amber given to him by Iulia? Her response gnawed at him. Why would she not leave with him? As he thought about it, he realized part of what she said was true. He did not know how to survive outside of Carnuntum. For his entire life, he had been kept by others, whether as slave, convict, or gladiator. He slept in quarters provided by someone else, ate food given to him, and fought fights arranged by others. And until Iulia gave him that damned amber sphere, the thought of running to the forest never occurred to him.

No wonder Camilla refused his request. Iulia's words were madness. What was this foolish prophecy, and why had he believed it? It was just a game played by the idiot daughter of a merchant, just to amuse herself at his expense.

By the time he'd finished breakfast, Avitus decided he would tell Camilla how ridiculous the idea was. He would even pretend it had all been a joke. He would deride the amber merchant's daughter, and they would laugh together.

His heart leaped when the door to his room opened. He had grown accustomed to being observed by Paula or by one of her assistants during the breeding sessions, and he looked forward to the first session, which was always with Camilla. When Paula entered not with Camilla, but with a new girl, his heart sunk. The girl stared at the floor and twisted a strand of hair tight around her finger. Her eyes looked red, swollen, and moist. She seemed to cower, while Paula entered proudly, her hair tied up high in a net. The chunk of amber hung from her necklace, shining rays of refracted and colored sunlight, one of them resting on the girl and seeming to pin her in place. Paula smiled broadly.

"Undress," she told the girl.

"But where is Camilla, ma'am?," Avitus asked. His chest felt tight and he badly wanted to see her.

The muscles of Paula's face flickered for a moment and then froze, mask-like, into a jubilant smile.

"Have you not heard then, my stallion? Why, Camilla is the first of our stock to be with child! Her cycle is long overdue," she said.

Avitus felt the room shake a little. The young woman next to Camilla now stood naked, her body willowy. Avitus cleared his throat.

"Will I see her today?" he asked.

"But why would you?" Paula asked. She disguised her delight poorly, gloating underneath her feigned confusion. Avitus wanted to choke her. "She has been bred. Why plant seed on a growing tree?" She pushed the girl slowly towards Avitus. "Present yourself to him."

"My lady, I wish to see Camilla first," Avitus said.

"Avitus, you will do as I say. Now. If you would be so kind. Impregnate this one," she said. She took Avitus by the arm and pulled towards the bed. He yanked his arm away from her. The girl lowered herself to lay on the bed, staring nervously between Paula and Avitus.

Paula stepped back and stared at Avitus, her brows lowered. She walked slowly backward, and when she reached the door, she smirked and clapped her hands.

The entrance of the villa guards did not surprise Avitus, but their number did. Paula slipped from the room as the dogs and guards streaming into the room. The girl cowered against the wall, but as Avitus picked up a chair, she wasted little time in flipping up the mattress to cover herself for protection. The guards carried only clubs and nets, and no swords or spears. The first two men fell quickly as Avitus swung the chair with sweeping blows. It felt good to have a fight, to feel his blood pumping and his opponents crumpling before him.

It was the dogs who changed the balance of the fight, their ivory jaws clamping into one calf and then the other. Avitus fought, trying to fend off the dogs, the guards landing blow after blow with their clubs, often striking from his blind side. He became dizzy and dropped the chair. He threw one arm around the neck of the nearest guard, the room a swirl of shouting and barking, flailing clubs and snapping jaws. Avitus wrested the club from the man's hand, slamming the end of the weapon into the guard's face until the room tilted in his vision. A bell rang in his ears and darkness flickered in his vision.

He was on the floor now, hands, nets, and teeth restraining each limb. As he felt himself lifted and carried, he looked at the ruin of his room. Four of the guards lay on the floor, most of them not moving. From behind the mattress, the girl's eyes peered at him. One slender hand rose, palm out towards him. Avitus smiled and tasted copper as blood trickled into his mouth.

Avitus awoke to coldness on his face. He opened his eye and saw Paula's face. She held a wet sponge in her hand and used it to wash him. His first thought was to grab her, but he could move neither hand nor foot. He looked around and saw he lay on some kind of rack, tilted at forty-five degrees from the floor. He felt a plank underneath, and another piece served as a footrest to bear his weight. Clamps held his ankles together, his legs extended straight, while other clamps held his wrists, his arms extended at forty-five degrees from his body. He was naked and could see a number of fresh bruises on his body, his calves lightly bandaged.

Avitus felt calm. In fact, he felt very little. He let Paula ladle watered wine into his mouth and enjoyed the crisp coolness in his throat. She smiled and looked across the room. Avitus followed her gaze, and saw the girl from his room, still naked, standing on the other side. Another nude young woman sat on a low bench, her eyes almost closed as she stared at the floor, hugging herself, her thick blond hair framing her face.

"They are for you, my gladiator," Paula said. "You will make them big with child, and give me more warriors. I have to tie you down, for you love the fight more than the fucking. What is it? Must you see blood to become excited?" Paula's eyes widened, her pupils expanding, and Avitus felt like a snake crawled through his belly. She leaned close to his ear. "I like it," she whispered. "I like to see the blood. I like to see men bleed. It's when they're at their best. The moment when their essence is leaving them, pouring out of their body, readying them for death, that is when they are truly alive. I can take as much, or as little, of your life from you as I want. I can take as much seed from your loins as I wish. I can take as much blood from you as I wish."

She leaned in very close now, gripping his head by the hair, tight, twisting his hair around her fingers. "I like the blood, Avitus." Avitus snarled as pain shot through his ear. He bellowed with rage as he realized her teeth were locked onto the cartilage of his ear. Insane laughter rattled out between her clenched teeth, until with a final sheet of pain, she stood up again, spitting the top of his ear into his face. It bounced off his forehead and onto the floor. She stared down at him, leering with blood-stained teeth and eyes not of the waking world.

She darted over to a table against the wall. Avitus glanced at the other women and saw terror masked by flat expressions. Paula returned to his side, an iron carding comb in one hand. The other hand held two bronze needles between thumb and forefinger. The carding comb consisted of a wooden handle widening out to a head like a brush, but instead of bristles it bore iron nails. Used to comb wool, Avitus had also seen its work on human flesh.

"Any sons of mine will grow to hate and kill scum like you," Avitus said. "I will die today, but the gods will see to your punishment."

Paula giggled like a madwoman.

"But you won't die today! No, I shall not give up my lovely pet, with his lovely milk and his lovely, lovely blood!" she said, her voice rising and falling unevenly. She tittered as she set down the comb and, pinching one of his nipples, jabbed a bronze needle through it. Avitus set his teeth, staring at the ceiling, and when he felt the needle stabbing through his other nipple, he steeled himself to not flinch. But when she twisted the needles back and forth, a gasp shot out of his mouth and Paula cackled.

She stepped back and wrenched off her own palla, her breasts heaving as she panted with excitement. Picking up the iron comb, she climbed onto him, straddling him, rubbing her wet pussy against his flaccid penis.

Chapter 7
Resurrection

"Fuck me!" she hissed, raking the comb over his shoulder. It felt like fire laid across his skin. "Fuck me!" she hissed, and now the comb raked across his chest. Again and again, the tool tore its way across his torso, as Paula jammed and ground her pelvis against him. Avitus clenched his teeth as he felt the comb catch on the pin in one of his nipples, feeling as much as seeing the white flash of pain as it tore out. He felt Paula working his cock into her vagina, shocked he could somehow be erect.

The wet pull of her hole gave a pleasure in parallel to the pain blazing across his skin. By focusing on the slick friction of her cunt, he felt some of the energy fade from the pain. Paula bounced on top of him, still occasionally raking him with the comb, but distracted by the sex. He could identify her orgasms only by the clenching of her internal muscles, for her expression masked all normal forms as she spluttered and spat. She leaned forward and rested her face against his shoulder. He felt her tongue lapping at the blood, and he was grateful at the cessation of the carding comb's attack.

When she sat up again, he knew his respite was at an end. He was surprised at how much blood covered her face. Crocodile-like, she grinned and this time carefully slipped the shaft of the remaining needle through the teeth of the carding comb.

"Your blood, your life, all mine," she cackled, snapping her wrist and tearing out the needle. Avitus groaned, the pain now all blending together, his mind confused by the feeling in his penis.

"Now, little bitch," Paula said, climbing off and dropping the carding comb with a chuckle. Blood was smeared across her face, breasts and hands. She turned to the girl from the room, her gaze changing from fire to iron. The girl walked over to the bench and set one foot on it, opening her shaking legs. The blond-haired girl turned with a rigid expression and stuck out her tongue, lapping mechanically at the smooth folds of the other girl's labia, spitting into her slit and working the saliva in with her fingers.

"Now," Paula said again, and both girls approached Avitus on the rack. Avitus stared at them, feeling as though he was not in the room but only observing them. His skin ached, and he almost laughed at the thought that part of his ear was gone. He wondered how much more of his body Carnuntum could take. The blond lowered her head and he watched as she sucked his softening cock into her mouth. He groaned with pleasure as the suction stretched his organ, but somehow he felt like two different people, both Avitus and someone observing Avitus. When his penis did not harden fast enough, Paula snapped the girl's bottom with a short strap, and the blond sucked with renewed vigor.

"Enough," Paula said, and the girl backed away, leaving Avitus' prick to bob in the air. "Now," Paula said, and the dark haired girl climbed over Avitus, straddling him. She bent her knees slightly and lowered herself, holding his cock with circled thumb and forefinger, aiming it inside. She lowered onto it, gingerly at first, until Paula's strap flickered against her, then grunted as she took it all the way in. She leaned her hands on the rack and stared at Avitus with her empty eyes, pumping her hips up and down like a machine. It bothered him, the way she stared and so he closed his eyes and focused on the wet pumping, allowing himself to feel only inside her until he came. He regretted looking into her eyes as he felt the white burn leaving his body.

Before his erection had time to soften, Paula goaded the blond onto him, who bounced hard on his pelvis with an erratic rhythm, eventually milking a second orgasm from him. Paula fed him wine, cheese, and mushrooms from her blood-stained fingers then, before a third girl mounted him later, clumsily jerking her hips and whimpering. Paula lashed her, heckling her with criticisms. When Avitus came, without pleasure and looking into the girl's sobbing face, it was because the whip had forced her into a spasm with each strike.

By the fourth girl, Avitus began to hate them, hate the way they sobbed and writhed on top of him, weeping as they stopped to suck him hard again. What did they have to complain of? Did they bleed, too? The rack seemed to sway and he demanded frequent drafts of wine, which Paula, laughing, supplied. The girl on top of him straddled him facing in the opposite direction, her muscular ass slapping against his hips as Paula's small lash flickered against her sweaty back.

"You can't even make him come?!" Paula barked at the girl. "Use this!" Paula, sneering at Avitus and letting him see it, placed a bulbous iron rod in the girl's hand, an object about the size of a dagger handle.

"I don't understand," the girl whined.

Paula grabbed the girl's hair, pulling her head close to her lips as though Paula wished to whisper in her ear. But Paula did not whisper.

"Stick it in his ass!" she hissed.

The fluids wetting his crotch did little to ease the pain as the girl, still astride him, pressed the device between his legs, pressing down on one testicle momentarily. Avitus spread his legs as much as he was able to, if only to shorten the process. Paula continued to lash and shout at the girl, and in her fear she jammed the tool against his anus, finally pushing it in at an angle.

"Wiggle it!" Paula shouted.

The girl jammed it back and forth, until Avitus felt himself convulse and come, like a painful reflex. He allowed himself to groan, lest Paula should fail to notice his orgasm.

Avitus closed his eye. He must have dozed, for he felt himself wake up to shrill laughter, coming from the girl on top. Her back laced with thin red lines, she turned her head to look back at him. He did not recognize her at first, for the blood covering her face. But when she turned further, he saw from the remaining half of her face it was Zari, the other half rent by tooth and claw. Her one eye fixed upon him as she reached back with a lacerated arm to lean on his belly.

"I died well, Avitus," she said, coughing blood. "By Hercules, I did not cry. I died well for you."

Needles of pain stabbed through his limbs as the guards lifted Avitus from the rack. They lifted him to his feet as they fitted manacles and leg irons. His legs throbbed as he stepped from foot to foot, but he was happy to be off the rack and did not ask where they were leading him. He gulped the watered wine given to him and even thanked them.

He walked, dizzy as they led him down a flight of marble stairs. It felt cool down there, even cold. He almost fell down the steps, stopped only by the guards' hands. When they came to a door, one guard unlocked it and stepped back.

"Go in," the guard said, his face pale. An acrid smell leaked from the door.

Avitus chuckled and pushed against the door. As he walked in, he felt a hand shove his back and heard the door slam behind him, the lock snapping shut. He looked across the room to see Camilla on tiptoes, her wrists fastened to chains suspended from the ceiling. Her naked body glistened with sweat, her long hair plastered to her face. She whimpered, lifting one foot at a time to relieve the pain. Avitus had seen people suspended enough to know her arms were already injured, if not ruined, from the way she hung.

He lurched towards her, forgetting his leg irons. He saw the floor rising up to meet him and put his hands up in time to break his fall. He looked up and noticed Gratianus and Paula each sitting on a chair to either side of Camilla, each with a massive black dog. Gratianus held a spear, Paula, a *flagrum*, its twelve straps flickering in the air as she bounced the handle of the scourge on her knee. He heard the tips, likely embedded with glass, bone, and metal, rattle against the floor.

A brazier, the source of the acrid smell, burned against the far wall behind the couple. Gratianus and Paula looked at each other, grinned, and stood up. Avitus felt his stomach squirm as he watched them approach the brazier. He struggled to his feet, feeling an urgency to do something, but he knew not what. Gratianus turned and sneered, pressing the tip of his spear against Camilla's belly, dimpling it.

"Stay," Gratianus called to Avitus.

Avitus stopped. Gratianus leered at him, making Camilla twitch as he poked her with the spear, just hard enough to make tiny wounds. Behind Gratianus, Avitus saw Paula drop the *flagrum* and open a wooden box. Paula took a number of metal objects out of the box, each the same size, about as large as a woman's fist and roughly square. They looked hollow and formed of iron sheets bent into cubes. Distracted by Camilla's suffering, he lost count of the cubes as Paula placed them gently on the floor in what may have been a pattern. He realized she was chanting or reciting something, though he could not make out the words.

When somewhere between ten and fifteen of the cubes lay on the floor, Paula pushed the box aside and squatted before the cubes, something small in her left hand. She lifted her face to the ceiling and a low drone climbed out of her lungs and into the air. She held the tone for a long minute, and then with a bark, clutched one of the cubes and tossed it across the floor. As it landed, it made a long clang, like a discordantly tuned bell, and he heard the sound repeated. When she threw another cube and he heard the sound echoed, he realized the noise came from Paula's mouth. She dashed forward, and with a piece of charcoal drew a strange symbol midway between the two cubes.

Again and again she threw the cubes, echoing the sounds in a way that made Avitus' skin twitch. Each time, she made a mark on the floor between the last two cubes thrown. When one cube struck another, the jarring sound coiled his stomach with nausea. That which burned in the brazier smelled worse now, but instead of producing smoke, a shimmering distortion rose from the device. It looked much the same as air quivering over an intense heat, but it took up too much space, thought Avitus. And it seemed to move away from the brazier, towards Paula. Gratianus tittered, hopping from foot to foot and snapping his head back and forth to look at Avitus, Camilla, and Paula.

The haze moved over Paula. Caught in the middle of singing out a metallic echo, her voice rose to a shriek and she leaped to her feet, her body convulsing without falling down. Avitus saw her as though she were a mirage, her form wiggling. She crouched down and snatched up the *flagrum* from the floor. She stood hunched over, her face distorted by the shimmering but also by a feral rage. She suddenly appeared to notice Camilla and sprinted towards her.

Gratianus darted backward, his giggling now shrill and idiotic. Avitus started forward as the first stroke of the *flagrum* hit Camilla's back. The girl convulsed as though struck by lightning, her feet flailing through the air. Paula drew the *flagrum* back, flicking blood across

Gratianus as he danced.

Gratianus started as he saw Avitus approach. He charged with his spear, feinting and tangling the spear in Avitus' leg irons, tripping him. Avitus fell to the floor, cursing his failure to spot the ploy. He felt a cord around his neck and realized Gratianus sat on his back. Every struggle brought blackness to his vision, and after one black-out, he looked up at Camilla.

The girl hung limply from the wrist chains, no longer struggling to stand, her feet trailing in a pool of blood, the pool growing from her dripping form. Severe lacerations marked the front of her body in places, and Avitus knew the back of her was far worse. Paula stood next to her, panting and sweat-drenched, staring at the girl and at the *flagrum* in her hand.

"So sorry about the girl, Avitus," he heard Gratianus say, still feeling the cord about his neck. "But there's nothing we can do about it now."

Avitus stared at the floor. It felt so cold in the room, impossibly cold. His ears rang and he felt himself shaking.

"Well," Paula said, catching her breath. "There is one way. And I would be willing to let him try, just to see it happen. How much do you love Camilla, Avitus? Do you love her enough to bring her back?" Paula stood up straight and walked over to the wall. She grasped a wooden wheel and turned it. The chains clattered through their brackets, dropping Camilla to fall wetly on her back.

"What do you mean?" Avitus wheezed.

"Can you *fuck* her?" Gratianus said.

"If you truly love her," Paula said. "And can summon the energy to spend yourself inside her, I can bring her back. I swear it."

"She's dead," Avitus sobbed.

"But only just," Paula said. "Here in the villa, Gratianus and I have the power to grant death *and* life. Yet, even we will be powerless to help you if too much time passes. As her blood cools, she will become rigid and her spirit will travel too far to recall it. But it is as you wish. It becomes tedious to explain what you cannot understand, and it becomes decreasingly relevant to do so."

Avitus felt the cord removed from his neck and Gratianus' weight lifted from his back. Gratianus walked forward and joined Paula, his hand on her back as they walked to the chairs.

"The guards will be here soon. Use your time as you wish," Gratianus called out.

Avitus started to stand.

"Crawl!" Gratianus barked.

Avitus lowered himself and crawled forward on knees and elbows, approaching Camilla. He crawled through the cooling pool of blood. He pictured Camilla laughing, smiling. He wanted to see her smile, if only one more time and decided he would do anything to make that happen. He tugged his loincloth free, dropping it into the blood as he climbed between her legs. Numbly, he was surprised to find himself erect as he pushed inside of her, quickly and deeply. She still felt warm. He pumped, vaguely aware of the snickering from Paula and Gratianus as he kissed her lips. Camilla's body slid on the wet floor as he thrust into her. He thought of the first time he saw her. He thought of what could have been, of their child, of an escape to the north. When he came he closed his eyes and saw her laughing again.

The orgasm fell from him like a curtain. Camilla's dead green eyes stared up at him, and his ears rang with the laughter of Paula and Gratianus. His tongue probed the piece of amber lodged in his tooth. It fell onto his tongue, almost like a living thing, and he swallowed it. He would kill them now. He would kill them both.

He tried to rise, but slipped in the blood and fell onto Camilla. More laughter, louder now. He slid off of her, his vision red with rage as he crawled towards the couple. He vaguely heard footsteps approaching him before the hood fell over his head, a noose around his neck, and hands on every limb.

Chapter 8
The Hounds

A dream, a foolish dream, Faustina thought. There would be no escape, no curse brought down upon the heads of her captors. Her hand had been cut in her torments, and a frivolous spirit must have woven this into a dream for her. If the amber merchant and his daughter could have saved her, and if they did remove her from this place, then why was she still here? It was nonsense. Nemesis would not save her now. She felt the cold floor underneath her body, her limbs cramping with thirst and the chill. *I will die here. All that remains for me is to kill anyone who falls within reach. One life, Nemesis. Let me take one life with me and I will happily die.*

Faustina immediately spotted the weaker of the guards when they arrived and opened her restraints. She felt the blood course into her limbs again as they lifted her, yet she let herself hang limp. When they fed her watered wine, she forced herself to be sick as they dragged her along the hallway, much to the guards' complaints.

There were three guards, two dragging her and one walking behind. Faustina noticed two of them, the one behind her and the one on her right, watching her. The one on the right pretended he was dropping her, perhaps checking her for a reflexive action. She barely resisted the attempt, but managed to sag towards the floor. The guards laughed then, groping her naked breasts and buttocks, probing her as they walked. But the guard on her left barely looked at her, apparently distracted and irritated by the others.

They stopped at a door and the guard following them stepped forward, unlocking the door. He pushed it open and turned, calling out to another guard down the hall.

Faustina felt the hilt of the weak guard's *pugio*, the broad-bladed dagger in her hand before she thought about grabbing it. In one movement, she drew it and severed the windpipe of the guard on the right. She spun, not stopping to look, and thrust the *pugio* into the lower abdomen of the weak guard, driving him into the room with both the dagger thrust and her shoulder.

Inside the room, she spun once more, shouldering the door closed and barring it shut. She turned to face the guard in the room with her. The man clutched the dagger, still embedded in his belly. Faustina heard a ragged laughter and realized it was her own. There was a rack of sorts in the center of the room, almost like a milking stand for goats. The man gasped and tried to keep the stand between himself and Faustina, but she quickly circled it and plucked the *pugio* from his belly.

She kicked his knee and he fell face-down on the floor. She heard him weeping as she knelt on his back. A strange warmth filled her. She could kill him instantly, as she had done before in the arena. A quick thrust to the base of the neck would end him. But for the first time in her life, it wasn't just about the win. It wasn't just about an order to kill. It was the giddy pleasure she now felt that surprised her. She wanted this to last. She heard the pounding on the door. They would soon break through the door. But she wanted the pleasure of making the man suffer.

Faustina felt herself drool a bit as she slowly sunk the *pugio* into the guard's kidney. He squealed with agony, and she with laughter. She looked up in time to see the door splinter, a guard kicking the door in, axe in hand. He stood still, his face flexing as though trying to comprehend what he saw.

Faustina raised the *pugio*, and with a shriek of joy sunk it into her victim's other kidney before she was knocked to the floor.

Faustina felt herself tumbling, as though in a crashing surf of kicking feet and leather straps, agony alternating with blackness. She sometimes looked up to see the room spinning with angry, shouting faces before falling again into darkness.

She opened her eyes again after the beating stopped. Broken blood vessels cast little threads over her vision. She felt herself lifted, the floor passing beneath her. Was Iulia with her again? She wondered until she felt herself dropped upon the wooden stand in the center of the room. She felt a guard holding each of her limbs, strapping them in place so her belly rested on a raised plank. Straps around ankles and knees secured her spread lower legs against the floor of the stand. Other straps fastened her forearms by the wrists and elbows. Faustina screamed in anger as the guards swiveled into place a vertical wooden bar against each side of her neck. The bars latched together at the top, preventing her from moving her neck. The belly-plank prevented her from moving forward, and now the neck bars stopped her from pulling backwards. She looked down and saw droplets of blood pattered on the floor, dripping from her nose and unknown cuts on her face or head.

"The most ill-behaved of all your bitches, Paula!" Faustina heard Gratianus say as he entered the room, but she could not turn to see him. "And she appears to be barren, no good even for breeding. Why do you keep such a dangerous and useless creature in your stable?"

"Ah, my dear husband!" Paula said, following him into the room. "Have you no mercy for poor beasts? This is a fine Persian bitch." Faustina snarled as she felt a hand slap her buttock hard. "But you cannot expect such a thing to come to Carnuntum with a civilized heart."

Three dogs walked on the floor in front of Faustina. One approached her, sniffed, and began licking the blood from her face while another licked the floor. A fear crept into her mind, but she pushed it back, unwilling even to identify it. She let herself enjoy her face being licked. It was like having a pet, and the one kind affection she experienced in weeks of torment.

"Mercy kills the innocent. Ask the guards about their fallen comrade. Ask them about mercy," Gratianus said.

"It is all a matter of understanding the creature," Paula said, the couple still standing behind Faustina. Faustina stiffened as she felt greasy fingers press gently but insistently into her cunt, into her anus. It was the mockery of tenderness that bothered her the most, the soft circling of a fingertip on her clitoris. Her body reacted against her will. The dogs paced in front of her, panting. She closed her eyes so she would not count more than the four she already noticed. She felt fingers making soft circles around her nipples, stroking the nubs as they hardened. *Focus,* she told herself. *Just feel the pleasure. Don't think. Just feel.*

The fingers stopped. Paula stepped in front of her, and Faustina's blood chilled as she saw the leash in the woman's hand.

"You see, Gratianus," Paula said, her face twitching, leering as she stared at Faustina. "You need to know the beast at hand." She lifted her fingers to her nose and sniffed. She walked over to the nearest dog and let it sniff her hand, its long pink tongue licking her fingers. Paula fastened the leash on the dog. "You say she is useless. Barren. But do you breed a lion with a house cat? No. You breed horses. With horses. Lions. With lions. Dogs." She showed all of her teeth to Faustina in one smile, and then slowly walked the dog around behind the rack.

"No," Faustina said, her voice hoarse. "No no no. You cunt. I'll cut you to ribbons. Let me *out!*"

"Dogs. With. Bitches! Hup!" Paula said.

"No! No! No!" Faustina shouted, groaning with the effort of pulling against her restraints. The fear in the back of her mind was revealing itself and nothing she could do would stop it.

Faustina felt the furry weight of the hound on her back. She tensed every muscle, the rack rattling and shaking as she fought, but holding her fast. The dog's toenails raked her flanks and she grunted with disgust as the moist organ squirmed into her vagina. She felt herself shaking uncontrollably as the cock sunk deeper and deeper into her, forming what felt like a hard knot inside her. The dog panted, wheezing through its nose. Again, Faustina felt a finger stroke her clit.

"No," she sobbed. The finger flickered against the nub. Faustina tried to push down the reflex rising inside her, tried to ignore the warm rub of the knot inside her, but the heat rippled out from beneath the finger. Faustina felt herself falling, letting go of something deep inside. It wasn't enough to just think of it as something being done to her body, though that had been her escape in the past. It was that she had to give in or go mad. And so she let the rush pulse through her, embracing it, enjoying it. She heard herself crying out as she felt the pulse inside. She felt the dog grunting, and in a few moments the knot inside her shrank and the dog dismounted her.

Faustina maintained her grasp on her mind for the duration of the second dog, her attention entrenched in the pure physical sensation, letting herself go and reaching orgasm without resistance as Paula stimulated her while the dog fucked her. Any intellectual activity, any thoughts of what was actually happening, where she was, who she was, all of these she locked far away.

But during the third hound, as her focus drifted down through a haze, something flashed before her. She looked up, and in the cold reflection of a large mirror placed before her, she saw herself as Gratianus held the mirror, giggling. Battered and bruised, hair clinging to her face with sweat and blood, it was not her dishevelment that made the blackness rise from her stomach, the cold self-loathing spreading through her body. It was the first second she looked in the mirror, and saw an expression of ecstasy on the face of the wretch within, mounted by a slavering beast.

This was the end. Someone had to die, and if it could not be Paula or Gratianus, it had to be her. Was this not what Aelius and Iulia had meant by the amber shard? The merchant told her she would know the time, when she would absolutely need to slay one who needs slaying. It would be her. The amber came away easily as she probed her tooth with her tongue. She felt it changing shape, reverting to its sharpened form. As she pressed it with her tongue, it slid easily into the skin of her inner cheek. She felt a sharp sting, like that of a bee, and then it was gone, embedded.

A cacophony filled her ears, every dog baying suddenly and frantically, the one on top of her scratching her back as it scrambled off, hurting her as he withdrew. The animals raced around the room, knocking the polished mirror over to rattle on the floor. They leaped at the walls, as though trying to reach something, running into each other, snapping at one another. The barking and howling echoed back and forth across the room.

Paula and Gratianus cursed, screaming at the dogs and trying to subdue them. All efforts to re-interest them in Faustina failed. Faustina did not know how long it went on. She no longer listened or watched, but felt an icy chill spread throughout her body. She waited for her heart to stop, waited for the darkness to cloak her vision. And when the end did not come, she screamed and screamed in the midst of the barking and did not stop until her voice left her and her sight fell into dreams of falling.

She awoke in dim light. She heard voices, females, the buzz of excited whispers rising steadily to talking, calling out, until a male voice
screamed at them to be silent. There were bars in front of her, and
heavy wooden plank walls to one side and stone wall on the other,
with more planks above to form the ceiling. She lay on straw on a
dirt floor, in a cell, just too small for her to stand or to stretch out. The
bars faced a wall, with what looked like a walkway between it and
the cell.

The whispers started again, rising in volume until once again, the
screamed command for silence barked out. Faustina listened in the
silent moments, and could now hear the sounds of struggle and violence from the villa above. And with each silent moment, the conflict
seemed to come closer. Again, the murmur of the voices grew.

"Shut up, you--!" the man shouted, but this time, Faustina heard
the wrenching and shattering of wood, and the man's voice turned
into a shriek of terror. She heard a sound of something wet being
slapped against a wall. A storm of screaming female voices filled the
air. The noise swelled, approaching her cell. She heard the sound of
cage doors opening, and looked about for anything to use as a weapon as she crouched in her cell, naked and empty-handed. She lay on
her back and started kicking the wooden cell wall, trying to dislodge
a plank.

A figure appeared in front of the bars and Faustina rolled to the
far side of the cell, reflexively moving to one aching knee and bracing to fight. But as she focused on the person, her stomach revolted
and she fought against the urge to retch. It was the girl, Camilla, but
something horrible had happened to her. Caked in dirt and dried
blood from head to foot, she crouched before the cell bars, holding
a long bloodstained bundle in her arms. Her hair stuck to her face in
spots, plastered by a crimson crust. Her eyes glittered like two lumps
of polished coal, all pupil. She tottered slightly in a way that reminded
Faustina of a puppet. This was not Camilla, she thought, but a blood
demon, something her grandmother spoke of.

"Faustina," the demon said. "I mean you no harm." The creature
spoke in Persian. "Your time has come," she said, unlocking her cell

door. "I merely offer you a choice." The demon held up her bundle and smiled, her teeth stained with blood not yet dry. She let the bundle's covering fall away. A trident and a *quadrens* clattered to the floor, followed by a bundled net, and the pieces of a *retiarius's* armor.

"If you wish, accompany me as I collect a debt from one Gratianus and one Paula. The final pleasure will not be yours, but I offer you the opportunity to witness their disposition, and, perhaps, bid them farewell. Or you may simply fight your way out on your own. You already know where to run. Do as you wish, but Gratianus' friends will look and find you should you take any direction but the Pole Star."

Faustina saw her hand shaking as it pushed open the cell door. The creature stepped back, giving her room to climb out and stand with her back to the wall. Faustina tensed herself, ready to grab a weapon should the blood demon attack.

"You were sent by Aelius?" Faustina asked, hearing her own voice crack.

The figure of Camilla smiled.

"In a manner of speaking," she said.

"You are a demon?" Faustina asked, spotting the corpse of the guard at the end of the corridor, blood smeared on the wall behind him. The cell doors all stood ajar, the girls all having fled.

"Tonight, some will call me such," the thing said, chuckling hoarsely.

"Demon you may be," Faustina said, picking up a tunic and belt from the pile and dressing herself. "But I cannot leave this place until I know the end of two other demons." Faustina picked up the shoulder armor and placed it on her right shoulder. Unlike the last one she used, the *manica* arm-guard was of chain mail, something she knew and used only far to the east. She pulled it over her right arm and smiled, the metal cool on her skin. "It all fits too perfectly, and that is strange," she said.

"And you do not run from me," the thing said. "That too would be strange, were it not for the loathing you must satisfy. I, too, know loathing, and that hunger must be sated."

Faustina heard herself laugh quietly as she tucked two prongs of the *quadrens* in her belt and picked up the trident and net. Simultaneously calm and coiled, she felt the old feeling she had before every big fight. Her mind took note of every injury in her body, calculating her strengths and weaknesses. Sound became crisper. Vision became clearer. She followed the demon down the walkway, abstractedly studying the ruins of Camilla's back.

"The *flagrum*," Faustina said. "That is the only thing I know to make such wounds."

"Indeed," the demon said as they walked past the dead guard. The shape of Camilla crouched and plucked the spear from his hands. The man's crushed head hung at a strange angle. "Ready?" she asked, her hand on the latch of the door. "They wait without."

Faustina held the trident mid-shaft in her right hand. In her left, she let the weighted net hang bundled together like a flail. She tensed, took her stance, and nodded, standing behind the demon.

Camilla's form threw the door open and darted into the corridor, spearing the throat of a wide-eyed guard as he thrust his spear into her abdomen.

Faustina did not stop to watch but moved to the demon's left flank, snapping the weights of her net into the face of a guard. He seemed so slow as she drove her trident past the man's spear, easily penetrating his chest, passive meat before her weapon. There were more guards behind the first pair. At her side, the thing attacked the men like an animal and Faustina felt herself splashed with blood as guards fell before the onslaught. Faustina's heart pounded, driving her trident reflexively into man after man, the smell of blood and fear soaking her nostrils. The men ran now, and Faustina raced behind her terrible ally as they pursued them, drunk with bloodlust. They ran over the bodies of those they killed, but also other bodies already present, men with pale eyes and skin like Camilla, armed and dressed like the guards.

The pursued men turned a corner and a hand grabbed Faustina's tunic, stopping her short. She wheeled to face the Camilla-demon who held her, Faustina's bare feet sliding in blood. The thing grinned at her.

"There is one other who may wish to join the hunt," she leered at Faustina. "Your comrade, Avitus."

Chapter 9
The North Star

Silence hung in the dark air. If Avitus did not sleep, he let his mind sink into a numb, gray void. He lay on the wooden rack, as inert as his thoughts. *Do not think. Do not imagine. But most of all, do not remember.*

When he slept, he dreamed he was a gladiator, a *secutor*, his feet churning warm, summer sand in the arena. In the dream, the amphitheater stands stood empty. But every so often, he heard the sounds of combat and realized he fought an opponent. His foes seemed mechanical and unable to fight back. They stood still while he gutted them or slit their throats. And when each new opponent arrived, the body of the last was already gone.

The sun grew brighter after the last fight. Two figures approached him, but now he could not move his arms. The light grew even brighter, the arena turning into the room within Gratianus' villa. But the figures approaching were not gladiators. What were they? It took time for Avitus to focus his eye upon them, but when he did, he recoiled, pulling at his restraints.

Lamiae. Blood-drinkers, the monstrosities who fed on life. The word rose heavily from his memory. One looked like Faustina, and her eyes burned with black fire. One looked like Camilla, and her eyes burned with green ice. Blood covered the naked form of Camilla, and Faustina stood equally soaked, wearing a crimson tunic along with her sparse *retiarius* armor.

"What is this?" Avitus heard himself croak. "Camilla."

Camilla shook her head with a crooked smile. She held a rectangular bundle in her arms.

"Sorry, friend," her voice rasped. "Not exactly, but I'm afraid I need to borrow her shell for the evening. Camilla is no more. Think of it simply as a similarity in appearance. A robe discarded may be worn by another."

Avitus felt a numbness in his chest and waited for his own scream, which never came. He saw Faustina look at the girl and frown.

Avitus let the feelings slip away from him. This would be a new game of Paula and Gratianus, but he knew not what. The restraints were falling from his limbs as Faustina bent over them. Should he kill these creatures who pretended to be his loved ones? His loved ones? He loved Camilla, but did he love Faustina? He realized he did. He was free now and the women were pulling him to his feet.

"Avitus!" Camilla clutched his face and shook him, too strong for a small woman. He stared down into her blood-caked face. She seemed wrong somehow, as though her face were not her own. "Avitus! Will you join us? We go to find Paula and Gratianus. Would you see their end?"

"Aye," he chuckled, trying to comprehend the dead face of the girl. "That I would."

"Then you will see, but it will not be your hand that ends them," Camilla growled. She shoved the bundle into his arms.

Avitus smiled, knowing exactly what was wrapped within. He set it down on the floor and slowly unwrapped it. He first took out the greave and fastened it onto his leg. Outside in the corridor, he heard the sounds of fights starting and ending. He worked faster, Faustina helping him into his linen *manica* armguard. The dried blood covering him crackled and flaked as he flexed.

"Can you still fight?" Faustina asked, nodding towards his bloody torso.

"Aye. What is this?" Avitus asked, pointing at Faustina's chain mail *manica*. He had never seen such a thing on a *retiarius*.

"It's what the true *retiarii* wear," Faustina grinned at him. Beneath the blood, Avitus could still see the ravages of the past weeks. Her face looked hard, swollen with bruising, tense with unrelieved pain. But in the terrible intensity of her stare, he saw something that made him wonder about the night of their fight. Was this the same woman?

He looked at Camilla. Camilla was certainly not the same woman. She was a thing of death now, horrifying in her malevolence. But as Camilla appeared transformed in death, Faustina throbbed with an overwhelming life. Looking upon this gladiator now, he knew he would never survive a second fight with her. He knew he looked upon the core of her being, the inner flame. It chilled him and boiled his blood in the same moment.

He felt the confusion sliding away from his mind. He knew where he was and who he was. It was time to get ready to die well. It was time to kill and perish and there was no difference between the two. As he pulled his helmet over his head, and lifted shield and *gladius*, the metal seemed to merge with his body. He felt his heart pump like the hooves of a horse.

"Now," Camilla said. "Now the real game begins. Now we find your most gracious hosts. Out in the villa, a raid takes place. The raiders know to not attack you. Please extend the same courtesy and do not pursue them. We kill any guard in our way. When we have Paula and Gratianus..."

"Run to the North Star. The tree," Avitus said, facing the door, balancing sword and shield in his grip.

"Indeed," Camilla said, chuckling, throwing open the door.

Avitus uncoiled his muscles as he sprang into the corridor, hitting two villa guards running. He drove his *gladius* into the first man's throat. Still charging forward, he pinned the second man to the wall with his shield and saw Faustina's *quadrens* dart behind the man's ear, sinking deep. The guard's eyes stared into Avitus' helmet, fading in death. Avitus stepped back and let him crumple to the floor.

Avitus turned to see the hallway blocked with guards, three rows of three men each, spears ready in a miniature phalanx. He held his shield and felt the cold hand of Camilla shove him forward.

"First row!" the creature barked in his ear. He saw the front row of men hesitate, and so he charged.

Too late, he realized his error. The front row of men dropped to one knee and readied their spears as the second row thrust forward. He stopped several with his shield but saw the rest lancing towards his chest. Before he had time to recoil, one of the men in the second row tumbled forward, his head wrapped in a net. The man was pulled forward, falling upon the shoulders of the front row.

Avitus took a step, dropped to one knee, and stepped again, holding his shield high as he stabbed at the forms struggling to rise. He saw a form dart past him as Camilla's form plunged into the chaos, ignoring spear thrusts. He saw her back, shredded from the *flagrum*. Avitus stabbed into the men, frenzied, his *gladius* competing with Faustina's trident, iron and bronze serpent fangs driven by reflex and instinct. His sword stopped when the last movement in the flesh pile ceased. He looked up in time to see Camilla locking her teeth into the last guard's face while snapping his neck.

At the end of the corridor, he glimpsed two robed figures running into a room. Camilla tossed aside the still twitching form of the guard and darted down the hallway. As the door almost closed behind the figures, Camilla threw herself through the air like a partially-flayed leopard, disappearing into the room.

Avitus sprinted down the hallway towards the door, Faustina's hot breath on his back. His shield held before him and *gladius* ready to stab upwards, he raced into the room, checked by Camilla's cold outstretched arm. A panel hung open in the far wall, and he saw the face of Gratianus turn to him and titter before disappearing into the passageway.

Avitus no sooner lunged forward than the iron-like arm of Camilla locked around his throat. From the corner of his eye, he saw Faustina likewise restrained, her eyes bearing all the rage of a tormented lioness as she plunged her *quadrens* over and over into Camilla's unbleeding form. His thoughts tumbled. Kill Camilla? It was not her. Camilla was dead. This was just another trick. He reversed his grip on his *gladius* and stabbed at the girl's pale leg, but a mist already covered his vision as he choked in the headlock. He was no longer sure if he stabbed Camilla, Faustina, himself, or the air.

He found himself on his knees now, empty handed, but with the arm still locked about his throat, loose enough to allow him to breathe now. He saw Faustina next to him, her face contorted with emotion, while the naked and tattered form of Camilla crouched between them, holding both gladiators. The handle of Faustina's *quadrens* stuck out, embedded in Camilla's chest.

A metallic taste soured the air, and before him he saw both Paula and Gratianus backing up towards him, both of them now back in the room. An orange light shone from the passageway in the wall, and the pair seemed to be retreating from it. Something flashed through the air, and Avitus now saw the *quadrens* bury its prongs in the shoulder of Gratianus. He heard Faustina bark laughter as the man looked back in pain.

Paula and Gratianus retreated to a far wall, each of them holding a *flagrum* before them as the light from the passageway waxed brighter. Something was tossed out of the opening to clatter and clang on the floor. Avitus recognized it as something like the small iron cubes used by Paula. Gratianus and his wife started at the sound. Another clattered and rang across the floor, soon followed by seven more in quick succession.

Avitus heard the snuffling of dogs and watched as the green eyes of one of Paula's immense black hounds appeared at the entrance.

"Come!" Paula called, her voice quavering, but the dog did not respond. It walked into the room, heedless of its master, followed by eight more.

"Come! Come! Come!" Paula yelled, over and over again, each time striking the floor with her *flagrum*, each time more shrill, her voice edged in panic.

The light grew brighter still, and in a moment, its source appeared. A guard appeared, his head hanging from a broken neck, his features twisted with mirth. In his hands, he held an amber globe, pulsing with the orange light, something writhing within it.

"You are well, Father?" the guard said, turning his body so his eyes could look at Camilla. The bend of his neck distorted his voice.

"Fairly well. Until these gladiators destroy this form completely, yes," Camilla said, chuckling.

A babble rose from Paula's mouth. She spoke incoherently, none of the sounds resembling anything Avitus knew as words. She waved one hand in the air, her eyes wide. Gratianus stared without expression, reaching back and grimacing as he tugged the *quadrens* out of his shoulder. He stared at it for a moment, then whipped his arm through the air towards Faustina. Avitus felt Camilla twitch and heard metal clattering onto the floor behind the trio.

Avitus looked at the amber dangling from the chain on Gratianus' neck. It glowed now, casting its orange light upward into the wearer's face. Paula wore a similar piece, and it glowed as well. Gratianus seemed to notice Paula's necklace first. His face twitched and he reached out, clutching it. He yanked it, breaking the chain, pulling Paula's neck down with the effort. She did not cease her babbling, but only grew louder, staring at the bauble with rolling eyes. Gratianus tore his own piece free, and threw both necklaces at Camilla.

"Take your fucking trinkets!" Gratianus screamed. "Do you think you can carry on without me? The trade stops without me! Carnuntum will close to the Amber Road without me! Do you think Diocletian's people will not come for you?"

Camilla laughed. The sound rumbled through the cold breast at Avitus' ear. He heard an audible puncture in her lung.

"If I was willing to come tonight without permission from anyone," she said, "then I would have come long ago. Truly, do you trust your own status to account for the ease with which you were permitted to pluck gladiators from the Imperial stable? Not just any gladiators, but these two? Your confidence eclipses your worth, my boy."

Gratianus' face slackened, his shoulders sagging. He stared at Camilla, and suddenly, as though in pain, he screamed and began swinging his *flagrum* into the ranks of the black hounds.

Avitus saw the guard raise the orb high and throw it down to the floor. It crackled as it shattered, bursting into hundreds of glowing fragments. Bitterness flooded Avitus' mouth and he felt himself gag with the taste. He saw Faustina likewise overtaken. Everything in the room took on an outline somehow both crisp and liquid, and tendrils of smoke rose from some of the luminescent pieces. Avitus renewed his struggles as he watched the tendrils move towards the dogs, wrapping around them, seeming to slide into their panting mouths.

Avitus did not then know if the room shook or if he himself convulsed. He saw Gratianus and Paula recoil, pressing their backs to the wall. The dogs twitched, their backs seeming to arch, legs growing longer and disproportionate. Some of them stood on two legs now, their forelegs thickening into arms, paws distending into misshapen, clawed hands. Avitus' feet churned the floor uselessly as he watched the hounds turn into hunchbacked monstrosities. Their jaws slavered and echoing growls almost resembling words bounced throughout the room.

The beasts bounded towards their former owners, ignoring the feverish strokes of the *flagrum* landed upon them. Their hands clutched Gratianus and Paula, lifting them in the air, their talons piercing their limbs. Nausea washed Avitus' stomach as he saw slimy red members jutting from the loins of each creature. And though he felt horror, he also heard laughter spilling from his lips as he watched tunic and *pella* torn away from his captors.

He saw Gratianus held horizontally, turned face down and held in midair as his kicking legs were parted. As one of the beasts thrust into Gratianus' rectum, Avitus heard the man scream with a mixture of outrage and pain seasoned with terror. Avitus heard himself laughing, his voice hysterical. While sodomizing Gratianus, the hound-demon's claws cut strips of skin away from his back. Paula, likewise, hung mid-air from the claws of her pets. While two of the creatures reduced her breasts to ribbons, another penetrated her rectum. Claws and teeth worked continually at the screaming pair, the floor soon becoming littered with severed extremities.

"They will lose interest in these two once their hearts stop beating," Camilla cried to Avitus and Faustina, yelling to be heard over the din. "And you won't wish to be the next object of interest. You know where to run."

Avitus fell to the floor as Camilla released him. He looked at Faustina, startled at the grin twisting her face. She nodded to him as they picked up their weapons and ran for the door.

Avitus sucked in the cool night air, letting it drench his lungs. He realized he had not seen the night sky outside of Carnuntum for years, nor had he ever gone this far north of the city. He and Faustina heard no signs of pursuit, yet they drove themselves on, not daring to stop. His legs burned. His stomach churned with hunger and a throbbing lanced through his head. Which was the North Star? He was not certain, but followed Faustina who did seem to know.

Something thumped ahead of him in the darkened trees, and he dropped to one knee. At Faustina's insistence, he discarded both shield and helmet at the villa. During their run, he was grateful for the advice. Too heavy and cumbersome, he would have ditched both items and left further clues to their route. Still, they made no effort to cover their tracks, and any effort to do so would be futile if pursuers used hounds. Avitus shuddered at what those hounds might be.

The pair reckoned their only hope to be putting distance between themselves and the city as quickly as possible. But now, with only his *gladius* for protection, Avitus sorely missed his shield and helmet. He remained on one knee so he might be less visible, so he might provide less of a target, but mainly because it cooled the fire in his legs for a few seconds. A few yards away, Faustina crouched, almost invisible in the shadows, her net draped over her face. Unlike himself, she retained all of her gear.

Avitus heard more thumping, and a slender form led a tall, white horse into a clearing ahead of them. The person looked female, and Avitus recognized the limp of Iulia. He exhaled his breath, and the girl turned at the sound, smiling in the moonlight. She waved him forward. He stood up, his legs cramping as he walked forward.

As he entered the clearing, Avitus saw two more horses, Aelius stroking one of them. He thought of Camilla as he saw the old man, and suppressed a gag. Aelius smiled at him. Avitus looked back and saw Faustina close behind him, trident held alarmingly ready. He checked his arm as he reflexively reacted to the stance. Faustina smiled at him.

"Why are there only three horses?" Avitus asked aloud, adjusting his grip and stepping away from Faustina. His chest began to pound as he watched Iulia scamper up a tree and climb out onto a limb, a pale creature in the moonlight, her white *palla* making her ghost-like. He felt himself placing his feet for a fight.

"Have you ever ridden a horse?" Iulia called down from the tree.

"No," Avitus said, scanning the tree line for enemies while keeping Faustina in his limited line of sight. So this was it. Having freed Faustina, they would now kill him or leave him behind. If they didn't kill him, he would have to kill himself before Carnuntum's troops found him.

"Then you'll ride with me," Iulia said. She stood up on the tree limb and made a clucking sound. The white horse walked beneath her. Iulia squatted, gripped the branch, and lowered herself to stand on the horse's saddle, sliding down until she sat on it. She stared at

Avitus and patted the horse's back behind the saddle. "You may sit here if you put your little knife away," she said.

Avitus heard Faustina and Aelius chuckling as he pulled himself up behind the girl, gripping the back horns of the saddle. By the time he was seated, he saw the other two already sat astride their mounts. Too tired to feel embarrassed, he watched as Faustina rode up next him. She leaned towards him. Without thinking about it, he reached out and traced the white scars of the letters on her forehead. KAL.

"I suppose no one will believe this, either," Faustina said, smiling. She held his hand.

"Faustina doesn't sound very Persian," Avitus said.

"Farnaz," she said.

Avitus leaned towards her and their mouths met, the *retiarius's* lips impossibly soft as they kissed. He heard Iulia cluck her tongue again, and the horse pulled away, Farnaz slipping from him. He held onto Iulia's slender hips as they rode, feeling her silently giggle. He watched Farnaz, regal astride her horse, trident still in her hand, and realized he looked upon her true form for the first time.

If you enjoyed this story, you can sign up for a free membership at ForbiddenFiction and discuss it with other readers and the author at the *Arena Breed* story page at http://forbiddenfiction.com/story/kh1-1-000160.

Author Notes

If you are reading this before any of the preceding stories, this section may contain spoilers.

It feels strange to reexamine stories I wrote over the years. They seem like recordings of my imagination from different times, serving as the literary equivalent of "that's what I looked like that year."

What would it look like if all my characters were in the same room? Who would get along? Who would fight? I doubt Sheldon would get along with Lot, and his daughters would be unlikely to find him charming. Folkvardr might get along fine with Avitus and Faustina. Would Hannah like Justin? I wonder. Jacqueline and Genesis remain wild cards.

Who would I get along with? It's easier to say who I wouldn't care for. Lot would likely grow tiresome. I picture Sheldon as someone, who, even if you didn't know his predilections, would still give off an alarming vibe. Maybe Justin would to some extent as well; not the same type, but probably an unsettling intensity. Unnr's viciousness would bother me. Gratianus and Paula would, who knows, use me for archery practice. Jacqueline and Genesis would probably both be fairly charismatic at a casual level. Andy from Frogger Says seems to lack character.

I sometimes try to find some overarching connection between my characters, but come up short. They all exist in social margins, I can say that much.

I end up writing a number of them into the Predator category. Pheine and Thamma, from Lot's Sin, behave as predators, intoxicating and raping their father. They rape Lot, however, to become pregnant. The rape is a means to an end. Sheldon from Glad Rags, on the other hand, enjoys his passive aggressively staged necrophilia as a goal in and of itself. Justin from Hunter's Tree leads an entire career consisting of predation. Tomb Brides contains a good deal of aggression, with various characters preying on each other. Unnr certainly victimizes Huld, but so does Folkvardr. Alrekr and the denizens of Ironwood, while aggressive and brutal, do not seek out prey; rather it comes to them.

Arena Breed holds less ambiguity, with Gratianus and Paula clearly taking predatory roles. I let Jacqueline and Genesis from All Consuming remain more ambiguous. While Genesis physically abuses Jacqueline, Jacqueline also manipulates Genesis in other ways, perhaps fostering dependence. In that couple, we might see that relationship dynamic of aggression, fostered in each other, but fed out of a self-destructive compulsion. With All Consuming, I think some of my observations of addictions, as they occur in couples or families, come into play.

Hannah poses a more complicated question (and returns me to the sense of Frogger Says being an unfinished story for me). I wonder how readers perceive her. A story, or any art, needs to stand on its own feet without the creator explaining what it meant. The interpretation of the reader is no less meaningful than that of the author, especially if the story doesn't present a clear explanation. However, Hannah is not the apex predator in that story. I left the ending ambiguous, and it may appear that she kills Andy, and if that works for you, so be it. But the story in my mind marks the choking of Andy as a transitional moment, a crossing over into Hannah's world. While Hannah exploits Andy, greater forces than herself also compel her, though where her own will begins and ends remains unclear.

Perhaps, though, the same may be said of Justin. He preys upon others, driven by his own nature, but in the sense that an attack dog does so, under the organization and ownership of another. He works on a contractual leash, nudged along by greater human powers and perhaps something else. But this opens up another line of inquiry, as to which of my characters aren't driven by an external force, and maybe no individual remains wholly isolated from his or her environment, as soil and climate nourishes or deprives a plant.

In writing a story, I've sometimes felt like a link in a chain of causality. I write the character, who is subject to my own inspiration, experiences, and knowledge. But what writes me? My genetics? My personal history? My environment? If genetics, then what made them fall into such a pattern? If personal history and/or environment, if is possible for me to trace different characters back to different events or perceptions? To this last question, the line of inquiry becomes extremely difficult to navigate, at least on a conscious level. If you write a story, and you have a moral to the story, a clear message you wish to convey, then maybe it becomes easier to write characters to play out the roles in your narrative. But I don't do that, at least, again, on a conscious level. In writing, my goal is to give as much free hand to my unconscious as possible, while creating a coherent story. How much do we think about the unconscious in modern life? It hardly seems to be mentioned anymore, just an obsolete concept to be replaced with more explicable and therefore more comfortable explanations. But I find it an important concept, one that should return to human awareness, and if I am exploring one small part of one man's part of it, then I am satisfied.

I wish to thank anyone who bought this book. It means a great deal to me. Thanks are also due to Fantantastic Fiction Publishing (FFP) and D.M. Atkins for indulging me in the content of my stories. FFP allows for a great deal of freedom of topics. If you are an author whose erotic story content may be a bit too difficult for other publishers, I highly recommend submitting work to FFP. I wish to also thank Lon Sarver, whose editing work proved invaluable for building these stories. I know I've said this before, but Lon excels at nudging me in the right direction. He doesn't tell me what to write. He never says, "You should make this happen." It's more that he asks, "What's missing in this scene? Why did this happen?" I want to also thank proofreader Todd Michaels for slogging through my abuses of the word "that," and for all his help in tweaking and unclunking my sentences. Finally, I want to thanks Siol na Tine for her fantastic artwork and cover design.

If you made it this far, thank you for your time and attention. I appreciate you reading my stories and hope you got something out of them. At the very least, I hope they entertained you and did not bore you.

About the Author

Konrad Hartmann writes erotica mixed with horror and action. Intending to write the sort of material not easily found in the world of sexual literature, he feels comfortable working in genre fiction to tell his stories. He accepts the human soul and the unconscious for what it is; he sees no duty to present justification. Hartmann enjoys learning about a broad range of topics including history (at the moment, 19th century U.S. and medieval European), folk magic, folklore, ichthyology, historic songs, mining, railroads, and all things maritime. He works under the influence of H.P. Lovecraft and Robert E. Howard.

Also by Konrad Hartmann

Spidermilk by Konrad Hartmann
https://forbiddenfiction.com/story/kh1-1-000086

Eddie Stover, private eye, lives in a future where artificial humans called LifeMates serve consumers as a purchasable commodity. When Stover takes a wandering daughter case, the search for the missing woman plunges him into a world of hijacked LifeMates, psychadellic milk, and a bizarre spider-worshiping cult. As the thrall of his old addictions and the enticements of the woman he promised to protect threaten to consume him, Stover is faced with the realization that he cannot escape the choice love forces him to make. (M/F, F/F)

About the Publisher

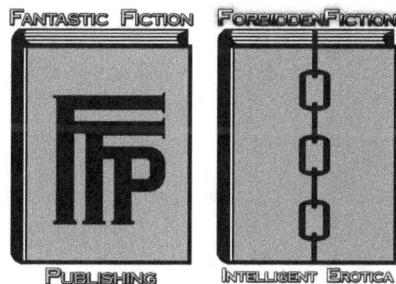

ForbiddenFiction.com is a publisher devoted to writing that breaks the boundaries of original erotic fiction. Our stories combine intense sexuality with quality writing. Stories at ForbiddenFiction.com not only arouse readers through sensations, but also engage them emotionally and mentally through storytelling as well-crafted as the sex is hot.

ForbiddenFiction.com is also designed to be a social reading environment. You'll have fun even if just reading the latest post each day, yet you will have the chance for so much more. Readers and authors can be part of ongoing discussions of specific works and individual authors as well as more general topics.

Sign up for a FREE Membership today at ForbiddenFiction.com

www.ingramcontent.com/pod-product-compliance
Lightning Source LLC
Chambersburg PA
CBHW072216170626
46813CB00003B/968